Cocktail at the Museum

Holly Witchey

Cocktail at the Museum

ISBN – 9781626130869

Published by ATBOSH Media ltd.
Cleveland, Ohio, USA

www.atbosh.com

For my husband, Curt, my son, Nick, and intrepid draft readers Billie, Dori, JoAnne, Kris, and Sarah.

Chapter One

"It isn't that," said Scrooge, heated by the remark and speaking unconsciously like his former, not his later, self. "It isn't that, Spirit. He has the power to render us happy or unhappy; to make our service light or burdensome; a pleasure or a toil. Say that this power lie in words and looks; in things so slight and insignificant that it is impossible to add and count 'em up; what then? The happiness he gives is quite as great as if it costs a fortune."

--Charles Dickens, *A Christmas Carol* (1843)

On the Wednesday after Thanksgiving, curator Joe Cocktail was surprised to find himself in the holiday spirit, but not in a good way. *I'm a modern day Bob Cratchit.* He warmed his hands and feet in front of the small space heater hidden beneath his desk. *Cold, underpaid, over-worked -* he ticked off the list of adjectives in his mind. *Bob Cratchit could have piled more coal onto the fire. There certainly isn't much I can do to change the amount of heat radiating from this postage-stamp-sized space heater.* Hands now warmer, Joe pondered the glass half full. *I do have a heater, and a space, no matter how small, and a job.*

Joe loved his job in the European curatorial department at the museum. He looked around the converted storage room. The museum facilities staff had somehow managed to wedge a desk, a chair, and a small bookcase into a corner for him. The rest of the space was dedicated to two massive wooden file cabinets and rack storage for some of the paintings in the museum's education collection.

He brought his hands to his mouth and tried blowing on them again. That wasn't much help either. He shrugged, pulled a folder from the top of the pile on his desk and opened it. It was another day and yet another endless pile of object folders to look through. Each of the folders on his desk contained the documentation associated with one of the works in the museum. His current task was to compare the information contained therein to the associated data in the museum's collections database. If they aligned, he validated the record. If not, he made a note of needed changes and moved on to the next folder.

Joe allowed himself a sigh. It wasn't that the work wasn't useful and important. The museum needed accurate and up-to-date information about the works in the collection. As Associate Curator of European Art, Joe had finished the process for the works in his own care weeks ago. *A victim of my own success,* he thought, and turned his head to look accusingly at the pile of folders on his desk. The chief curator had been both pleased and annoyed with her junior associate's efficiency, so she added the task of attending to her collections as well.

He bent down once again to try to warm his hands at the space heater; it was so damn cold and he felt distracted. He thought about his boss, Prudence Fenn-Martin, and grimaced. He'd been a curator at the museum less than a year and he truly liked most of his colleagues, but it hadn't taken long to become weary of his immediate supervisor. "Prudence Fenn-Martin," Joe spoke her name out loud. When he said her full name, he always heard her voice as she introduced herself to people she didn't know. "That's Fenn-Martin with a hy-fenn." She over-emphasized both the "fenns" when speaking and then finish with her horriblc braying laugh. Close friends and colleagues called her Prudence or Pru. Staff beneath her on the career ladder were instructed to refer to her as Dr. Fenn-Martin, or by her initials PFM, both options she considered as appropriate for use by subordinates.

A sharp knock on the door at the end of the storage room resulted in a sharp rap on his skull as he raised his head, forgetting he was positioned underneath his desk. And as if he had summoned her with his thoughts, he heard PFM's voice. "Cocky, Cocky, are you there?" PFM called him Cocky. It wasn't easy growing up with Cocktail for a last name - but as a guy you learned to deal with it, first in grade school, then in high school, and later in college when the jackasses who just wanted to fight decided your name might be good for a round or two. Joe had learned a lot about choosing which battles to fight, and fighting with PFM over a nickname wasn't worth the effort...yet.

"Here, PFM," he called out as he came up from under his desk, rubbing the back of his head. "What can I do for you?" She was a majestic

3

woman - tall and solid with a magnificently shaped head. Her hair was always perfect, a deep chestnut brown cut and styled in an immaculate older-woman bob. She strode up to his desk and looked pointedly at the pile of folders.

"Aren't you finished with those folders yet?" She sounded like Cinderella's petulant stepmother enquiring about the housework. "I told the Director I'd have the 16th and 17th century collections completed by the end of the year and we've barely made a dent." She didn't wait for a reply or even give a thought to how she conflated his work with her accomplishments before blithely switching topics.

PFM always spoke a mile a minute. "Before the end of the day I need to talk to you about the painting we brought in last week - the Pseudo Pierfrancesco Fiorentino *Madonna and Child.* We've decided to purchase it and I need to seal the deal tomorrow morning at the latest so the Director can officially present it to the guests and the board of trustees at the gala on Saturday evening."

"You can't be serious, PFM?" Dumbfounded by her words, he was quick to register the annoyance that crossed her face. She stared coldly at him.

"I am always serious about the collections. Surely you know that. If I learned anything at...". PFM continued her dressing-down of her junior colleague by reminding him of her important degree from an Ivy League university and of her mentorship by a respected art historian who had retired from teaching long before Joe was even born. Joe was all too familiar with her spiel. She always described her relationship with her famous mentor as "sitting at the great man's knee." Joe suspected, given the gentleman's reputation, that knees were definitely part of the picture, but refused to allow his imagination to go any further.

He snapped back to the present when he heard the question, "When will these be finished?" Pointing again at the pile of folders, she had returned to her original topic. "I have a meeting with the Director now and I need to give him a status update. He wants everything complete for the gala. So, when will this work be done?"

Joe struggled to keep his frustration in check. First PFM had directed him to drop his other work in order to reconcile the data for her collections. Now, she wanted the monumental task completed by the end of the week. December 31st had been an optimistic deadline, Friday was next to impossible. It might be doable, if he put all of his own work on the back burner. The second, and infinitely more disturbing issue, was PFM's rush to purchase a painting in time for the museum's 100th anniversary, just a few short days away.

"Cocky! Are you listening to me? I asked you a question."

Again he was startled out of his thoughts. *The cold is clearly making my brain sluggish.*

"PFM, last week was a short week due to Thanksgiving. I need a good two to three solid weeks to complete the work. The project should be completed by mid-December, December 31st at the latest. There isn't time between now and the gala to get it all done."

"Weeks? It can't take weeks. I'm going to tell him it will be finished by the celebration and we'll just have to get it done."

She's still using the term we but she's not offering her own help with the project.

She looked narrowly at him as if she could hear his thoughts. "I'm not having your collections finished and mine still incomplete, is that understood? Get a couple of interns in from the university to help you this week, but get the work done."

Joe didn't bother replying to her last suggestion. His graduate students were in the final frenzied weeks of the semester. With papers to be written and exams to be studied for, they were unlikely to have the time to drop everything else they were doing and give their full attention to the job on Joe's desk. He made a mental note to talk to a couple of the students who lived in town and might be available during the holidays.

PFM glanced at her watch and gave a small squeak. "I'll be late for the meeting," she wailed. Like a dervish, she spun on her heels and headed for the door. She turned back before leaving and gave her final orders: "Be ready to talk about that painting this afternoon."

She sailed out of the office, failing to shut the door behind her. Joe was too cold to get up and close it himself. He sat there, hoping some warmth from the rest of the museum would waft through the opening. *The painting. She wants to talk about the painting.*

Chapter Two

PFM had discovered a painting during a gallery visit to New York with some of the trustees. The dealer had identified the painting as the work of a late 15th century Italian master, so if it were accessioned into the collection, it would technically become his responsibility. Late last week, PFM had belatedly remembered to call him into the process. On the Friday after Thanksgiving, he had been surprised to get an early morning call at home asking him to come into the museum to look at the painting. He had found PFM and her good friend, Rita Avi, the president of the museum's board of trustees, in the conservation lab.

The two women had been excited to share their story. In the gallery of a well-respected dealer, they had been shown a painting of the *Madonna and Child.* A talented artist had created a lovely, young, blond Virgin Mary, set against a trellis of pink, white, and red roses. Mary was impossibly slim and elegant - a virgin to make other virgins weep with envy and renew their resolve to diet. In the bend of her elegantly rounded arm, she tenderly supported a slender baby Jesus, teetering on a low ledge of marble.

The child, in his turn, held a European Goldfinch in tiny hands with nails as pink and delicate as miniature snails. Mother and child smiled mournfully at one another - ignoring all others - absorbed in their all-too compelling prettiness.

"The perfect early Renaissance painting and the perfect purchase for the museum's centennial celebration," Rita had cooed over the panel in the museum's conservation lab that day. Rita was an astonishingly thin woman in her late fifties. A fashion model in her late teens and twenties, she'd married and buried three husbands and enjoyed being the focus of attention. Her role as president of the museum's board of trustees provided her with plenty of opportunities to bask in the limelight and, if current museum gossip was true, she had plans to make the Director husband four. Privately, Joe thought the Director's stunning and much younger wife wouldn't give him up without a fight.

"Isn't she just the prettiest thing?" Rita trilled rather than talked as she pointed to Mary. Rita had an annoying little girl voice, charming in a child, and vaguely creepy in women over fifty. "Dear Prue thinks she, Mary, I mean, looks a teensy, weensy bit like me." Rita bowed her head slightly and turned her profile to the right so Joe could compare and admire the likeness.

Joe put on his poker face, looked at the trustee, looked at the painting and commented, "The artist certainly had a lovely model." Rita purred but PFM had given him a rather sharp look. PFM avoided giving underlings the chance to show off any skills they might have; this typically would have annoyed Joe, but this time it had come as something of a relief. A few minutes later, PFM and Rita sashayed off to a cocktail party. Joe was now alone with the painting in the conservation lab.

He studied the painting from various angles and was still looking at it thoughtfully when Al, head of paintings conservation, entered the studio. Al was one of the nicest guys Joe had ever met. Close to retirement and unfailingly courteous, he was a favorite with the whole staff. He was particularly popular with the young professionals whom he quietly mentored. "What do you think, Joe?"

"I think it's 19th century not 16th century, to be honest, and I don't know what to do. PFM's gonna hit the roof."

"What makes you think so? I'm not saying I disagree with you, I'd just like to see it through your eyes, Joe."

Joe trusted Al. "I've seen her type before, this blonde virgin and her beautiful child. It's a lovely painting. The only problem, I don't think it's a Renaissance painting. To be more accurate, Al, I think the best way to describe it is a 'Renaissance-style' painting. If I had to guess, I'd say that this little beauty was painted sometime in the late 19th century probably in or around Siena. A wealthy American traveler on a grand tour of Europe had probably been convinced he was getting a bargain for his Manhattan brownstone."

Joe continued, "The gallery owner might or might not be aware of the problems with the painting. Paintings like these usually come with a stunning pedigree." Al nodded his head in agreement.

"I'm on your side in this one, Joe. I've seen a fair number of paintings like this myself through the years. Any museum with a gallery

9

named for a 19th century robber baron has a score of these kinds of paintings, some hanging on the walls, some tucked into the darkest corners of storage."

Joe and Al spent another quarter of an hour discussing how to break the news to PFM. Over the long weekend Joe had rehearsed various scenarios and today he needed to decide exactly how to phrase it. The problem - few of the scenarios involved happy endings for PFM and the museum, and he knew that none of the scenarios would result in a happy ending for him. He knew his analysis would prove distressful for both PFM and the president of the board of trustees - assuming they'd even listen to him. Joe still didn't have a clue about how to broach the topic with them.

He came back to the present and looked sadly at the pile of folders on his desk. It wasn't getting any smaller while he worried about the painting upstairs in conservation. He glanced at the open folder on his desk and bent down, once more, to warm his hands before getting started. Again he was startled by a voice, in falsetto, calling "Oh Cocky..." This time he did not hit his head on the way up, but as he came up from beneath his desk he grabbed a cellophane tape dispenser. He lobbed it in the direction of the voice, which he recognized as belonging to Charlie, head of information technology for the museum, the main IT guy, and a good friend. The tape dispenser hit the doorframe as Charlie ducked back behind it for a second only to pop his head back around, his familiar smirk plastered on his face.

Joe glared at his friend. "Call me that just one more time and you'll find yourself without a drinking buddy on Friday nights - and then whose sloppy seconds will you strike out with?"

"You can't use that kind of scare tactic on me. How would I survive in the dating market without you? Hmmm, me an information technology professional with marketable skills and a salary to match, and you a guy with a Ph.D. in art history and no chance of ever earning a real living. I'm shaking in my shoes. C'mon, Joe. Heave yourself out of this ice tray and come have a cup of coffee with me."

As Charlie ribbed his friend, they both heard the unmistakable sound of a door being slammed at the end of the hall. Charlie looked over his shoulder and then stepped inside the office, leaving the door slightly ajar. "Uh, oh, trouble brewing. It's your boss and she looks mad. Her face is the color of a candy apple, the old-fashioned kind, not the caramel kind."

They listened to the footsteps approach; Joe hoped they weren't headed in his direction. PFM halted a few steps before Joe's door. A second set of footsteps signaled someone else had rushed to join her. The exchange was an angry one and even though the voices were muted by the door, Joe and Charlie both recognized the second voice as that of PFM's longtime crony, the Curator of Decorative Arts, Bradley Boehm. The two men in the office listened shamelessly to the conversation. Sometimes gossip overheard proved the best, if not the only, way to learn things at the museum.

"Prue, you cannot honestly be surprised at what he's doing. Why are you getting so angry? You know what he's like. You know they are sleeping together."

"Shut up, Bradley, stop talking about that. It's my painting. I found it and I ought to get credit for it. He gets all the press all the time. It's always about him."

Either Boehm didn't answer or they just couldn't hear him.

"He didn't go on the trip." Her voice started to rise hysterically. "He doesn't visit galleries. He didn't find the painting. He hasn't even really looked at the painting. He just had a tête-à-tête with Rita over drinks." There was the sound of a snort, presumably emanating from Boehm. "Now all of a sudden she's giving the painting to the museum as a gift in honor of his enlightened leadership and he's accepting it. My painting and he's accepting it!"

"But darling, we know it's your painting. Rita knows it's your painting. What does it matter about the silly old gala? Be reasonable Prue; part of the pecking order here is we do things and others get credit for them. After all, when you are not..."

"I swear, Bradley, if you quote that stupid paperweight that sits on your desk to me one more time I'll scream. I'm not in the mood."

"Well, it's true, Prue. When you aren't the lead dog the view never changes. You are not the lead dog here. He is. And you'd do best to remember that he's the director and you aren't."

"Bradley I've outstayed, outplayed, or outlived four directors of this museum and I'll outlive this one – even if it kills me or I have to kill him to do it."

Chapter Three

Joe looked at Charlie; Charlie grinned back and whistled softly. Joe shushed him. PFM and Boehm continued walking and the sound of their footsteps faded. Charlie peered around the door, and pretended to wipe his forehead. "Boy, that was close. I'm not sure if I need a coffee or a drink after that."

"Well, since it's still before noon, let me suggest coffee; yes, definitely coffee. Let's try the Design and Installation Department. They usually have a pot brewing. I'm not getting much done here anyway." They threaded their way through the museum's labyrinthine basement to the Design and Installation office only to find the door locked tight.

Charlie swore. "We missed them. They must all be upstairs dusting off the knick-knacks for the big party."

Joe heaved a melodramatic sigh. "Once again let me remind you that museum professionals do not refer to objects in permanent collections as knick-knacks."

"Right, right. Memo to self. Not knick-knacks. Not trinkets. Not stuff. Anyway the doors are locked and there's no chance of coffee here. How about the café?"

Joe glanced at his watch. It was only 10:30 a.m. Too early for the ladies that lunched to be in the museum café and school groups would be in mid-tour. "Okay, but just a quick cup. I've got a ton of work to get through today."

They retraced their steps and went up a flight of stairs, exiting through what might have been a hidden doorway into a public hallway. It was definitely a door, but was kept locked on the public side because it didn't lead anywhere useful for museum visitors. Museum staff used the passageway as a shortcut to the café. Pushing open the double doors, Joe wasn't surprised to find that everyone else on staff seemed to have had the same idea. The café was packed with staff members, drinking coffee and gossiping. Obviously, little work was getting accomplished.

The café was on the small side and after they'd purchased their coffee, and after Charlie had managed to make the young woman at the cash register blush and laugh, and blush again, they turned to find a seat. There was only one table free.

Joe and Charlie both groaned aloud. Charlie spoke first. "Oh no, not a table by the horribles, I was having such a good day." The woman behind the cash register giggled.

Three middle-aged women were huddled around a two-person table, with an extra chair drawn up, along the far wall of the café.

Joe stifled a laugh. "Shut up, you moron. Someone's going to hear you say that sometime and you'll get hauled into human resources for sensitivity training."

The women represented a powerful triumvirate in the museum. Vanessa, head of the education department, was a short, stocky, solid woman with yellow hair. Ivy, the head librarian, was Vanessa's opposite - the Jack Spratt to Spratt's wife - she was dark, tall, and Whippet skinny. Ivy was the kind of woman who invariably looked as if she needed a sandwich but couldn't eat because of some bad taste in her mouth. The third woman, the museum's chief registrar, bore the unfortunate name Fanny, and looked for all the world like some bizarre cross-production of the other two - a head and a pear-shaped torso on top of skinny stork legs.

Curled over their coffees like crones over a cauldron, they didn't look happy. *But then, they're never happy,* Joe thought. All three were occupationally unhappy and had become bullies, though in different ways. Like many bullies, they wore their victimhood proudly and enjoyed nothing more than congregating and regaling one another with their tales of woe or to complain of their treatment by the world at large. They were miserable and determined to make everyone below them on the totem pole miserable too. Joe had witnessed the remarkable transformation of these women in different company. In proximity to the Director, museum trustees, or important donors, they became charming and efficient.

He had to admit all three women were good at their jobs. They had mastered the skill of managing up. They knew how to please the big boss, but could not themselves be considered good managers. All oversaw staffs that contained a significant number of employees - talented, idealistic young women at the beginning of their professional museum careers, and a kind of man

15

Charlie sarcastically referred to as a "belly-up boy." Joe wasn't sure exactly how Charlie defined it, but he seemed to be referring to a man who turned over on his back and displayed a soft belly when faced with authoritative women.

He knew that all three women worked hard for the institution, and that their jobs - like his own - were relatively thankless. He wondered yet again how with marked employee turnover and the general unhappiness in the people who worked for them, they managed to hold onto their jobs. "Just another of the great museum mysteries of our time," he muttered to himself as they headed to the empty table next to the women.

"What did you say, Joe?"

"Nothing worth repeating, Charlie." Both felt the full impact of their collective icy glare as they dared take seats at the adjoining table. Joe gave a great sigh. "Life is too freaking short for this."

"Ain't that the truth!"

They sipped their coffee in silent contemplation. A sudden change in the café environment caused Joe to look up. Seated opposite a mirrored wall, he simultaneously saw exactly what Charlie saw. Charlie stiffened and sat rigid in his chair. The Director had just entered the café accompanied by the attractive new young curator of contemporary art. The long-limbed, graceful silver-haired Director appeared to glide rather than walk - as a newspaper once reported, "the cultural savior of our city enters a room like he's walking on water."

The Director was smiling as usual. He almost always smiled and staff members were obsessive about identifying his smiles and what they meant. He currently wore his "I am the great and beloved director of my staff" smile - which was not quite as deep and full as the "You must love me because I am one of the truly great directors and you are privileged to be in my inner circle" smile. He trotted that one out when he interacted with certain core trustees and patrons. Joe wondered what type of smile the Director wore when he was with his peers. Did he have an "I'm from a bigger and better museum than you are" smile, and a "you are from a bigger and better museum than me" smile? It was something to consider.

The Director gazed around the room, still smiling. There were no free tables. His smile diminished only a fraction, and then he turned his gaze toward the central table occupied by two of Charlie's user-support staff. The face of the one man Joe could see had the glazed look of a deer caught in headlights. Both men hurried to pick up their unfinished coffees and scurried out of the café. Joe looked at Charlie. Charlie frowned and continued to watch the action develop. Joe turned his gaze back to the mirror.

The Director hadn't moved. He allowed events to transpire. He continued to stand while a member of the wait staff hurried to clean off the already clean, vacated table. Then the Director's long suffering personal assistant - a pleasant, rather old-fashioned woman named Mabel – emerged from the serving line carrying a tray with two cups of coffee. She placed one on either side of the table and retreated. The Director, still smiling, crossed to the table and waited until his subordinate sat down before settling himself into the opposite chair. He crossed his long legs before

17

repositioning the razor-sharp creases in his impeccable trousers.

A moment later everyone in the room began breathing again, and normal, somewhat hushed, conversations ensued.

Charlie finished his coffee in one last gulp. "I'll catch up with you later, Joe. I'm not feeling the love in here anymore."

Chapter Four

No reason not to get a little work done while I finish my own coffee. Joe pulled his fountain pen and a small quad notebook out of his pocket and began jotting down some ideas for an article about art historian and connoisseur Bernard Berenson and some of his shadier friends - who were actually much more interesting than his non-shady friends - and they were pretty interesting. *What was the name of the woman who put live frogs in her mouth as a party trick? You just can't buy fun like that these days; unfortunately, The Friends of Frogs Coalition would hunt you down and sue you. Hmm...The Friends of Frogs Coalition - the FFC.* He wrote for another minute or so before sensing the women at the next table seemed to be in a stew about something.

It must be my day to eavesdrop on conversations. Without turning his head, he directed his attention to the table next to him.

One of the women commented. "She's a tart."

"A tart, what kind of word is 'tart?' You make her sound like a costermonger."

"And you think costermonger is a better word? You need to stop reading those Regency romances, Fanny. You don't like tart? Fine then, she's a slut. Look at the way she's flirting with him."

"She flirts with all the men at the museum."

Joe understood. The topic of conversation was Sandra, the new curator of contemporary art. He glanced up and into the mirror for a moment. He could only see the back of Sandra's head. Long, shiny, jet black hair hung down and over the back of the chair. She was little too gothic for his taste. If only for the unrepentant black clothing, she'd have been a real beauty. Yep, the ladies at the next table had every reason to be jealous of this one, and not only for her looks; Sandra was smart too.

Joe suddenly found himself skewered by a pair of grey eyes in the mirror. The Director. Joe looked directly back, allowing his lips to turn up briefly in acknowledgement. He was careful not to show his teeth and bent his head to his notebook again.

All in all it was rather like working for a wild animal, not that anything about the Director could be considered wild. He was, if anything, cold and calculating, although only staff saw that side of him. The Director was a chameleon, much loved by the demographic that funds museums. *I have a good reason for disliking him. I don't believe he gives a hoot about art. He talks a good game in front of audiences. But where's the passion? Where's the animation? He rarely looks at objects and I've never seen him in the galleries. Though, I gotta be fair, he does have to spend a fair amount of time schmoozing and fund-raising.* Joe concluded his internal discussion. *He's not excited by the collection, just by the power.*

Joe looked up again. The Director had finished his meeting with the lovely Sandra. She got languidly up out of the chair, flipped her hair and wiggled her shoulders a little. She turned around and caught Joe watching her. She opened her eyes very wide and, glancing back over her shoulder to make sure the Director saw her, she gave a little wave to Joe and crooned, "Hey Joe, whaddya know?" *Like a beautiful chipper vampire.* Joe nodded in acknowledgement because he couldn't think of anything else to do. She walked past him to the door, turned and waved to him again, and then with hips and hair swinging she strode to the doors, pushed open one side, and slipped out of the café.

Joe looked back in the mirror. The Director was up and out of his chair and almost at the table. *Oops, he's headed my way.* Joe didn't like the look of the Director's current smile with its implied "Don't mess with my toys" message.

Joe was saved from an immediate encounter by an unlikely source. Fanny, who, of the three women, had known the Director the longest, smiled slyly up at her boss and made an attempt at a joke: "The new curator's a little young for you, isn't she?" It was rumored that Fanny sometimes called the Director by his first name. Few staff members ever took that kind of liberty with the man.

The Director stopped in his tracks. He turned slowly to look at the small table of women, his grin almost feral. "Well, well, if it isn't the double, double toil and trouble crowd." Joe was stunned for a moment to realize how closely the Director's thoughts had paralleled his own. The Director continued, smiling down at the women,

"What, no babies to eat? No youthful heroes to kill?"

The head librarian, in this case slightly quicker on the uptake than the other two, looked taken aback and sat up very straight in her chair. "That's hardly an appropriate remark to make to three senior staff members."

Still looking at them with smiling malice, the Director bowed slightly from the waist. "Ladies, if the pointy hats fit..." He allowed his comment to trail off. Joe was so surprised that he swallowed his coffee the wrong way and spurted hot coffee through his nose, drawing the Director's attention to him once more. He smiled at Joe, the evil "you'll get yours, don't worry" smile, and addressed Joe directly.

"Tell your friend Charlie that I expect him to resolve the problems with my home computer with dispatch, I'm growing tired of inefficiency. I'll see you in my office at 2 p.m. today, Cocktail." The Director approached the double doors leading to the hallway and pushed them both at once, so that they stayed open. The ever-faithful Mabel was waiting for him and fell in behind him as he strode off down the hall.

Joe wiped his mouth and face and attempted to hide his consternation. He needn't have bothered. The three women weren't paying any attention to him anyway. They had more important things to worry about and were consumed by their outrage, their faces pale with anger. As Joe left the café he heard one of them hiss, "If I was a witch the first thing I'd do is drop that man into a boiling cauldron and cheerfully listen to him scream."

Chapter Five

After a drama-filled coffee break, Joe returned to his office and buried himself in his work. At lunchtime, he ran back up to the cafe, grabbed a bowl of soup and a sandwich, and ate at his desk. He managed to put in a good couple of hours demolishing most of his tower of files before meeting the Director. The timing of this meeting was unfortunate. One of the quarterly convenings of the museum's accessions committee - members of the senior staff and board of trustees who made the decision about the works to be acquired by the museum - was scheduled at the end of the week. Before each quarterly meeting Joe had separate meetings with PFM and the Director. This time around his meeting with the Director had been scheduled prior to his meeting with PFM. Joe was nervous about having a conversation with his big boss before one with his immediate supervisor. Twice that afternoon he had put aside his work and attempted to call PFM to cover a few issues, but she was either out of the office or not answering her phone.

Just before the appointed time, Joe headed upstairs to the Director's suite of offices on the main floor of the museum. The Director had annexed the series of rooms that now served as his offices from the senior curators and trustees. All in question were still unhappy about their exile from prime office real estate. The view of the lakeshore from The Director's suite was magnificent.

The outer office - the domain of Mabel, the Director's executive assistant, reminded Joe of the lobby of a boutique hotel. Mabel sat on a tall seat at a large semi-circular mahogany counter. Her work surface was spotlessly clean, except for a phone, a glass cube with perfectly sharpened pencils resting in it, and a clean notebook in which she kept notes in immaculate shorthand. Natural light fell through the large windows behind her. There were several seating areas around the room consisting of wing chairs and small tables meant to provide visitors to the inner sanctum a place to rest for what was often a long wait.

Mabel was something of an enigma to Joe. She looked and dressed like his grandmother, always in a neat skirt and pastel blouse, with a jacket or sweater. She was everything efficient in a personal assistant and seemed to have absolutely no interest in the museum or museum politics at all. She was kind and helpful, knew the name of everyone's wife or partner, and children or grandchildren if they had any. She looked up and smiled at Joe as he came in. "Take a seat, Joe. His wife is with him, but they should be finished momentarily. I don't expect you'll have to wait long for your meeting. If you don't mind, I'll just step out for a minute and powder my nose?"

Joe's eyes drifted to a door in the north wall, parallel to the counter, glad the door was closed. He had no desire to over-hear conversations between the Director and his wife. Before finishing his thought, fate intervened. The door to the office was wrenched open, rather violently, and he heard two raised voices. It was just going to be one of those days, he decided, and picked up a recent copy of *The Art Newspaper,* which he'd already read, more for camouflage than anything else.

The Director's voice was taut with controlled anger, "I want this to stop and stop now. You aren't on stage anymore Elizabeth. This is real life and you aren't the star."

"Thanks for the tip," her voice dripped with sarcasm. "I'm not the star because the big museum director always has to be the star. You and the entire museum can all go straight to hell as far as I'm concerned. I'm not going to your damned gala and you can't make me. I'm sure darling Rita will be more than pleased to act as your whore for the evening."

A long silence followed and Joe tried to focus upon the text in front of him. He realized he was holding his breath and exhaled softly.

The unseen Director spoke slowly and clearly as if to a child. "You'll be there, Elizabeth, and you'll be on your best behavior. This is the last time we will discuss the topic; this scene is finished. Run away now and make someone else's life miserable for awhile."

"Drop dead, you bastard." She slammed the door behind her. The sound echoed through the office. Joe couldn't help himself as he glanced over the newspaper and watched Elizabeth as she stormed across the outer office, her head up, eyes flashing, an enormous purse clasped to her side.

The Director's wife was a gorgeous creature and knew it. Tall and slender, with small hips, lovely breasts and long, long, long legs. Stunning by anyone's estimation, she had a head of fantastic, and absolutely natural, pale blond hair. Together, the Director and his wife were a handsome pair. They could be counted upon to play the roles of perfect husband and wife at museum functions. Staff and insiders, however, gave the couple a wide berth outside of formal events. When they weren't attempting to woo trustees and donors, the two were oil and water, constantly sniping at one another. He would turn icy and condescending, and she vacillated between virago and victim, playing whichever part suited the situation. Today was clearly a virago day.

They hadn't been married for all that long. Elizabeth was a local girl with a degree in theater from a small private liberal arts college in a nearby town. Elizabeth had been a floating staff member working on special projects in the department of performing arts, and later in events planning. The Director had noticed her - and it was hard not to notice Elizabeth. A few months later the two had married. Everyone in the museum was taking bets about how long the marriage would last because neither of them seemed happy.

Elizabeth didn't pause in her stride to the door. Clearly furious, she glared at Joe as she swept out of the office, just as Mabel was making her return. The two women barely glanced at one another; Mabel stepped out of the way, letting the angry woman pass. Mabel's face was perfectly placid. She stepped into the office, looked at Joe, and commented, "I'll see if he's ready for you now."

Chapter Six

Joe had his own reasons to be wary of the Director's wife. Elizabeth liked attention and she liked men. He'd only been at the museum a couple of months when he'd run into her at a cocktail party at the home of a staff member. The martinis had been large, and his conversation with her had started innocently enough. Elizabeth had been sitting alone on a settee and he asked her if he could get her anything. She asked for a fresh martini, and Joe, not realizing she'd already had more than one, fetched another for her and she asked him to sit down. He did and she'd launched slowly, but inexorably, into a conversation about how miserable she was in her marriage. How unsatisfied she was. Joe had been embarrassed for her and for himself. With no graceful way out of the situation, he'd simply excused himself and escaped. Elizabeth seldom deigned to notice Joe after that evening. *I wonder if she even remembers confiding in me. Probably not.*

       While he waited for Mabel to return, Joe considered the number of upset staff he'd seen in the first part of the day. *The staff are all on edge. With preparations for the gala in full swing, everyone is stretched too thin and none of us seem to be at our best right now. Museum professionals are a skittish bunch during the best of times, and under pressure, tempers flare and words are said that cannot be unsaid, or forgotten.*

On top of preparations for the gala, the quarterly accessions committee meeting was scheduled for this week and the thought of this meeting was making Joe tense. He was in the Director's office today to discuss a small group of problematic paintings in his part of the collection. The paintings fell into one of two categories - suspect or clearly fake. He wanted to move most of them out of the galleries and into storage until he could research them more thoroughly. The topic of the new painting PFM wanted to bring into the collection was yet another issue Joe now felt compelled to address as well.

Chain of command politics was the battleground of museum work Joe liked least. He wasn't very good at it. He'd minored in political science and philosophy as an undergraduate and had a finely tuned sense of dialectic. Joe constantly found himself evaluating and re-evaluating his options and decisions. For example, his meeting to discuss accessions and deaccessions for his part of the permanent collection was taking place prior to his meeting, later this afternoon, with PFM. *Should I wait to bring up my doubts about the panel painting with her first, or should I bring it up now, given the topic relates directly to the discussion I'm going to have with the Director?*

Mabel had returned from the Director's office. "He's ready for you now."

"Thank you, Mabel." Joe went to beard the lion in his den, as his mom was fond of saying when approaching an onerous task-and what a den! The room that was now the Director's inner sanctum had originally been the trustees' private meeting room - created in the early 20th century so the captains of industry responsible for determining the fate of the city's art collection didn't actually have to ever meet or mix with the *hoi polloi*. Later, the office became the domain of the chief curator.

The current Director had required a suite of rooms, as a part of his contract with the museum. Thus, he had this private office, the outer office where Mabel ran interference for him, and on the other side, a boardroom that was used by the director and the executive committee of the board for smaller and more intimate donor cultivation parties. The office in which Joe currently stood had, he'd been told, a private bathroom and a private bar, both hidden behind paneling. He'd never seen them. In meetings with the Director, Joe found he generally needed all of his wits about him, so he spent little time glancing around the room for hidden doors.

The Director's office was like the Director - sleek, elegant, cold, and austere. The Director's desk was clear of paraphernalia except for his phone, his laptop (closed), and two mahogany desk trays. Each tray held a few folders, nothing at all like the piles of paper in Joe's own office. A pedestal next to the desk held a Brancusi *Male Torso*. Its highly polished surface reflected the surroundings.

The defining feature of the office, however, was the bank of windows which looked out onto an icy winter landscape. The view was fantastic. A snowy, cold October followed by a frigid November had left the lake waves frozen into giant stalagmite-shapes. *I like it,* Joe thought, *it's the perfect setting for this guy. He's an evil Jack Frost, an ice lord, sitting in his splendid office, ready to freeze the will to live of those who disobey him.*

Joe's face must have reflected something of his thoughts. "Something you find amusing about my office, Mr. Cocktail? Something you'd like to share?"

"No, No, I was just thinking how much the winter landscape of the lake reminded me of Narnia in eternal winter," Joe extemporized, quickly recovering.

"Did you come to chat about children's literature or to discuss the accessions committee meeting?" The Director reached for a file. "I've got a full schedule today and I don't have time to waste. Sit down." The Director opened the file, looked down at the thin sheet of paper on top and then at the checklist of objects below. He frowned slightly.

"What's this about, Cocktail? You want me to agree to remove a significant number of the paintings in the galleries for study. Why? What's wrong with them? Have they been damaged?"

"No, the works are," and Joe hesitated, choosing his word carefully, "problematic."

The Director looked at him, and then looked down at the list again. He scanned the first page of the checklist, then the second page - there were 30 objects in all on the list, some of them extremely popular with the visiting public.

"What do you mean 'problematic?'"

Joe opened the necessary conversation. "These works all entered the collection, or at least entered collections in this country, between 1890 and 1930."

"Yes, I can see that. I do know the collection, Cocktail, and I know how to interpret accession numbers. Get to the point."

"The point is, sir, it is likely that a significant number of these paintings probably aren't actually 15th century paintings at all. I think they are pastiches, fakes, painted for rich Americans traveling in Italy."

"Cocktail, have you noticed the family names of the original donors of these works?" He rattled off a series of prominent family names, whose descendants were still major players in the business and cultural scene.

"Yes. I know there arc political implications for this kind of project."

"You have no idea." The Director spoke each of those words clearly and precisely as if Joe was a child. Joe felt himself blush.

The Director continued, "What happens if you discover these paintings are not authentic? What then? Make an announcement to the press? Are you hoping for headlines? 'Noted scholar exposes fakes?'"

The Director's tone was scathing and he was clearly working himself up to deliver a massive dress-down to his employee.

"Mr. Cocktail, I'm going to ask you two questions. First," and he held up a long narrow finger, "Are the paintings in question in good condition?"

"In some cases, yes, but," Joe started to explain.

"No, no buts - just answer my questions, Mr. Cocktail. Are the paintings good paintings? The technique."

"Well, yes of course, but," and Joe tried again.

"Fine then. They stay as they are and they stay where they are." He looked at the list again. "Many of these paintings are favorites with the community and with the donors. Our audiences accept them for what they are and I do not intend to have this museum put in jeopardy so you can indulge your fondness for intellectual one-upsmanship on past art historians and collectors. You know a great deal about art, but very little about people and how museums work in the modern world. A study like this and the potential results would cause mayhem."

"But, but," Joe stuttered and his face was definitely beginning to feel hot as he tried to deal, internally, with what he felt was the injustice of the conversation.

"Cocktail. Do you like your job?"

"Yes." Joe's voice sounded sulky even to himself. He was being treated like an adolescent, and to his dismay he found he was beginning to act like one as well.

"Then do as you are told. Now, was there something else on your mind or can I get back to the work of running this museum?"

Frustrated, Joe decided he might as well throw all his cards on the table. "The painting Rita Avi wants to give in your honor is probably a 19th century fake as well - I don't think we ought to rush into accepting it in committee until we've looked at it more closely."

Joe had been looking squarely at the Director as he made this statement. The Director's lips thinned and his eyes narrowed.

"Cocktail. We aren't ever going to speak of this again. You are not to express any doubts whatsoever about this gift at the committee meeting tomorrow. In fact, you are not to speak at all about the painting. I have already asked Prudence to present the case for the gift." The Director removed a pen from his breast pocket, drew a heavy black line through Joe's study request and closed the folder, placing it on top of the desk tray closest to the edge of his desk. *The 'done' box,* Joe supposed.

"Cocktail. You have stepped over the line in this matter and more distinguished scholars than you have approved the painting, you with your Ph.D. from a mid-western university. Consider this an official warning, you are on notice for insubordinate behavior and I'll be drafting a note to human resources with regard to the matter and discussing your behavior with Prudence. You may leave now."

Joe stood up. *Is there anything I can say that will redeem this situation or at least make it less confrontational?* He opened his mouth to speak and the Director spoke, "I asked you to leave."

As Joe turned on his heel and headed for the door to the outer office, the Director addressed him once more, "I don't want to hear any more about this, Cocktail, or you can look elsewhere for employment, do you understand?"

Joe turned and regarded the Director for a moment. "I understand completely, sir." And he did.

Chapter Seven

Joe opened the door of the Director's office and let himself out. Joe did not slam the door, but closed it, gently, perhaps more gently than he would have normally shut the door because his mind was whirling. It took him a moment to realize there was drama in the outer office as well. Mabel was under siege.

"Mabel, I've just got to see him. Now! He's in there and this is important." Joe detected a note of desperation in the voice of the woman at the desk.

Uh, oh. Dragon-Lady in the house. Boy, there sure are a lot of combative women in the Director's immediate family, business and social circles: his wife, PFM, Rita Avi, the three witches, and, the Dragon-Lady.

The Dragon-Lady was the not-so-affectionate nickname Charlie had given to the museum's marketing director. It wasn't really a fair nickname, Joe reckoned. Lori didn't breathe fire, at least not in the literal sense. She was just hard-driven and humorless. Lori took a dim view of curators in general, because they interfered with her marketing plans - what she characterized as populist seemed more like pandering to the least common denominator. Several of the senior staff felt that Lori over-simplified their ideas, and more often aggrandized projects, producing copy that made the staff cringe with embarrassment. In Lori's world, exhibition titles needed to include phrases like "gold of," "treasures of," "masterpieces of," or "mysteries of" in order to be successful. The curatorial staff had quickly learned there wasn't much point in openly fighting Lori – she usually got her way - and until recently she'd had the Director squarely in her pocket.

But something had gone wrong. It might have been related to the Director's developing relationship with Rita. In any event, the dynamic had changed, and in more than one meeting over the past few weeks, the Director had been openly dismissive of his head of marketing. Lori wasn't going down without a fight, and today she didn't look like she was moving from the office until she had some face time with her boss.

Mabel, however, was more than a match for anyone, staff member or trustee. Mabel was unmovable. "He isn't available this afternoon. He's in a meeting right now." She looked directly at Joe over Lori's shoulder. He smiled a trifle grimly. Lori whipped around and stared hard at Joe. She was, he realized, processing the fact that he had just come from the office and thus the Director must be free. She started across the soft carpet and headed for the door to the Director's office when all three of them heard the sound - the sound of the door behind Joe being firmly locked shut.

Lori paused for a moment as if she might try to force the door, or at least relieve a little tension by banging her fists on it or perhaps

36

screaming to get the Director's attention. Her face was red with anger. She gave her head a shake and her shoulders drooped slightly for just a moment, and then she drew her head up, pointed her chin, and turned back to Mabel.

When she spoke, she was overly formal. "Please give him the following message for me. I'll wait until you are prepared to write." She waited until Mabel had picked up a pencil and opened her notebook to a fresh page. Mabel looked at Lori. Lori said, "There's a matter I need to discuss with you before the gala this weekend. We need to make a decision." Mabel finished writing and looked up from the notebook.

"Is that the entire message?

"Yes."

Mabel was unflappable. "Let me just read it back to you." Mabel read the short message back word for word. "I'll make sure he sees this today."

"Today?" Lori sounded as if she didn't quite believe Mabel.

"Today." Mabel was firm in her assurance.

Joe felt compelled to try to lighten the mood. "You're probably better off not seeing him right now, Lori. He's not in a great mood today."

"For the record, I'm not in a terribly great mood today myself." With that, she left the office, slamming the door behind her.

Joe winced. "Museum employees are hard on doors around here."

Mabel regarded him placidly. "Yes, so are museum spouses. Luckily, old museums were built to last. Is there anything else you need, Joe?" She stressed the pronoun.

"No, no. I'll wander back to my office and lick my wounds before my meeting with PFM." He smiled sheepishly at Mabel and left the perfect executive assistant sitting at her desk. The moods and little idiosyncrasies of museum employees and their spouses troubled Mabel not at all. What troubled her was not knowing how long she might have to stay in the office because she would stay at her desk for as long as she was needed by her employer.

Chapter Eight

All too soon for his taste, Joe was standing outside of yet another office into which he had no desire to go. *This is the longest day ever.* He knocked and received permission to enter. PFM may have had to give up her lake view office to the Director, but she still had a great office. Joe envied the floor-to-ceiling bookcases, not to mention the actual working radiator. PFM was seated behind her desk. Bradley Boehm occupied the only other chair in the office that wasn't stacked high with piles of books and papers. Boehm had an embroidery hoop on his knee. He embroidered as he talked, and talked as he embroidered. Joe's entrance barely merited a pause in the incessant sound and motion. Boehm had an agile mind, chiefly occupied with new acquisitions, research, travel, museum gossip, and discovering new and inventive ways to get others to complete any task he felt beneath his dignity as a curator.

Boehm never worked if he could gossip, and if he had nothing to gossip about, he complained. If he really had nothing to complain about, he generally sat in the museum library reading *The New Yorker,* the *New York Times* or

The Art Newspaper, or one of the wide variety of decorative arts journals to which the museum subscribed.

Boehm greeted Joe effusively as he came in.

Uh-oh. That's worrying.

"Joe. How fortunate that you should arrive just now." He paused to take a breath, continuing to stitch rapidly. "I had just approached Prue about a great opportunity for you." He beamed at Joe. "I was going to suggest Prue temporarily assign you to the Decorative Arts Department. You could assist me in reviewing the object data. It would be good experience for you and it's high time we introduced you to the decorative arts collection in a more significant way."

Here we go. I bet he's got several big stacks of folders on his desk and needs help. With the Director all set to enforce a deadline for completion of the work, Joe imagined Boehm was a long way from being finished with his work. However, if he'd hoped his friend Prue was going to bail him out this time, Bohem was sadly mistaken.

"Sorry, Bradley. It can't be done. Joe's hands are full with the European paintings collection. You'll just have to figure out another way to get the work done, but it needs to get done. The Director is standing firm on this one - our merit raises are dependent upon the work getting done."

"But, Prue, I need help." Boehm whined.

"No means no this time, Bradley. Besides, Mr. Cocktail is soon going to have other work to occupy him. He's been quite a busy boy already this afternoon." She gave Joe a dark look. *She must have already had a conversation with the Director, yipes.*

Boehm got up and began to grumble aloud, "I don't know why I am expected to review this information myself. If the Director wants to make sure the information is accurate he ought to be able to put up some funds for us to hire some capable and knowledgeable curatorial assistants. This is not a good use of my time as a curator."

Joe nearly laughed out loud. *If he isn't going to take responsibility for the accuracy of his own material, who is? Curators don't generally have regularly assigned fact checkers in this day and age.*

Boehm continued with his complaints, "It's not as if I have time for this project. I have to watch everything that happens in my department. The woman assigned to me while Claire is on maternity leave is always forgetting to use my private notepaper for letters and insists on using the museum letterhead - as if I can write to the Duchess of Kent on cheap paper."

The litany might have continued if PFM hadn't interrupted him. "Bradley dear. As fascinating as your stationary woes are, I have a meeting with Mr. Cocktail right now."

Second time she's referred to me as Mr. Cocktail. That can't be good.

"Well, alright Prue," Boehm continued as he neatly folded up his embroidery and dropped it in an over-sized scarlet Fendi tote at the side of the chair.

"I'm going to talk to the Director about this at length after the gala weekend is over. Prue, I'm thinking of having a little brunch on Sunday to celebrate, well, just to celebrate." Boehm hummed happily to himself and made a tent of his fingers, clearly chuffed to bits at some secret. "In fact, I'm off to speak with the Director about a little something I've discovered." Boehm rose from the chair - he was a bulky little man, more Weeble than anything. He slung his tote over his shoulder and sang, "Au revoir, mes petites" as he departed the office without closing the door behind him.

Chapter Nine

Joe hesitated for a moment. PFM frowned at him. "Shut the door and take a chair, Mr. Cocktail." She waited until he had seated himself before she continued. "Would you like to explain to me why you felt it necessary to go over my head with your discoveries about possible fakes in the collection?"

Joe did not pretend to misunderstand her question. "My intent wasn't to go over your head. My accessions meeting with the Director had to be rescheduled and earlier this afternoon was the only time he had free. I did try to call you to discuss the issues before the meeting, and I sent you both the same set of documents."

"Pray tell, Mr. Cocktail..." The words she used to begin her sentence distracted Joe. *Pray tell, nobody actually uses the phrase "pray tell" except in books.* He missed the rest of the sentence and had to ask his boss to repeat what she had just said. "I'm sorry, what did you ask?"

"What is wrong with you today, Cocktail? Are you losing your hearing? Or are you simply uninterested in your job? I asked you how the topic of my painting and your notion that it is also a fake came up in a conversation with the Director?"

"PFM, if this was a normal week, you and I would have had the meeting we are having now before I had my quarterly accessions meeting with the Director. We didn't, and I had to cover issues with him before I covered them with you. I wasn't comfortable doing it, and as I said a moment ago, I did try to call you about my concerns earlier today, but was unable to reach you. I had no choice, PFM, if I was going to get some kind of decision on my collection before the accessions meeting. Oh, and I did get a decision, by the way."

"I am aware of the decision. I've had a thoroughly unpleasant discussion with him about the matter and I cannot tell you how disappointed I am that you circumvented me in this issue. He also tells me you don't have a high opinion of my judgment in acquisitions."

"What?" Without being aware of it, Joe leapt up out of his chair and leaned towards PFM, placing his hands on her desk to steady him.

"Do not raise your voice to me, Mr. Cocktail! And do not hover over me in that threatening manner." Joe took his seat again. "You are already in enough trouble as it is. You will sit down now and listen to me. Here's how the next few days are going to go, and for your sake you need to listen carefully to what I am saying."

Joe nodded his head, completely confused. *I don't think I said anything derogatory about PFM in my meeting with him. What the freak did he tell her?* "Tomorrow, as you well know, is the accessions meeting. You will speak only to answer questions directed to you, or in the event the Director asks you to comment. You will not offer opinions. Most importantly, you will not allude to any doubts you may have about works currently in the collection or those offered as gifts or for purchase. The topic of the Pseudo Pier Francesco Fiorentino painting is strictly off limits. Do you understand?"

"PFM. You need to listen to what I have to say about the painting."

"I don't want to listen to what you have to say about the painting. I don't need to listen to what you have to say about the painting. And furthermore, I don't intend to have a conversation now or ever about the painting. You will do as you are told or face the consequences. There is a hierarchy here. You are the Associate Curator of Paintings. I am the Curator of Paintings, as well as Chief Curator. You are my junior here, but this fact seems to have escaped your notice. I'd like you to go back to your office now and do the work you've been hired to do and stop causing problems."

"PFM, please listen..."

"Cocktail! What part of this discussion haven't you understood? You can leave or I can call HR and have you escorted from the premises. Your choice."

He was angry. This whole situation had spiraled out of control. He felt, he had, been unfairly treated in both meetings. He wasn't some kid just out of college, he knew what he was talking about, and neither PFM nor the Director wanted to listen. *I need to calm down now. I'm not thinking straight.*

He got up to leave and as he was leaving PFM added, "And if you are unwilling to learn how to become a team player, I'd suggest you start getting your c.v. in order. I'm not sure you have a real future at this museum."

Chapter Ten

Outside PFM's office Joe paused to gain control of his temper. It was a difficult task. *I'm angry. I started this job full of excitement. What the hell happened? My plans to look more deeply into the history and condition of the works in my care are reasonable. I can understand and even sympathize with the Director's concern about negative publicity and a need for managing the donor relations part of the issue. But, we ought to be able to manage expectations and relations in a positive way.* Joe had imagined getting a new generation of donors excited about discovery and visual analysis, training a new type of audience. And, for freak's sake, both the Director and PFM were in absolute denial about this proposed painting of the Virgin. *How can that be ethical? I have knowledge, actual knowledge, and experience of these works. I'm trying to do my job; I'm trying to keep the museum from making a huge mistake.*

PFM is worried about how she is perceived by the director. The Director is concerned about how he appears to the board of trustees and donors. Doesn't anyone at this crazy institution care about the difference between right and wrong, about authenticity, or is it all about appearances? I've been torpedoed through the looking glass. This isn't what museum work is supposed to be like. That's enough. Time to stop feeling sorry for myself. He needed to get his head together and figure out how to save his job. Time to channel this energy into getting something done. *Wonder if Charlie would be up for a drink after work? Some decompression time with a friend might not be a bad idea.* Joe turned and headed off in the direction of the IT offices.

The Information Technology Department was a different world from the rest of the museum. Joe had discovered, at least from his experience at this museum, there was a reason for all those stereotypes about IT guys and the characters from Star Trek. Sure, they could be grumpy and even anti-social, but taken as a whole it was a pretty effective department. On his way to Charlie's office he popped his head into the two outer office areas to say hello. The help desk office was empty, everyone out solving browser, laptop, or printer issues, he guessed. Then he went on to the small server/hardware room. The IT staff - minus Charlie - was gathered around a computer screen. Ted, one of the hardware guys, was having an argument with Madeline, one of the help desk associates.

"I tell you it is the real thing," Madeline pointed at the screen.

"Nah, it can't be. They wouldn't be allowed to sell it."

"It comes with a guarantee of authenticity," she insisted.

"Big deal, Khan King chess pieces from the Franklin Mint's 25th Anniversary Chess Set come with guarantees of authenticity and they made close to a zillion of those. What does authenticity mean if it's one of one billion made? If I've got a printer I can make you any kind of guarantee of authenticity you want. The design and installation people can probably make you a copy of one of those if you asked them."

"What's for sale?" Joe asked.

Most of the group turned around to acknowledge Joe's question. Sam, one of the software guys, answered for the group. "It's possibly an authentic Dilithium crystals prop used in the original Star Trek show."

"Oh, it is not," scoffed Ted.

"Yes, it is," insisted Madeline, "Look, it even says it's from Jimmy "Scotty" Doohan's family collection. Guys, the bid's only $19.95."

"Good luck with your auction." Joe walked away shaking his head, heading for Charlie's office. He knocked on the door and Charlie looked up from his screen.

"Your staff's contemplating buying some possibly authentic Dilithium crystals from an auction site." Joe dropped into a chair. "Building a department starship in your free time?"

"No, probably just acquiring another object for the IT Collection."

"What IT Collection?"

"Oh, it's not a big collection and it is totally on the QT. Mostly just odds and ends from science fiction movies and television series, a few comic books, and some models, but everything has a label. Madeline is in charge of the documentation. She is our curator/registrar/treasurer. We have an accessions fund. We each kick in a few bucks when we think of it and there's a can on Madeline's desk where we drop spare change and fines for massive goof-ups. We keep the collection in those big locked shelves next to the ink cartridges. When someone leaves the department we take a vote and deaccession an item as a going-away gift."

"Remarkable."

"You think that's remarkable, you should ask Madeline to show you the Peeps collection."

"You mean Peeps as in marshmallow candies?" Joe was skeptical.

"That's right. My people are resourceful. And if they find that the company hasn't made a shape they need, they create their own. You should see the Darth Vader Peeps they made. A box of purple rabbit-shaped Peeps and a little creative surgery with the assistance of the guys in design and you can't tell that they weren't intended as Darth Vaders from the beginning. We keep them off view in a secure area in server storage - it's cold in there and keeps the insects away." Charlie pause, looked at Joe, and said, "You didn't come here to talk about Peeps did you? What's up?"

"Drink after work?"

"Sure. Having a bad day?"

"I don't know about Joe but I am." Katherine, the head of performing arts, entered the office. "I need this day and this whole gala to be over, with a capital O." She came and sat on the edge of Charlie's desk.

"We're heading off to the Fox for a drink after work. Join us?"

"Why not. Can we make it a little later? We won't finish here until around 6pm."

Joe looked at Charlie. Charlie shrugged. "Suits me. I've always got stuff to do. Speaking of that, do either of you need anything or are you here just wasting my time and yours?"

Katherine tipped her head to one side as if thinking about her answer. "Depends, I guess, on what you consider a waste of time. We've got problems with the you know who and the you know what for the gala."

"I can sense my presence is going to prove an obstacle to this conversation," Joe offered, "So, I will get back to my own work."

"Sorry, Joe. We want to tell you. We are dying to tell someone, aren't we Charlie? I know that after Saturday night we will look back on this and laugh. But it's not even remotely amusing right now."

"Okay. I'm off. See you both this evening." Joe got up and Katherine slid into the chair he had just vacated. Within moments, his two friends were bent over a schematic that Katherine was holding, and they began muttering about timings and tolerances. Joe hurried back to his office and was soon engrossed in his work.

Chapter Eleven

Towards the end of the day, Patsy from the mailroom came around with the mail cart. She set a pile of mail on Joe's desk, including various inter-office mail envelopes, post cards announcing art auctions, sales catalogues, and a call for papers for an annual conference. She also handed him a copy of the *Chronicle of Higher Education.* He tried to hand it back to her. "Hey Patsy, I don't think this is mine."

"It's got your name on it."

He turned it over and looked. Sure enough, a printed label read *To the immediate attention of Joe Cocktail, Associate Curator of Paintings.* "So it does, hmm. Wonder how I got on their list? I'm not really an academic; must be looking for new subscribers."

"I hope you aren't asking me those questions. I just deliver the mail. I don't try to explain it."

As she started to leave the office to complete her rounds, Joe thought of something he wanted to ask her. "Hey Patsy, has Toby's indoor track practice started yet?" Joe was a runner, and he knew Patsy's only son was a runner too. Joe and Toby had run into one another at several 5K runs during the fall.

"Yep and he's doing real well this year, Joe. There aren't many meets during the winter, but it keeps him in shape for regular track. He's one of the team captains this year and coach thinks he might earn a college scholarship if he keeps improving his times."

"That's great, Patsy. Tell him I'll be seeing him at some of the winter runs."

"Will do, and thanks for asking about him." They chatted for a while longer about holiday plans before Patsy departed to make her last deliveries of the day. Joe put the *Chronicle* on the top of his in-box and went back to his work. When he next looked up, he realized it had gotten late - almost 6:30 p.m. *Yipes! I better get moving if I'm going to meet Charlie and Katherine on time.*

He shut down his laptop and closed the screen, then straightened the papers on his desk. He glanced at the *Chronicle of Higher Education* sitting neatly in his in-box. In graduate school, he had loved to look at the advertisements for jobs in the *Chronicle;* that was when he was still trying to decide whether he would move into museum work or try to stay in the academic world and teach art history. There had been something almost magical for Joe about the journal. Any one of the jobs advertised could take him off on an unexpected adventure and possibly lead his life down an alternate path.

Funny the paper came today, of all days, when both of my bosses suggested I start polishing my resume. Is this a sign? Wonder if there's anything interesting in it. Perhaps, I should polish my resume. Or, perhaps, I should go grab a drink. Joe decided on the latter course of action.

He shut down his computer, grabbed his coat off the hook behind the door, flipped off his office lights, and headed towards security.

Charlie was already there when he arrived. They both handed the security guard their keys and walked out to their cars. Neither man spoke until they'd left the museum proper and were walking toward the employee parking lot.

"That guy is such a douche-bag." Joe didn't have to ask who Charlie was talking about. "He's a museum director, not the almighty Emperor of the Known Universe. Just wait until Saturday night, Joe. If this were a novel you'd know he was going to come to a bad end. He is so unbelievably arrogant." Charlie hauled off and kicked a block of ice off the wheel well of his SAAB with rather more violence than was absolutely necessary.

"Hey, don't take it out on the car. C'mon, it's freezing and I want to be somewhere warm with a beer, don't you?"

"Yes, I do." Charlie gazed down at his phone. Joe was used to that. The IT guys were always multi-tasking. Suddenly, Charlie said, "Oh shoot, wait a minute, something has just come up I need to deal with. It shouldn't take long. I'll meet you there in about 45 minutes. Okay?"

"Sure, sure. Is Katherine still coming?"

"Yeah, she was just going over a few items with the Director and then going to give the contractors final instructions for the evening. She's probably looking at the same time frame as I am now. I have to run. I'll see you in a few." Charlie turned around and headed back into the museum.

Joe wondered what was up. As head of IT, Charlie was always on call and constantly being called for some reason or another - security issues, problems with staff, someone being let go. Joe hoped it wasn't his own position being eliminated, but he wasn't going to pry. Charlie and Katherine would show up at the bar sooner or later, probably later. In any event, after the day he'd had, Joe was fine with sipping the first beer on his own.

Joe headed towards his car. He liked Charlie's SAAB, but he liked his own car even more. The cherry red 1985 Alfa Romeo Spider was his pride and joy, a legacy from a favorite uncle. He got in, started the car, and pulled slowly out of the parking lot. *Best to drive carefully in museum parking lots. Museum employees are not the best of drivers because they are usually thinking about something other than driving. And to be honest, museum patrons weren't a whole lot better - usually talking to one another and not paying attention to what other drivers were doing.* Joe cautiously maneuvered the twists and turns of the parking ramp, swiped his identification badge to exit the gate, and was on the road.

A light snow was falling. There had been snow on the ground since late October, and there was enough fresh snow to make the area around the museum scenic - the street lights with their snowy halos made the whole place look a lot more romantic to the visitor than it actually was from an insider's point of view. Joe turned onto the major artery that would take him most of the way to the Fox Tavern. Traffic was light, partially due to the snow, partially because it was the week after Thanksgiving. *I might still have some time to kill at the bar while I wait for Charlie and*

Katherine to show up; that's okay. I can use some down time to just sit and relax on my own.

Chapter Twelve

He parked in the lot across the street from the Fox. There were almost always spaces available and tonight was no different. He plugged the meter with a few hours worth of time, pulled his collar up around his neck to avoid the cold, and waited at the light to cross the street to the tavern. He glanced around the parking lot while he waited and then crossed the street.

Joe pushed through the two sets of doors into the restaurant/bar. On a cold winter's night, the Fox was a cozy, intimate home away from home. There was a friendly hum and buzz, the bar was comfortably crowded, but with enough free tables that he didn't feel like he needed to try to save one for himself and his colleagues just yet. He started towards the bar and stopped suddenly. Scott Theodore, head of special events for the museum, was seated at the bar. The only open seat was right next to him. He didn't really want to join Scott, but what the hell. *Scott's probably had a tough day, too, with the gala almost upon us.* He walked up behind Scott and thumped him on the shoulder. "Hey Scott?"

Scott turned to look at Joe. Scott's eyes were red and bleary; he was more than half in the bag. Nevertheless, he smiled at Joe and welcomed him with an over-hearty and somewhat slurred greeting. "Joe. Sit down. Have a drink. Have a few drinks. We're all just sitting here drinking trying to forget our mother f'n jobs and bosses." Joe looked around. Others seated at the bar were obviously ignoring Scott.

"Whoa, buddy. Sounds like you've already had a few drinks. What happened? Bad day today? Gala got you down? Tomorrow will be better."

As the museum's special events planner, Scott was in charge of overseeing all the details for the gala. It didn't bode well for the museum to have Scott sitting at a bar, drunk, just a few days before a major event was due to take place.

"Tomorrow won't be any better, Joe. The bastard told me I was out of a job come Monday morning."

"What?" *This seems to be the only word in my vocabulary today.*

"Yep, that's right. You heard me. Have to get through the gala to get my severance. Four bloody weeks of severance, after 15 years at the place, and then I'm out. Well, that's fine-j'esh fine." Scott was noticeably slurring his words. "Les see how well his big ol' party goes. I'm there days, nights, and weekends. I barely see my wife anymore." He slumped over his drink. To Joe's horror, tears began running down the man's cheeks.

"Scott, buddy. It's going to be okay."

"It's not gonna be okay. How'm I gonna pay the bills, Joe? I got two kids in college, Joe. How'm I gonna pay the bills?" Scott pushed his drink away, folded his arms on the bar, and dropped his head down onto them.

Joe looked up. Sylvia, one of the bartenders, caught his eye. "Friend of yours, Joe?"

"Work colleague. How long's he been like this?"

She moved slightly farther away from Scott and dropped her voice, which was probably unnecessary since Scott didn't seem to be listening to their conversation. "He came in around 4:00 and has been drinking steadily ever since. I cut him off about a half an hour ago. He's drinking water and thinks its vodka. I'm not charging him for them," she added.

"Can you get him a cup of coffee – one for me, too? He might drink one if I do. I'm going to step outside and try and get hold of his wife."

He turned to the drunken man. "Hey, Scott. I'll be right back. Sylvia's bringing us both a cup of coffee. Drink some of it for me, would you?"

The man raised his head. "Don-wanna-cupa- coffee," he muttered and dropped his head back down on his arms.

Joe hoped he could get Scott out of the bar while the man could still walk. As he stepped away from the drunken man, Joe was already dialing the Director's office. There was every chance Mabel was still at her desk if the Director was still in his office. Joe breathed a sigh of relief when she picked up.

"Mabel. Do you have Scott's home number? I'm here at the Fox Tavern and he's not doing real well."

"I was afraid of that. He was upset when he left the office. He didn't look like he was heading home."

"He didn't."

"Do you want me to call his wife again?"

"Again?"

"I've known Scott and Judy for years, Joe, and I know how he reacts to bad news, of any kind. I called her when he left the museum today, I wanted to give her a head's up."

"Mabel, you are one in a million. HR must hate you."

She chuckled. "What they don't know doesn't hurt them a bit, but that's between thee and me, Joe."

"Yes ma'am. Why don't you give me Judy's number, there's no reason for you to play go-between. Right now, I just need to get him out of here and home." Mabel read him the number and he wrote it on his hand, thanked her again, and hung up. He dialed Scott's home number. Joe had met Scott's wife, Judy, only once or twice in his time at the museum. She answered the phone on the first ring.

"Judy, it's Joe Cocktail."

"Is Scott okay?" She knew why he was calling.

"He's fine, he's just in no condition to drive. I dropped in at the Fox for a drink and found him at the bar." He hesitated. "He's in pretty bad shape, Judy."

She sighed heavily. "Don't worry, Joe, you don't need to candy coat anything for me. He's had this problem for a long while."

"Would you like me to bring him home?"

"Oh Joe, would you? I've been so afraid and when the phone rang I assumed the worst. I'm shaking so hard I'm not sure I'm in any condition to drive." She gave him directions to their house; it wasn't far away. He could drive Scott home in his car and walk back to the Fox.

Proximity to home had probably been part of the Fox's appeal for Scott in the first place. He had to know he was going to the bar to get purposefully messed up.

Chapter Thirteen

Joe walked back to the bar. Scott was sitting with an empty glass and an untouched cup of coffee in front of him. Joe sat down, briefly, and took a swig from the mug Sylvia put down for him.

"Okay, Scott. Time to go home."

"Donwannagohome. Wanna drink more."

"Nope, you've had enough."

The bartender was watching the drunken man knowingly. As a bartender she'd seen this particular scene a hundred times and knew just exactly how ugly a drinker could get.

"Hey, Sylvia. How about a go-cup for the coffees, if it's not too much trouble?"

"Right you are, Joe."

While she was gone, Joe managed to coerce his colleague into something resembling standing and helped him get his coat on. It was like trying to dress a scarecrow, Scott's arms flapped and flailed in different directions, and his knees seemed liable to give way at any moment.

Joe was aware of the covert glances of the other bar patrons. Just his dumb luck that he arrived early and got the job of Prince Valiant. "Scott. Help me out. Where are your car keys?"

"I can drive."

"Nope, no you can't. It's my turn today. You can return the favor some other day."

"You're a nisch guy, Joe. Whaddyawanna stay at that crappy museum for?" Scott asked mournfully. Joe didn't think the question required an answer. He'd gone to college with guys like Scott, the mournfulness could easily turn to anger or violence and he didn't want a scene in the bar. As if the drunken man had read Joe's thoughts, Scott suddenly hissed, "Someone should poison the bastard, or maybe shoot him. Right in the middle of his big damn gala. That'd show him."

Geez, what did I do to deserve this today? Joe turned to Scott and spoke sharply. He used the command voice that he'd used as captain of the cross-country team in college. "Shut up, Scott. You don't mean that. C'mon. We're out of here. Now." Joe knew the effect of his voice would only last a moment or two. While Scott was trying to regroup and respond, Joe began hustling him out of the bar.

Sylvia came out from behind the bar and hurried in front of him to open the door, balancing two cups of coffee in one hand. "You aren't going to need these, are you?"

He looked longingly at the cups in her hand. Suddenly, he wanted coffee more than a beer. He shook his head sadly. "No, guess not, not enough hands." As he passed through the door, half carrying his colleague, he said in passing, "Charlie and Katherine are due here in a few minutes. Will you tell them I'll be back in a few?"

"Sure thing Joe. Be careful."

"Oh, I think the danger has passed. My big fear now is he'll pass out or get sick."

Supporting Scott, almost carrying him, Joe felt the man's car keys in the side coat pocket of his heavy parka. Joe slipped them out. The cold air hit them at the same time and Scott seemed to recover a bit.

"Where are you parked Scott?"

"Cross the street. The blue Malibu."

"Right." Joe got them to the other side of the street and leaned Scott against the rear passenger side of the Malibu as he fumbled to open the door. His fingers were freezing and he hadn't taken the time to put on his gloves. Scott started to slip sideways and Joe dropped the keys in the slush as he grabbed and steadied the man. "Just hold still, Scott," Joe snapped. He bent down and fished in the cold snow and slush for the keys. Once he found them, he opened the car door and somehow managed to maneuver Scott into the passenger seat. He got the seatbelt across the man and then shut the door, a trifle harder than he ought to have, and walked around to the driver's side.

By the time Joe let himself into the car his passenger had passed out, or fallen fast asleep. Scott's head was down on his chest and the man was breathing loudly through his nose. Joe sighed and got out of the car again. Walking around to the passenger side, he opened the door and tipped the passenger seat slightly so that Scott's head was resting at a comfortable angle. He closed the door a second time; this time much softer - he didn't want Scott waking up and getting sick. He walked around the car yet again, let himself in, and started the car. As he approached the exit of the parking lot, he saw Charlie's car approaching. Joe stopped for a moment and rolled down his window to talk to his chum. "I've gotta drive Scott home. I'll explain when I get back."

"You don't need to explain. I know the situation. How are you going to get back?" the ever-practical Charlie asked.

"I'll walk, it's not far."

"Naw, I'll follow you. Just had a call from Katherine. She'll be at the museum for another half hour or so, we'll be back in time to meet her."

"That's great. I can use the help. Looks like Sleeping Beauty here isn't going to get into his house on his own two feet."

"Poor Judy. Let me turn my car around and I'll be escort. I know where Scott lives and I've been through this with him a time or two before."

Charlie turned his car around and the unhappy little caravan started out. The drive didn't take more than five minutes. Judy had the garage door open and was standing in the doorway leading into the house when they arrived.

Joe drove into the garage and parked the Malibu next to a cheerful red Honda CRV, presumably Judy's car. Charlie parked in the street and walked up the driveway to help Joe. Judy was nearly in tears. "I can't thank you enough, Joe, Charlie." She looked at each of them in turn.

Charlie spoke in a soothing voice to the woman and patted her a little awkwardly on the shoulder. "It's okay, Judy. He's home with you now. We're both as sorry as we can be about what happened today."

Of course I should have realized that Charlie, as head of IT, would have had advance warning about Scott being let go. Probably why he'd had to go back into the museum earlier. One of Charlie's jobs was to evaluate how likely it was that an employee who was let go was going to do damage to the museum's systems or try to make off with secure information or property.

"He's just been so miserable, and with the added pressure of this gala, I've been afraid for weeks that he was going to spout off at some point about something. Apparently that's what happened today?" The rising inflection in her voice transformed her statement into a question.

The two men glanced at each other and both shrugged their shoulders. Joe spoke. "I ran into him at the Fox and he told me he was being let go on Monday; I don't know any more than that."

Charlie nodded. "I got word from HR to cancel his security access as of Monday morning. Sorry Judy, it's part of my job and not a part that I'm crazy about. Lay-offs, or terminations, it doesn't matter, they are never pleasant."

She seemed to take a moment to gather herself. "I understand, Charlie. Well, let's get him inside. Wait here a moment, let me see if I can wake him up." She went over to the car door and squatted down. The two men watched her gently tapping her husband's shoulder and speaking. Getting no response, she stood up and shook her head. "It's a no go, I'm afraid. I'll need your help to get him inside and into bed."

The two men went over to the car. Charlie got his shoulder underneath one of Scott's arms and essentially bench-pressed him out of the car. This was no mean feat; Scott had to weigh at least 200 pounds. He wasn't big, but he was taller than both Joe and Charlie. Joe got underneath the other arm and then both men picked up a leg, and they carried their colleague up the garage stairs and into the house.

"I made up the sofa bed here in the family room," Judy explained. "There's a bathroom close by and this way you won't have to carry him upstairs, and I won't have to deal with him in our bed." She pulled down the covers and the two men gently deposited Scott on the clean white sheets. "You go on now. I'm sorry this interrupted your evening."

Charlie hugged Judy. "Now, don't worry. Will you call if you need anything? You have my number?"

"Yes, I'll call. Thank you, again." She walked them to the garage. Charlie hugged her again, and Joe did, too, feeling the occasion merited a little warmth. She watched them until they cleared the area of the garage door and as they turned to wave goodbye, the door slowly closed. Judy was left with the unenviable task of dealing with a spouse destined to wake up in the morning with a nasty hangover and two or three more days of hard work ahead of him, followed by unemployment.

Chapter Fourteen

Joe and Charlie didn't speak as they walked to the car. Charlie started up his car and shifted into first gear before speaking. "That wasn't much fun. How drunk was he?"

"So drunk he couldn't decide whether it would be better to poison or shoot the Director."

"I don't have an opinion on the method but I'd pay money to see him get his just rewards after today," Charlie joked.

"Me, too. This has been one long day."

Charlie turned on the radio and they listened to Michael Stype singing about *The End of the World as We Know It*, until Charlie turned back into the parking lot across the street from the Fox, scoring the last free space.

Inside Katherine had arrived and staked out a place for them at their favorite 4-top table in the corner. She waved and they wound their way through the now-crowded restaurant area, sinking gratefully into chairs. Sloughing off coats, hats, and gloves, they piled their stuff on top of Katherine's in the extra chair. Sylvia came over to the table to get their orders. "Thanks, Joe. That's one less patron to worry about tonight."

Charlie, Joe, and Katherine all ordered beers and the three friends decided to see if they could polish off one of the Fox's famous wing-buckets. The beers arrived with incredible speed, and Sylvia murmured, "First round is on me."

Joe and Charlie drank as Katherine spoke, "Okay, spill. All Sylvia said was you had to take someone home from the bar."

"Scott Theodore." Joe began the story. "When I got here he was at the bar and, according to Sylvia, he had been drinking pretty steadily since late afternoon. Scott told me the Director had called him in on the carpet and told him to be prepared to clean out his desk first thing Monday morning."

Katherine was incredulous. "I can't believe it. He fired his event planner effective just after the gala? Why didn't Scott just walk? It's what I would have done in that situation."

"Ah, that's the diabolical part - the Director said Scott will only get a severance package if he does a good job on the gala."

"Can that be legal?"

Joe shrugged.

Katherine turned to Charlie. "Did you see Judy? How's she doing?"

"Well, it isn't the first time she's had to wait for someone to bring him home in that condition. Hell, it isn't even the first time she's seen me bring him home in that condition. I think, to be honest, she was so worried about him that the whole losing his job aspect of the situation hasn't even kicked in yet. I wouldn't want to be a guest at breakfast tomorrow in the Theodore household."

About that time, a member of the wait staff arrived with a monstrous pick-up-truck-sized bucket full of meaty, juicy chicken wings that had been marinated and flash-fried, and then dipped in the cook's tasty but lip-numbing secret hot sauce. The bucket came to the table with a load of accessories - crisp celery, carrots, and green onions; a pint of blue cheese dressing; extra sauce to dip; bone plates and a stack of napkins. It certainly wasn't date food, but it was very satisfying. Charlie and Katherine had been friends for a long time, and they'd welcomed Joe into their group soon after his arrival at the museum. There was no uncomfortable dynamic - all three were hungry and thirsty after their long day. They dug in and attacked the food with gusto.

A short while later, their hunger sated, the three relaxed with their beers in companionable silence. Again, Katherine was the first to speak. "Who wants to begin with their version of the *Ballad of the Bad, Bad, Day?*"

Joe smiled and bowed his head. "Ladies first." Charlie nodded in agreement.

"No. No. I couldn't possibly, and besides, Charlie was privy to a lot of my bad day. Why don't you start and give us some reason to think 'well at least my day wasn't as bad as Joe's?'"

"Where do I begin?" Joe told his friends about the initial morning run-in with PFM, and related the conversation he and Charlie had overheard in the hall. Then Charlie and Joe gave a joint retelling of the morning's cafe adventure that ended up with all three of them laughing so hard that a swallow of beer went down Katherine's throat the wrong way. Joe pounded her on the back until she stopped coughing. She wiped her eyes with a napkin and motioned him to continue.

"I'm all right now."

"After his verbal assault on the ladies at the next table, he came over to give me a message for you Charlie. Let's see if I can remember his exact words. 'Tell your technology friend he better stop messing around and get my home computer fixed, pronto.'"

Charlie flushed and said a rude word. He bitterly resented any slurs on his own effectiveness or that of his department.

Joe picked up the narrative again. "Later in the afternoon, I duly arrived at his office a few minutes early, unfortunately, just in time to witness some very unfriendly husband and wife sniping. Elizabeth came out of his office in a fury and sailed past me as if I didn't even exist."

"She's as bad as he is, if not worse." Katherine's unkind comment surprised Joe. Katherine got along with almost everyone.

"Not really her fault, is it, Kathy?" Charlie asked. "You'd be that way, too, if you were married to him."

"First of all, Charlie, I wouldn't be married to him. Second of all, I've known Beth for a long time. We were in high school together. Beth's pretty to look at, but every bit as mean and nasty as the Director. She and her older brothers were the kinds of kids who tortured animals - rocks, sticks, BB guns, slingshots, magnifying glass - whatever they could use to make something or someone miserable. They practiced until they were perfect. And if there were no animals to torture, they turned their attention to the other kids in the neighborhood."

Charlie stared at Katherine with his mouth hanging open. "You never told me that before!"

She turned and glared at him and in an unusually cold and clipped voice replied, "You never asked, did you? Beth and I weren't fond of one another in school and now that she's a grand lady and I'm a peon, she doesn't acknowledge our public school past or the fact that she got her start at the museum as a part-timer in my department. The guys in our high school couldn't see beyond those legs and that chest, and it's been my experience that grown men who should know better aren't any different," Katherine trailed off.

Joe and Charlie were both astonished. This was not the Katherine they were used to on an every-day basis. Charlie tried to lighten the atmosphere with a joking "Meee-owww."

Katherine turned on him. "Get screwed, Charlie. All a good-looking woman has to do is open her baby-blues wide and you assume she's helpless and in need of rescuing. Beth has never needed rescuing in her entire life. She's a blood-sucking parasite." Katherine had her face close to Charlie's, nearly hissing the last words. Charlie's face had flushed, again, a sure sign he was going to fight back, and Joe decided it was time to step in.

"Hey, guys. Woo-hoo, remember me? I'm telling this story. Can we forget the Director's wife for the moment and move on?" His friends leaned back in their chairs and picked up their beers. He saw them minimally relax, but they weren't looking at one another. He wondered, not for the first time, if there was or had been some kind of relationship other than friendship between the two.

"After Elizabeth stalked out, Mabel ushered me into his majesty's office, where my request to do further research into early acquisitions was denied." His friends commiserated with him - they knew how much the project meant because he seldom stopped talking about it. "Not only am I not to do the work, I'm never to mention my doubts about any of the paintings ever." He went on to tell them about his conversation with the Director about Rita's centennial gift and his own doubts about the painting. "And then," he finished this part of the story, "as I left his office he suggested that if I wanted to keep my job, I should keep my mouth shut."

Sylvia came up to the table at that point and they all ordered another round of beers. She cleared the empty glasses and the remains of the wing massacre and took herself off to fill their order. Charlie gave a low whistle, "So that's why you looked so angry when you arrived at my office."

"But wait, I'm not finished yet. Later in the afternoon I had my weekly meeting with PFM, who'd already been briefed by the Director on my bad behavior. She ripped into me and she too suggested it might be a good idea to get my resume in order. So, Katherine, to return to your earlier request for a ballad, it looks like the chorus of mine is 'I woke up with a job I thought was sweet, and at the end of the day it's no better than dog meat.'"

Katherine laughed. "Don't leave your day job anytime soon to work as a lyricist, Joe." The next round of beers arrived and Charlie excused himself to go to the men's room.

Joe decided to ask Katherine a question he'd been thinking about asking her for the past few days. "Katherine, are you invited to the gala?"

"Who, me? I'm basically at the hired help level, no invites for me, although I don't have any duties to perform once the whole shebang gets started - at that point the producer takes over. Why?"

"Would you be my date for the gala? I'm allowed to take a guest."

Katherine looked at him curiously. "Really, Joe?"

"I'd like to go with someone who is a friend, who understands the museum, who feels a part of the museum, and who is fun to be with. And besides, if I have to choose between you and Charlie, I'd bet you look a darn sight better in an evening gown than he does. What do you say?"

Katherine smiled at him. "I say, yes. What the heck, I'd love to be your date, Dr. Cocktail."

Joe saw Charlie heading back to the table and said quickly, "We can discuss the details tomorrow at work, okay?"

"Sure," agreed Katherine as Charlie eased back into his seat.

Chapter Fifteen

Joe drank. "I'm finished with my story. Who's next?"

Charlie raised his glass to Katherine. "Your turn, lady."

"Thank you."

Joe was relieved; all seemed to be forgiven. At least for now the two had decided to let bygones be bygones.

"I'll tell my story, but Joe, you will just have to understand that there are cryptic bits I have to leave out. Part of my story is also part of Charlie's story, so he can jump in when necessary. This gala is a huge event for the Director. Not every museum director has the opportunity to celebrate a museum's centennial, so this is a big deal in every way. He is sparing no expense to have every detail just exactly the way he wants it and, as we all know, he is a demon micro-manager. Of course he knows he can do everyone else's job as well or better than they can because otherwise he wouldn't be the top dog.

"Without giving you too much information, Joe, the Director had a BIG IDEA a few weeks ago," Katherine heavily emphasized the words as she spoke. "And without discussing it with staff, or "as far as I can tell with anyone familiar with productions and how they get done, or with the head of Information Technology," she nodded here at Charlie, "or any of the people who know how computers and high-end technology systems work - he went ahead and hired a firm out of New York City to come in and design a stage set for a production, or rather a 'happening' as an opener for the gala. Last Friday - probably around the time you were being introduced to your pseudo-renaissance Virgin, Joe -Charlie and I were called into a meeting with the Director and this truly annoying consultant from the New York firm."

Charlie interrupted her. "Wait, wait. You aren't supposed to call him a consultant - he's the Producer."

"This means," and now Katherine's voice was heavy with sarcasm, "that Mr. Producer sits in MY office with his feet up on MY desk, ordering take-out and talking on a cell phone that is permanently attached to his ear. His backside is clearly and permanently attached to MY chair. I am called in to deal with the pissy little details, and, meanwhile, my crew is close to rebellion. They had to work double overtime over the Thanksgiving weekend, and the outside contractors are treating them like know-nothing hicks. And, in addition to the staff issues, I haven't been able to get the representatives from the city hall down here to actually approve the construction taking place. Because the construction is only temporary, the Producer tells me 'not to worry about permits and things, baby doll.' Baby doll, grrr."

Katherine stopped to take a breath and a drink and went on with her story. "Meanwhile, the Director is sticking his aquiline nose into construction areas every 5-10 minutes and asking for regular progress updates. And if that isn't enough, the entire project is so insanely arrogant that I am embarrassed to have anything to do with the production. Professionally, I am going to have to go hide under a rock for a year or two until all my colleagues forget, and I'm afraid they'll never forget. I was late getting here tonight because one of my last instructions from the Producer was to round up 30 costumes for... Wait, I can't tell you what kind of costumes they are or what they are for." She put her hand over her eyes for a moment.

"The whole thing is just insane, and the only upside I can see right now is at least I don't have to go back tonight, so I can get a little sleep. Tomorrow is going to be grueling, and the only thing that is keeping me from losing my mind completely is the fact that the Director will be occupied with the accessions committee meeting for most of the afternoon. If you told me to jump off a cliff right now, I probably wouldn't do it, but if you told me to push the Director and his producer friend off the cliff, I'd gladly oblige."

Both men laughed at that, and Joe couldn't help but feel empathetic. *I don't want to push him off a cliff, but I wouldn't mind the opportunity for a fair fight.* He quite fancied the idea of popping him one across the jaw and wiping the smile off that superior face. Joe guessed that Charlie felt the same way, if not more so - he'd been around the museum longer and had just as many reasons to dislike the Director.

Meanwhile, Katherine had finished her story and she looked toward Charlie. "How was your day? Anything you'd care to add to our list of complaints?"

"Well, there is actually a lot I'd care to add, but I'm not sure it would mean anything at this point. The list of crimes perpetrated by the Director today, at least in my book, include: running two of my guys out of the cafeteria, because he wanted a place to sit; snarky comments about me to Joe; and belittling Joe and threatening his job when certain ethical suggestions were floated towards him. But I guess my primary complaint about this guy is bigger than the sum of all these individual complaints. He's not a leader. He's not someone who motivates or inspires others to excel at their jobs. And, I think he's a bully. Yep. That pretty much covers it. Not only is he a bully, but he's an even bigger bully than the bullies he surrounds himself with."

Joe considered his friend's statement. "You know, Charlie, you've hit the nail right on the head. He is a bully. Most of us began working at museums," here he nodded at Katherine, "or in the performing arts, because of a love and passion for our disciplines. Our jobs at the museum ought to be fantastic. And they ought to be fantastic on a daily basis. We are privileged to work with the cultural heritage of the world." Joe realized he had stepped up on a soapbox, but he had just enough alcohol and adrenaline in his system to keep up the momentum, and he was excited about what he was about to articulate. "Part of what I object to about this guy is he doesn't seem to even like the collections. He takes no joy in that pivotal part of his responsibility.

"What did Scrooge's nephew say to Scrooge about his feelings for Christmas? *'And therefore, uncle, though it has never put a scrap of gold or silver in my pocket, I believe that it has done me good, and will do me good; and I say, God bless it!'* That's the way I feel about working with art - and I assume everyone who works in a museum at least started out feeling that way or they wouldn't stay there. The pay isn't great, but the rewards of doing something you believe in are worth something. Working at an art museum is a labor of love for most of us."

Joe continued, "He doesn't care about the art and he doesn't pay any attention to the people who work for him, unless it's negative attention. How fantastic would it be to work for someone who cared about the people, the art, and the institution? Someone who came in to work cheerful most mornings, looking for opportunities to showcase works and people."

Charlie was smiling at Joe. "Dude. You need to be a director."

Katherine added her piece. "The Director doesn't want you to talk at the accessions meeting tomorrow, Joe, because he's afraid of you. You're a natural leader with a passion for objects and stories and you can communicate it to others. The Director and Prue are both terrified the new guy is going to come in and make them look bad. It's probably worse for Prue than the Director, because you're the next generation curator snapping at her heels, and she's not ready to lie down and let you run over her. And speaking of being run over, I feel like road kill after the day I've had and I'm going home to try to get some sleep. I'll see you guys tomorrow." She opened her handbag to get her wallet out and Charlie put his hands over hers. "Put it away, tonight's on me, guys."

"Thanks, Charlie. You are a good guy. Mostly." She grinned at him as she put on her coat and gave both of them quick hugs, then was out the door and into the night.

Joe considered having another beer. "What do you think? One more? Or shall we call it a night?"

"Let's call it a night. We have to maintain some stamina for tomorrow; it's going to be a long day." Charlie looked over at the bar and caught Sylvia's eye. "Check," he mouthed, and made a signing motion with his hand. She nodded, and in a very few minutes the two were out the door, in their cars, and on the way to their respective homes.

Chapter Sixteen

Joe pulled carefully into the narrow driveway that separated the building he lived in from the adjacent Mexican restaurant. Once in the back yard, he had to get out of his car to manually open the tiny garage. Since his car was a prize possession, some kind of living arrangement with a private garage had been a necessity. Joe wasn't taking any chances with big apartment parking lots where careless owners slammed their car doors into his carefully maintained paint job. He knew he was a trifle neurotic about his car, but it had been a gift from an uncle, one of the few family members who understood Joe's desire to study art history. His family, on both sides, had engineers, scientists, and finance people - all those left-brains loved him, but didn't really understand Joe's obviously right-brain way of thinking.

He pulled his car into the garage and threw her cover over her. Joe thought of the car as a woman and had even named her "Kate," one of his favorite names, after the character in Shakespeare's "Taming of the Shrew." Kate was a temperamental car and Joe did everything he could to keep her on an even keel. He closed and locked the garage and then headed back across the yard to the rickety old staircase that led to his apartment above a charity thrift store in an old 1920s building. Joe's was one of three apartments in the building - one tiny apartment, not much more than a studio, behind the thrift store, and a pair of two-bedroom apartments above, each running the full-length of the building over half of the store. Both the studio and one of the two bedrooms had been available when he was looking for a place to live. Joe had briefly considered the studio, but in the end had chosen the roomier apartment above.

He quickly ran up the stairs to his back door. The lights were off next door. Mr. and Mrs. Watson, who managed the thrift store for a local charity, lived in the larger of the two apartments, and now used the smaller apartment behind the store for storage, a small office for book-keeping. They had even carved out a space for Joe to keep his free weights after he'd nearly frightened Mrs. Watson to death one morning when he'd lost his grip and let the heavy weights fall to the floor. She had been certain a meteor had struck the apartment next door.

The Watsons were good neighbors. Mrs. Watson was always trying to fatten him up with some goodie or another that she'd baked. She didn't actually believe that a single man was capable of caring for himself and was constantly introducing him to a niece or daughter of a friend who she thought might be a suitable partner for a bachelor. And an unanticipated benefit of living next door to Mrs. Watson and above a thrift store had been the significant improvement in his wardrobe. Mrs. Watson had a keen eye for what might fit Joe and since moving in he'd been able to purge his wardrobe of a lot of cheap clothes purchased as a graduate student and replace them with finely made clothes purchased at a fraction of the original price.

Joe unlocked the door and entered the apartment. *I really did luck into a sweet situation here.* The rent was minimal because the Watsons simply wanted nice responsible neighbors. The fact that Joe was gainfully employed at the art museum had seemed to reassure them that he would fit the bill. Joe's back door opened directly into a tiny kitchen, not much room to move around, but good enough for his needs. He set his laptop bag down on the small kitchen counter.

Directly through the kitchen was the dining room. It had huge windows, which overlooked the wall of the Mexican restaurant next door. Not much of a view, but they let some light in on sunny days. Located on either side of the windows were built-in storage cabinets with leaded glass shelves. A doorway adjacent to the kitchen door led into a smaller bedroom that Joe used as his study or a guest room when there were guests to be accommodated. On the opposite side of the room yet another doorway opened to a long hallway that led to the living room at the front of the apartment. Two doors opened off the hallway, one to his bathroom with its antique claw-foot tub - a pain to try to shower in, but very impressive to look at -and another to his bedroom, which didn't allow space for much more than a bed, a dresser, and a tiny closet.

The selling point for this apartment had been the living room. A large bow-front window overlooked the street below. The room was wide and gracious, and best of all it had more built-ins, this time bookshelves, and a working fireplace. The only downside - he had to carry firewood up from the storage area beneath the staircase leading to the back door. On the wall opposite the fireplace was his front door. The door led to a small landing. Across the landing was the front door to the Watson's apartment, but neither used the front staircase except to pick up mail.

Joe kept a few Duraflame logs in the bottom of a capacious storage closet at the top of the front staircase. Both he and the Watsons had keys to this closet and they used it for odds and ends. Though it had been a long day, it wasn't really late. Joe grabbed one of the commercial logs and started a fire. He opted against pouring himself a nightcap. *I could check my email, or better yet take a quick hot shower.* His muscles felt tight and he needed to work out; no time for that over the next few busy days. He moved into the bedroom and set his alarm clock for an obscenely early wake-up call. *I'll get up and run.* The location of his run would depend upon the weather. He didn't mind running in the cold, but he hated fighting cars and slush. With that decision made he headed for the tub.

A few minutes later, he toweled dry and made a dash for his bedroom, keeping close to the wall. There was a place in the hallway, near the bedroom, where he could see out the front windows of his apartment. And if he could look out then someone else could look in. Just across the street there was a high-rise apartment building for senior citizens. He'd forgotten his bathrobe and he had no interest in providing peep show opportunities. He found a pair of flannel pajama bottoms and a long-sleeved t-shirt and grabbed the Inspector Appleby mystery he was reading. To do so, he had to reach over a tall stack of scholarly journals, which sat on the floor next to his nightstand. *The journal stack stands as a grim sentinel of my laziness. The taller it gets the worse I feel. Stacks of work to read at home, stacks to read at work.* Joe sighed.

Instead of a nightcap, he poured himself a glass of milk, tossed the empty carton into the trash, and grabbed a handful of cookies. Then he realized what he'd done. *Empty carton no milk for coffee in the morning. Why didn't I remember to pick up milk at the store earlier this evening? Rats.* He took his late night snack into the living room, placing them on a small round occasional table kept just for that purpose. He pulled his one significant luxury, a burgundy leather wing chair and ottoman, close to the fire.

Joe's living room was also his library. The bookshelves on either side of the fireplace were populated with his favorite books - both those he used for reference and those he read for pleasure. The top of the bookshelves was at the same height as the mantel, and in the same wood -the builders had made one continuous display shelf across the entire wall. Joe had found a severe-looking antique mirror in the thrift shop and stripped off the white paint to reveal a dark cherry finish that just happened to match the bookshelves. The tops of the shelves were finished with a plate groove at the back, and Joe, for the first time as an adult, had a place to display his small collection of 20th century French prints, pride of place going to Erik Desmazieres' meticulous, fantastic, and sublimely ridiculous *Wunderkammer II.*

He had just settled in and was reading one of Michael Innes's evocative descriptions of a country manor house, when the phone rang. Joe looked up at the clock on the mantel, 11:15 pm. *Wonder who could be calling me at this hour?*

He picked the phone up. "Joe Cocktail here."

"Joe. It's Charlie. Can you come down to the museum?"

"Right now? What's wrong?"

"I'd rather not discuss it on the phone. Will you just come? Security will meet you at the gate and escort you in."

"Charlie? Is everything okay?" Joe felt his adrenaline rise.

"Joe, just get here."

"Okay, I'm on my way."

Chapter Seventeen

Joe quickly discarded pajama bottoms, replacing them with a pair of blue jeans. He threw a heavy sweater on over the t-shirt and grabbed a ski jacket. Whatever had happened Charlie hadn't sounded as if Joe needed to be in a coat and tie. He decided it was okay to let the log burn down - he moved the fire screen in front of it to block any sparks that might fly. No sense in burning down the apartment house. He left a couple of lights on and headed out to his car.

On the way to the museum, he realized he'd left his phone at home. *No matter. There are phones at the museum.* Randy, one of the museum's security staff, was waiting for him at the parking garage entrance. He got into the passenger side of the car when Joe drove up and called ahead to the security desk.

"Okay, I'm with Joe, raise the gate to the parking ramp would you? We'll be right there."

"What's up, Randy?"

"I better let Sarge and Charlie tell you - I haven't seen the mess yet."

"Mess, what mess?"

"Oh, damn. Didn't Charlie tell you anything? There's been an accident in your office."

"Accident? In my office? What kind of accident? Has anyone been hurt?"

"No one has been hurt. Just relax, Joe. We'll get it all sorted."

Joe parked in a spot close to the security entrance, locked his car, and the two men walked to the door where they were buzzed in by the night staff. Charlie and Sergeant Pat, the head of museum security, were waiting for him in the secure lobby area, where visitors to the museum normally waited until their escorts from the museum staff came to fetch them. Both men were looking grim and Joe felt his stomach flip.

"Charlie, Pat, for God's sake, will somebody tell me what's happened?"

Sgt. Pat answered, "We aren't quite sure, Joe. Sometime during the late afternoon the security cameras stopped recording traffic in office areas - and my staff seems to have been so busy escorting the various contractors for this event on Saturday night, that no one knows exactly what happened or when. What time did you leave tonight, Joe?"

"Sometime just around 7:00 pm - don't you know that from my security swipe?"

"Yes, I'm just checking. And everything was okay when you left? You didn't see anything or anyone in the halls near storage area four, I mean your office?"

"No, no one. My sense was that everyone had pretty much gone home."

"Somebody did some serious damage to some of the files stored in your office and, because of the security camera glitch, we don't have anything on tape. There were still lots of people at the museum after 7:00 p.m. because of this blasted gala, any number of whom might have had access to that hallway, some who had required escorts, some who didn't."

"Can't you tell who entered my office via the keypad lock?"

"Well, we could, except your office was originally a storage room with general administrative level security, not to mention the maintenance code."

"What maintenance code?" This was the first Joe had heard of a special maintenance code.

"The override that all the cleaners have so they can get into offices."

"What?" For the umpteenth time that day Joe voiced that word.

Both of the other men looked sheepish. Again Sgt. Pat answered for the pair, "It's a widely-known secret code, guess no one bothered to tell you about it yet. It doesn't work for actual permanent collection storage, but your space is now considered regular office space."

"But my object files are in there." Joe was aware of a big silence in the room.

"Not the object files, please tell me it's not the object files?" He looked at the two men pleadingly.

Charlie said, "Don't worry, Joe. You put all the relevant information in the database already."

"Charlie. You don't understand. The object files aren't about data. I can't explain now. Let's go. I need to see what's happened." He looked to Sgt. Pat. "Who else have you called? Have you checked any of the other curatorial offices?"

"Charlie called you, while I called Al. I figured you'd maybe want someone from conservation here. He's on his way. We are continuing to check each of the areas of the museum, office by office - as of right now your office is the only place we've found a problem. Charlie, you go on with Joe and I'll wait here for Al."

Charlie opened the door leading into the museum and the two set off for Joe's office. "Charlie, why did security call you first?"

"They called me when they discovered the glitch with the security cameras. Thought that maybe the computers had gone down and that had shut the cameras down too."

"Was that what happened?"

"I don't think so, Joe. The cameras were shut off on purpose. You knew people were pissed at you today. Hard to believe any of them would take measures to this extreme."

"How extreme?" Joe was starting to feel light-headed and he barely remembered the walk to his office. He punched in the code on the security keypad and opened the door. The smell of cleaning solvent was so powerful he reeled back for a moment, and then Joe held his breath, and walked in. Joe glanced at his desk, still neat and ordered, as he'd left it, but moved quickly to two large, wooden file cabinets, with copper-paneled fronts. The file cabinets were so old they'd probably been part of the museum's original furniture. Joe loved them and loved keeping his files in them - it made him feel a part of the continuity of history at the museum. The cabinets were tipped forward like a pair of old drunks. The drawers were standing open - all of the drawers. These cabinets were old enough so they either didn't have the mechanisms, like newer models, that allowed for only one drawer open at a time, or the mechanisms were broken.

Next to one of the file cabinets was a large, empty container that must have held whatever had been poured onto the files. It certainly hadn't been there when Joe had left for the day. There were pools of liquid on the floor. He started to pick up the bottle and thought better of it. Joe turned around and walked to his desk. He opened one of the drawers and pulled out a couple of pairs of white art-handling gloves he kept inside.

Charlie explained the situation. "One of the security guards on his rounds noticed the smell when he opened the door and the puddles at the bottom of the file cabinets. He opened a couple of the drawers, noticed that the papers were soaked, and immediately alerted Sgt. Pat. I was already on my way back to the museum by the time they discovered the mess here. Sgt. Pat called me and I called you."

Joe turned back to the files. The folders and the documents within them were soaked with solvent; the smell was so powerful he had to back away from the drawer and felt like retching - for any number of reasons. There was a puddle of liquid spreading out from the bottom of the file cabinets. He had an idea. *There might still be some way to salvage this situation.* He turned to his friend.

"Charlie. Find out from Sgt. Pat if I can start moving stuff out of these cabinets. If I can, I need a mask so I don't have to breathe this stuff, and some rubber gloves. Oh. And you know those towel-drying racks down by the washers and dryers where the cleaners work?"

Charlie nodded and headed toward the door.

"See if you can get Sgt. Pat and his night guys to bring me a couple of those, and drying equipment, fans, dehumidifiers, and vacuums. And Charlie..."

Charlie turned back.

"Charlie, thanks for calling me as soon as you did. We may not be in as bad a shape as I think."

"That's great, Joe. I sure hope you're right, but I don't like the looks of this one bit."

Joe turned serious. "I know what you mean. Whoever did this is crazy - even if they don't like me personally, why would they try to destroy the museum records?" Joe was talking to himself at this point as Charlie had started off to find Sgt. Pat and get the rescue effort moving. Joe looked at his watch, 12:15. He spoke out loud to himself, "Well Joe, it's past the witching hour, you better get to work. Looks like it's going to be a relatively long night for me."

"But at least you won't be alone." Al stood in the doorway.

"Al, boy oh boy, am I glad to see you."

"I'm sure you are. I saw Charlie in the hallway - he told me what he was off to do. Let's see what the situation looks like." Joe offered him his gloves, but Al declined, pulling a pair of latex gloves from his pocket. "Never without my own, you know, it's an occupational habit."

Joe pointed out the empty solvent bottle on the floor. After seeing what it was, a look of concern swept over the conservator's face. "Someone sure did want to do some damage here." He read from the label, "Cohesive Ink and Dye Stripper. Must have come from the design and installation workshop. Let's hope we are in time to minimize the amount of damage done. We will do what triage we can tonight, and then tomorrow, I'll get the paper conservator to examine the documents to see what, if anything, further needs to be done. In a worst-case scenario, Joe, if this stuff starts eating through the papers, we may have to line up some volunteers to scan everything so at least we have a record of what existed. But, let's not worry about that until we have to.

"The good news is your files are packed in so tightly that the solvent may not have been able to seep between the individual pages. And, it's a quick-drying solvent so that ought to work in our favor. If it had been water, we'd only have 48 to 72 hours to dry things out before mold would start to set in - that's not a concern with this solvent, but I am concerned about it eating through the paper. Some of the documents are going to be completely lost. Some have suffered damage, but most of them will still be legible and useful. My big fear now is that there might be solvent pooled up at the bottom of these drawers and eating into folders from the bottom up, so here's what we are going to do." And Al quickly outlined his triage plan - as soon as supplies arrived, Joe would start carefully removing folders and hand them to Al, who would do whatever first-level intervention was necessary to save the bulk of the papers.

Soon afterwards Sgt. Pat arrived with several of his security officers, carrying fans, a wet vac from the installation department, the drying racks, and a couple of industrial-size trash containers. When Charlie arrived half an hour later with cups of coffee and a box of donuts from the local shop, Al and Joe and the two security officers that Sgt. Pat was able to spare from the night duty by doing their rounds himself, had an assembly line in place. "Caffeine and sugar for us all," announced Charlie. "We've got a long night ahead. Joe, if you don't need me here, I'd like to do a little more digging to see what I can find out about the security cameras?"

"Go ahead, Charlie. We've got things under control here," Joe answered on behalf of his team. They all stopped briefly to drink the hot coffee and eat the doughnuts, while Al outlined a strategy to deal with the disaster. Charlie's caffeine and sugar did the trick; a few minutes later the newly energized salvage team set to work.

Chapter Eighteen

Just before dawn Joe handed Al the last of the folders. Every usable surface of the room was covered with drying papers. Only one of the two industrial size garbage containers had been necessary for unsalvageable papers and debris from the clean-up effort.

Joe helped the two security guards return the fans and the wet vac to their appropriate locations in the museum. He thanked both men profusely, and they assured him it had been a nice change from walking through the galleries all night. Nevertheless, he resolved to do something nice for them. The security guards took the garbage bags off with them and Joe collapsed in the chair in front of his desk; Al was seated in the desk chair. "Al, I don't know what to say. You saved the day."

"We saved it, Joe. It was teamwork. You'd already started making the right decisions when I arrived. I suggest we tell Sgt. Pat to lock this room up and, just to be safe, I'll have him change the code for your office. I think it's safe now, but wouldn't want to take any chance of losing tonight's work. Now, it's time to get home and grab a few quick hours of sleep; we'll both need to be back in here in a few hours." Companionably, they finished the last dregs of the now-cold coffee and Al took his leave. Joe put the sweater he'd shed back on and picked up his coat. He wondered if Charlie was still around.

He made his way to the Information Technology offices. The hallway was dark, but he could see a dim light burning in Charlie's office. He found his friend, head down on his arms asleep at his desk, with some kind of program running on his desktop. "Hey Charlie, wake up."

Charlie came instantly awake. He yawned widely, stretched his arms, and asked, "Hey Joe, what time is it?"

"Almost dawn, time to go home for a few hours."

"Is everything okay? Where's Al?"

"Already gone. We managed to salvage almost all the important bits - due in large part to the fast thinking of you and Sgt. Pat."

"That's great, Joe." Charlie yawned another enormous yawn. "We better get home and grab some shuteye. Hope today is better for both of us than yesterday."

"I don't see how it can get any worse," said Joe, but as he left the office he made sure to knock on wood.

A few hours later, following a brief rest, another shower, and after swallowing a double-espresso and grabbing two extra-large coffees to go, Joe was back at the museum. He left one of the large coffees with Charlie's assistant and took the other one to the security office. Sgt. Pat was sitting at his desk, looking tired but in command. "How'd it go last night, Sarge?"

"I learned something, Joe. I learned I've got to bring some more comfortable shoes to work.

I've been sitting at a desk too long and I wasn't prepared for my late night hike. I'm out of shape. How are you? Are you feeling better?"

"Well, I'm still angry and puzzled, but with Al's help we managed to save the most important papers. Can I get someone to go with me and let me into the office?"

"Sure, but I think Al and his team are already down there. He came back about an hour ago, and they've been ferrying loads of papers up to the conservation lab while you snoozed, Sleeping Beauty. I'll walk down there with you, then I'm off to my home and my own bed."

Joe's small office was a beehive of activity. Al was directing a couple of conservation interns about the order in which remaining items were to be removed from the office. "Hey, Joe. Welcome back. We've got almost everything upstairs at this point. I'm going to need you to spend some time up in the paper studio next week organizing things once we get everything dry and stabilized. There's a tiny silver lining to this situation. I've an idea that this might just make a useful case study in disaster preparedness protocols for the American Institute for Conservation."

"I doubt that too many museums have 'accidents' with industrial solvents and wish we weren't the test case, but you're right. We certainly managed the crisis efficiently once we got started."

"We did, but it does raise a lot of questions about what we could have done even better." Al was clearly in full diagnostic mode this morning. "Let's have lunch next week and go through this all again. I think there is really a lesson here that can be shared with colleagues in the field. By the way, if I were you, I wouldn't work in here this morning. I don't think there is any danger from residual fumes, but my people will probably be in and out, and security too. Got somewhere else to go? The library, perhaps?"

"Sure, why not, a change of scenery might be helpful." Joe looked around and thought about what he needed to get done. The accessions committee meeting luncheon started around 1:00 p.m. *No comments to prepare for the accessions meeting. I'd like to do a little more due diligence on the new painting even if the Director and PFM want me to keep quiet about it in the meeting today. I can call Gianni.*

He looked at his watch. It was early afternoon already in Italy; Gianni should still be at his desk, unless he was off drinking an afternoon coffee or having a long lunch. Joe looked through his in-box until he found the small batch of papers relating to the painting that PFM had given him. He sat down at his laptop, turned it on, found Gianni's contact information, and made the call. His friend was happy to hear from him. They spent a few minutes catching up and then Joe moved on to the reason for his call. He asked his friend a series of questions, and a serious conversation ensued.

At the end of the phone call, Joe was more convinced than ever that the museum was in grave danger of accessioning a painting that wasn't what it was supposed to be. The origins of the painting were unclear. It was supposed to have come from a private collection belonging to a certain member of the impoverished Italian nobility. This kind of history, or provenance, was a classic front for doctored paintings in the early 20th century. Wealthy Americans traveling in Italy had loved the idea that they were acquiring works that had spent centuries in the great country villas and urban palazzi of the wealthy.

His friend wasn't familiar with this particular painting, but he knew of a half dozen similar cases in which private citizens or museum curators had purchased, or accepted as gifts, dubious works like the painting Joe described. Joe felt himself heading for a right or wrong moment, and he hadn't had enough sleep to feel like he was at the top of his decision-making game today. He thanked his friend and ended the phone call, turned off his laptop, and put it and several of the folders from his desk (enough to keep him busy throughout the morning) into his briefcase; he then headed for the library.

Chapter Nineteen

The library was Joe's favorite spot in the museum outside of the galleries, even if it was a little modern for his taste. The reading and study room was a clean space, long and sleek, with private carrels for the curators that held the books necessary for their immediate research needs. Joe's carrel, as one of the newest curators, was not in a prime spot, but he could see a bit of a view from a window by craning his neck around the side of the carrel, and the skylight let in natural light, a light tempered by the soft grey of clouds promising to dump more snow. The accessions meeting might go long, so at least he would miss rush hour.

He nodded at a couple of colleagues who looked up as he came through the door. The elderly and quite shy curator of Asian art, Shu, acknowledged him briefly, as did Kristina, the curator of prints and drawings, a terrific older woman, who gave Joe a big smile of welcome.

Wonder of wonders, Bradley Boehm was sitting at his carrel, concentrating on the book propped up in front of him. That was odd. Boehm's cubicle was crammed with books and magazines piled upon more books and magazines, bookmarks with brief notes in his indecipherable scribble hanging out at all angles - but as far as Joe could remember this was the first time he'd actually seen Boehm in the library. Must be something to do with the accessions committee meeting - Boehm was probably boning up on some colorful details for a presentation he was due to make. He didn't look up as Joe walked past.

Arriving at his own cubicle, Joe unpacked his laptop, plugged it in, and brought out the folders. He wasn't quite ready to launch into the followers of Caravaggio, so he decided to write up notes on what had happened the previous day. He opened a blank document and began typing everything he could remember about yesterday, not the early parts of the day, but what had happened after he'd gotten the call from Charlie and arrived at the museum the night before. He realized he hadn't really had time to think about what had happened until now. He pushed the laptop away for a moment, rested his chin on his hands, and considered the situation.

Everyone, or at least all the curatorial, conservation, and education staff, knew that he kept his object files in those old file cabinets in his office. That wasn't unusual - all of the curators kept object folders. As far as he knew nobody else's office had been vandalized and, in fact, his office hadn't been vandalized; only his object files. Joe couldn't escape the central issue - his object files had been the targets of the attack. Why? He'd been through all the documents in all those files, at least twice. There weren't any deep dark secrets in the folders about past donors, or insurance values, or shady dealings. The only secrets in those folders were the secrets that might be revealed by the further research he had suggested to the director yesterday, and obliquely to PFM, before she'd ordered him out of the office. Could either of them have been looking for any notes he might have made about the Pseudo Pier Francesco Fiorentino painting?

Surely, neither the Director nor a curator would have a hand in destroying object records. Besides, he wasn't even sure the Director knew where his office was. And PFM, as angry as she was with him for getting her into trouble with the Director, was too conscious of her duty to have a hand in this kind of vandalism. He shook his head. *Who had he angered so badly?* The three witches weren't his biggest fans - but he refused to believe that a registrar or librarian would ever sabotage a document, and he really didn't think the head of education disliked him any more than she disliked everyone else in the museum. He'd talk to Charlie later, if he got a chance, to see if he discovered anything. Right now, he was just spinning his wheels.

Just at that moment an excited graduate student who had been engaged in some research for him walked over to Joe. She'd discovered an alternative identification for the figure on a Renaissance medallion depicting *Mary, Queen of France*, by artist Jacopo de Trezzo. Joe, infected by the student's obvious enthusiasm, pushed last night's incident out of his mind and spent the better part of the next hour working with the student, and a reference librarian, to pull a selection of books and journal articles for the student to review. By lunchtime, Joe was feeling thoroughly refreshed - new research had that kind of impact on him. He was pleased to encourage any student with an interest in research. Bethany's ideas weren't unreasonable, and part of his job as a curator was to mentor the next generation.

Joe looked at his watch. He had just enough time to drop his stuff at the office and make sure he looked presentable before the accessions committee luncheon got under way. The Director required staff to put in an appearance in the boardroom a few minutes prior to an event for any last-minute instructions. As he headed downstairs, he decided to take a detour to Charlie's office to drop his laptop bag off, since it would save him a trip back to his own. There was no one around, but Charlie's door was open and Joe ducked inside.

There was a cabinet just inside the door that Joe had used for just such occasions in the past. Joe opened the cabinet and used his arm to make a space to place the case flat. The bag wouldn't sit flat and Joe reached in and felt a piece of fabric. He pulled it out only to discover he was holding a rather outrageously sheer woman's bra. He shook his head. *Naughty Charlie, or maybe it's a gift for a girlfriend? Oh well, it's none of my business.* He returned the garment to the cabinet, tucking it out of sight, and headed off to the boardroom.

Chapter Twenty

Joe was among the last of his colleagues to arrive in the boardroom. He slipped in the door and quickly into a chair. He looked around, slightly confused; almost the entire senior staff was present - not just the curators, registrars, and conservators, those who normally attended the accessions meetings - but the entire senior staff. He grinned at Charlie across the room. Soon the Director and PFM entered. The Dragon-Lady was right behind them. The Director was smiling, but not in a good way. Neither the Dragon-Lady nor PFM looked happy.

As the Director opened his mouth to begin speaking, the door next to Joe opened. Shu, the curator of Asian Art, and Kristina, the curator of Prints & Drawings, entered. The former looked embarrassed, the latter not at all. The Director watched them and the room was silent until the two had settled into their chairs. "Now that you've all decided to find time in your busy day to join the rest of us," the Director began his remarks. *Jerk,* thought Joe. *Nothing like gratuitous sarcasm to show real leadership.*

"After the accessions meeting there will be a press conference where I will be making some significant announcements with regard to the future of this museum. Some unprecedented decisions were made at a special meeting of the Executive Committee of the Board of Trustees this morning. These decisions may come as a surprise to many of you." Here he stopped and grinned, a little maliciously, at his staff. "So let me remind each and every one of you that you are at-will employees. You can leave at any time if you aren't happy." Joe noticed that Linda, the director of human resources, was nodding her head approvingly at the Director's statement. "I'd like all senior staff, even those without accessions committee responsibilities, to remain in their offices at the museum for a communication at the end of the day. No one is to leave early." A few staff members nodded their heads, while others simply look puzzled.

The Director continued, "Let me also remind you that the staff serves the museum, the museum does not exist to serve staff." Around the room, people's faces started to change, expressing outrage, fear, or concern depending upon the personality of the individual.

"That's all. And curators, your presence is requested in the private dining room at once. Those of you who have roles to play at the accessions committee meeting today, please keep your remarks brief and to the point." He looked around the room and let his eyes rest on Bradley Boehm for a moment. "Boehm, I am speaking specifically to you." Boehm flushed and managed to look both outraged and obsequious at the same time. The Director continued, "No displays or emotional tantrums today. Is that understood?"

Boehm muttered what might have been an affirmative.

110

"I'm sorry, Mr. Boehm, what was that you said?" The Director's voice was sharp.

"I will contain my remarks to those absolutely necessary," Boehm stated haughtily.

"Thank you. See that you do. And, before the end of the day tomorrow will you and the registrar please bring the *Helt Diadem* to my office?"

The room got absolutely quiet.

The *Helt Diadem* was a curious object from the museum's collection of decorative arts. Joe had never actually seen it on display. He'd only heard about it and seen pictures of it in early catalogues of the museum. The piece had come into the museum as a gift. Thin sheets of gold and gold wire had been used to create a vine of laurel leaves; woven among the leaves and wrapped in more gold wire were a series of rough, uncut emeralds. The diadem had been passed down through the donor's family, ostensibly since the late Middle Ages. In the photographs Joe had seen, the item looked like the kind of crown a Gaulish warrior prince might have worn proudly into battle, if Gaulish warrior princes had been silly enough to wear gold crowns into battle.

The diadem was seldom on display, because there were doubts regarding its authenticity. Most museums have objects that fall into this kind of gray area. Some come into collections with overly optimistic attributions, some are fakes or forgeries, others are simply not of a quality or in good-enough condition to display and, so, they languish in storage, carefully stored and wrapped in soft cocoons of acid free materials.

Gossipmongers at the museum whispered amongst themselves that the diadem was not actually kept in storage. Rumor had it that Boehm, with the permission of the registrar, kept the diadem in his office. Some even speculated that behind his closed office door, Boehm could often be found wearing the diadem.

"Why do you need the *Helt Diadem*?" asked Boehm.

Joe was a bit surprised at Boehm's boldness in challenging the Director.

"That's none of your business, Mr. Boehm."

The assembled group continued to collectively hold its breath.

"With all due respect, I'm the curator responsible for the object so it is precisely my business."

The Director replied silkily, "I don't think we are going to have this conversation in a public setting, Mr. Boehm. You will please do as directed. The rest of you have things you need to be doing as well. Please disperse."

With that, the Director turned around and left the room. He took no other questions and allowed for no other comments. PFM headed in the direction of the simmering Bradley Boehm and was joined by the registrar. Both women spoke rapidly in lowered voices, in response to which Boehm was shaking his head vigorously. The rest of the staff gave the little group wide berth.

Charlie walked across to join his friend. "Well, well, I wonder what that was all about?"

"Which bit?" asked Joe. "The request for the diadem, or the special meeting?"

Charlie responded, "Well, I can pretty much imagine why he wants the diadem. I'm more concerned about this special meeting.

Seems pretty clear that some of us are going to be looking for jobs in the near future. Happy 100th Anniversary to us." Charlie started humming the familiar birthday tune.

Joe wanted to ask Charlie about the Director's plans for the diadem, but had a more important question on his mind. "Listen, Charlie. I have to go to this luncheon and accessions meeting. Have you managed to find out anything about what happened last night?"

Charlie's expression became serious. "Three things. First, someone purposefully turned off all the cameras - and it wasn't a computer glitch - it was an upper-level admin command. Second, whoever it was hasn't left a trace that I've been able to find so far. They used an admin password and a security key, and I haven't been able to check if someone has hacked into the computers, or if some idiot was just a little too free with passwords. But, I'll find out. And three, whoever did it, was clever enough to cover their tracks. I found residue of some kind of sticky substance, maybe from a stamp or a mailing label, on the camera in the security office and the cameras in the halls leading to your office, as if someone had just slapped a temporary cover on the eye. I'd say it's definitely an inside job, but inside doesn't mean much right now with all these contractors wandering around the museum - not to mention you, me, and Katherine. The cameras in the security office and the halls were disabled early yesterday evening and Sgt. Pat discovered the problem around 10:30 p.m."

"I didn't attempt to destroy my files. Did you?"

"No!" Charlie sounded confident, but looked worried.

Just then, Katherine came over and joined the two men. "Wow, that was something else, wasn't it? You think we will all be out there looking for new jobs with Scott come Monday morning?"

"I'm pretty sure I will be," Joe replied glumly.

"Oh, lighten up, Joe, at least there's the gala to look forward to. Hey, would you mind picking me up around 5:00 p.m.? I have to come in to do a final sound check. Or, would you rather just meet here?"

Charlie was looking at them both curiously.

"I'll pick you up and I can get a little work done while you're tending to your duties. How 'bout I pick you up at 4:00 p.m., and we can grab a cup of coffee before we head in and give the folks at Starbucks a treat. They'll think we're off to a homecoming dance."

Katherine laughed. "That's almost a perfect plan. Instead of risking spillage on our fancy duds, let's bring them and change here at the museum?"

"Good call. That's a perfect plan." As she started to leave, Joe remembered a question he needed to ask her. "Wait, Katherine, what color are you wearing?"

She turned and looked down at her neat trousers and blouse – "Uh, black and white."

"No, goof, not now, Saturday night?"

"Oh," she laughed again, "blue."

"Right. Thanks."

"No problem," he said and made his way towards the door.

114

Charlie looked at Joe. "What was that all about?"

"Katherine wasn't invited as a guest to the gala, like we were, and I'm not dating anyone right now. I thought it might be fun to have her there. Is that okay? You and Katherine aren't an item, are you?"

"No, that's all in the past. I just wondered. I'm glad she's going to get to be a part of the front of the house; she's put in enough hours on this fiasco."

"Any chance you are ready to give me a hint at what you mean by fiasco?"

"Nope. My lips are sealed and, anyway, shouldn't you be headed off towards that luncheon?"

"Oh shoot, yes." Joe noticed that the room was almost empty of staff and certainly all the curators had cleared out. "I'd better get going. See you later."

Chapter Twenty-One

Joe hurried out of the boardroom and over to the private dining room. The wait staff was busy putting salads in front of everyone as Joe slid into the remaining chair. He glanced around the room and saw that both the Director and PFM had their eyes on him disapprovingly. *Screw it. I'm a good employee and I'm going to enjoy this lunch.* He re-introduced himself to the trustees seated on either side of him. On his right was an elderly attorney from a prominent law firm, partially deaf, and interested mostly in his meal. On his left, the youngish scion of a wealthy family, known more for her social connections than her interest in art, who was being groomed by the museum for a more prominent position on the board.

Having greeted the elderly attorney, no more was required from him on that front, except for an occasional response to a request for salt & pepper, or to pass the butter dish for the fresh popovers being handed round. A waitress offered to pour Joe a glass of wine, but he declined, feeling like he wanted all his wits about him for the events of the afternoon.

He and the youngish scion discussed mutual acquaintances and compared holiday schedules. She asked him about the collection and he, remembering she was a pet lover, asked about her dogs. This conversation carried them through the salad and main course - the ubiquitous breast of chicken with *chevre*, baby vegetables, and mashed potatoes that had been forced into an unnatural shape. Unfortunately, the potatoes looked to Joe like a fanciful pile of intestines.

With the advent of dessert, miniature petits fours and the coffee service, the Director stood and reviewed the schedule of events for the remainder of the afternoon. After luncheon, he intoned, the group would repair to the education gallery where all of the works under consideration were on display. Trustees and accession committee members would have a chance to look at the objects, and curators would be on hand to point out salient features and answer questions. After 30-40 minutes of this activity, the group would return to the boardroom and proceed through the agenda, voting on items to accession and, in a very few cases today, to deaccession. Afterwards, the curators with new works, and trustees on the accessions committee, would take part in a brief press conference. Staff members were reminded that after the meeting they were to return to their offices and hold themselves in readiness for a late afternoon announcement. With his comments finished, the Director gave the signal for all in the room that the luncheon meeting was at an end.

Joe hurried over to Kristina and asked for a moment with her. "Kristina, I don't have anything in the education gallery and the Director and PFM have asked me to keep a low profile at this meeting."

"Really, why? Is it about the new Renaissance painting?" Her eyes sparkled; he could see she was curious.

"Too much to go into right now. Let's do lunch soon and I promise to tell you all about it. I'm going to run down to my office. Will you ask security to give me a buzz if I'm not in the boardroom when you all reconvene?"

"Of course, Joe." One of the trustees claimed Kristina's attention. Joe felt bad for bothering her with his little task; Kristina, as always, had a number of objects for consideration, but he also knew that most of the trustees would be paying attention to the larger objects -the paintings, and sculptures, and decorative arts.

Some of the board members still considered prints, drawings, and photographs as examples of lesser art forms. Joe could never understand why people felt that way, but thought it probably had to do with the fact that most of them failed to understand the process. Take printmaking, for example. The skill needed to capture an image in the mind and then create the same image in reverse so that the inked image that appears on the paper is exactly as it had been originally conceived had always intrigued Joe. Most people just don't understand that print-making requires a high level of skill comparable to the skills of the painter or sculptor.

Joe hung back as the others left the dining room and then headed down to his office. He got there only to remember he'd left his computer in Charlie's closet. Blast. He'd have to go back up and get it. He looked down at his desk and noticed *The Chronicle of Higher Education* was centered there. He was certain he'd left it on top of his in-box yesterday afternoon. Perhaps Al or one of his people had been looking at it this morning. Joe sat down and started flipping through the pages. A piece of bolded text caught his eye: "Are you an energetic curator stuck in a frustrating museum job?" *Yes, I am. How do you suppose they knew that? And who are they?* His curiosity piqued, Joe read on.

"Historic estate seeks an energetic curator to mount small exhibitions, do comprehensive research on objects, and become a part of our museum family. If you are looking for an adventure, if you love objects, if you like people, if you are curious about history and art history, if you want to make a difference, this might be the job for you. We don't want your curriculum vitae - we want to know who you are. Fax or send an email answering the following questions to the address given at the end of this advertisement. If you're the right person, we will know, and we'll get in touch with you.

- What is the last book you read? Why?
- What are you reading now? Why?
- Describe a favorite work of art.
- Describe your perfect physical office space.
- Describe a favorite holiday memory.
- Describe an object of material culture, something that had belonged to someone, that captured your fancy."

Wow. This may be the worst museum in the world, but the job posting is great. It wouldn't hurt to send off an email answering their very interesting questions, he thought. *Maybe this is the right job at the right time and I'm the right person, looking for the right job, at the right time.* He snorted at the ridiculousness of the idea but emboldened by the thought of doing something positive, he tore the job posting out and stuffed it into the inside pocket of his suit coat. All he really needed was the email address; the questions were already etched in his mind.

Chapter Twenty-Two

Joe swung by Charlie's office, picked up his computer, and headed to the boardroom, which had been reconfigured following the earlier senior staff meeting. The accessions committee meeting was a hierarchical affair - important folks, like the Director, PFM, senior curators, and the trustees sat in the center of the room around the big conference table. Junior curators and others in attendance sat in chairs around the periphery of the room. The room was empty when Joe got there. He picked a chair in a corner of the room, pulled a notebook out of his computer case, closed the case and stuffed it under his chair. He found his favorite fountain pen in his breast pocket and began to think about the questions. He'd draft now and type later.

What was the last book I read? Well that one is easy at least. They are probably looking for something particular, but even if they are I don't know what it is, so here goes. He wrote:

"The last book I read was John Cowper Powys's novel 'A Glastonbury Romance.' Earlier this year, I happened to pick up a book about the Canadian novelist, William Robertson Davies, a favorite author of mine. Davies considered 'A

Glastonbury Romance' the greatest novel ever written in the English language. I'd never heard of the book or the author and I was intrigued. It's a long book and a tough read, or at least it was for me. It was written during the 1930s and deals with the conflict between Christianity and Celtic mysticism in the modern world. Like I said, the novel was a difficult read at first, but now that I am used to Powys' style, I'm a convert. I'm even planning to try to read my way through some of his other novels.

'What am I reading now?' After Powys, I felt I needed something a little lighter - also I wanted a paperback book that I could tuck in my coat pocket and have with me - so I'm reading a mystery by the British author Michael Innes, 'Appleby's Answer.' I'm not embarrassed to admit that British cozy mysteries are the junk food of my reading collection. As a curator, I spend a lot of time with my nose buried in a dusty book or dustier journal, and at the end of a long day, I like nothing better than to settle down in front of my fire with a good mystery. Mysteries are my stress-relievers."

That, Joe decided, *is a decent draft in answer to the first question; it still needs a little polish but it's a good rough draft.*

Question number two: Describe a favorite work of art. Joe wrote:

"It's quite difficult for me to describe a favorite work of art, because often my favorite work is whatever work I'm currently standing in front of at a museum or art gallery. I do have favorites, however. From the time I was a college student, I have been a fan of Albrecht Dürer. I went to Germany for study abroad in college and on the weekends we used our Eurail passes to visit other towns and cities. On Friday and Saturday evenings, we would find any overnight train traveling to a destination six hours or more. This way we could sleep in train cars and avoid spending our limited resources on hotels and youth hostels. I can remember arriving in Munich early one morning with my friends. After a trip to a bakery to refuel our engines, we left to explore the town. I was the only art history major and the other guys had no interest in visiting museums, so I headed off on my own. For whatever reason, the Alte Pinakothek had few visitors that day, or at least that's how I recall the situation. I can still remember walking through rooms, having a fine, if not memorable, experience, and then coming into the gallery that held Albrecht Dürer's great 'Self-Portrait in Fur-Collared Robe' and having one of those 'wow' moments. I stood absolutely stunned in the face (if you'll pardon the pun) of Dürer's technique.

I had a similar experience a few years later, in graduate school, during a history of printmaking class. On a visit to the Cleveland Museum of Art, the curator of prints & drawings brought out Dürer's 'Saint Jerome in His Study.' Again, Dürer's technique was overwhelming, but, rather like the painting, the overall experience was a sort of awed quietude - if that makes sense? As I looked at the impression, I felt somehow as if I were being transported into the elderly scholar's study. I could actually feel the sunlight coming into the chilly room through the Medieval coke-bottle-bottom windows and that I needed to be quiet, so I didn't disturb either the lion or the dog asleep on the floor. Or the scholar at his reading. It's the transformative moment I crave, and I think that is probably why I'm in the business of historical inquiry in relation to the arts."

At that point, the door to the boardroom opened, and some of the museum's cafeteria staff started setting up the coffee and cookie service intended to get the members of the accession committee through the long meeting ahead. Joe looked up briefly and continued with his draft. Describe my perfect physical office space. He gave the matter some consideration and began to write:

"I've never really thought about my perfect physical office space. For most of my professional career, I've been happy to have an office or a cubicle to call my own. In general, the more bookshelves and file cabinets there are the happier I am, but if I were asked to describe an ideal scenario, I think my perfect space might look a little something like the study Dürer created for Jerome, but with three significant differences. I imagine the third wall of Jerome's study, one of the walls we can't see, is lined with floor to ceiling bookshelves complete with a rolling stepladder to access the items highest on the shelves. There may possibly even be a balcony with another full story of bookshelves. Second, I'd need a more comfortable chair to sit on than the one currently in use by Saint Jerome. But most important is the desk. When I was in college, I went home for the weekend with one of my suite mates, a guy from Mansfield, Ohio. When his mother found out I was interested in museums, she insisted on taking me (and dragging him) on a visit to Malabar Farm, the home of the Pulitzer Prize-winning author Louis Bromfield. Bromfield had the greatest desk I have ever seen - a 10-foot circular desk with bookshelves all across the front. It's difficult to describe except perhaps by imagining Bromfield at work, encircled by a desk that had acres of flat surface space for notebooks and pens and reference books. A visitor, a friend perhaps, or a guest at Malabar Farm, enters and Bromfield, I imagine, looks up and says, 'I just need a couple of more minutes on this paragraph, sit down and find something to read.' The visitor sits down in a comfortable chair placed on the opposite side of the desk and, instead of a plain wooden front facing him/her, the visitor discovers an array of titles and interesting volumes. Bromfield designed the desk himself and I've never been able to imagine a better work surface to write from - a desk that is as convenient for the visitor as the owner."

Trustees and committee members were beginning to enter the room. They busied themselves with procuring coffee to fortify them for the meeting and with finding seats. It was time to put the notebook away, no matter how much fun he was having. So Joe stood up, put the cap on his fountain pen and put the notebook, face down, on his chair. Smiling with satisfaction, he also went to get a cup of coffee to help him weather the hours ahead. He spoke for a few minutes with a trustee whose family had given several fine works to the museum. Soon the Director arrived and everyone took their seats.

Chapter Twenty-Three

In general Joe quite liked accessions meetings, particularly when he didn't have to talk and wasn't worried about an important gift or purchase for his own part of the permanent collection. The majority of his colleagues were passionate about their collections and articulate in discussing the finer points of objects under consideration. The elderly Asian curator, Shu, gave a soft-voiced encomium on a Shang bronze wine vessel, a *Guang*, that he wanted to purchase for the collection. Joe was interested to learn that, historically, the wealthy of the Shang Dynasty, who lived in China more than 3000 years ago, had preferred their wine - or at least their ceremonial wine - spiced with cinnamon. *I wonder if they drank their wine heated or cold?* He wouldn't interrupt the flow of the meeting with that kind of question, but made a note to ask Shu about it later.

Shu was followed by Kristina, who spoke both quickly and economically about the prints she wanted to acquire, including Roy Lichtenstein's massive set entitled *Wallpaper with Blue Floor Interior,* which the committee had not been able to see in the gallery due to their large size. Joe was really fond of Lichtenstein's work and loved the whimsy of the large prints that, because of their size, functioned as wallpaper, offering a view into a post-modern interior with windows to an abstract urban skyline. Joe loved the entire concept and only wished he was able to afford one or more of them for himself.

A couple of trustees who were more conservative in their tastes objected to the prints. Boards often had one or more members who weren't really keen on anything made after 1900. Kristina listened patiently to their objections, answered their questions, and tried to provide her critics with information that might make them more responsive. In the end, it didn't really matter because the prints were offered as a gift from an anonymous (not to Kristina) donor, and the artworks would be accepted by the museum, notwithstanding complaints.

The registrar, Fanny, sat with two of her assistants at a table at one end of the large room and kept track of the proceedings. She had a large notebook in front of her and followed the discussions closely, making notes on the pages and giving instructions to the two young women on either side of her who worked on laptops. They would keep immaculate minutes of this meeting. Accessioning and deaccessioning are part and parcel of the legal business of the museum and Joe gave Fanny credit - she was prepared for these meetings. She never smiled, though, and neither did the young women. Perhaps they all thought it was too serious a business to smile.

Perhaps I'm not serious enough. Sometimes, particularly when the museum got a great gift or made a significant purchase, like the

Lichtenstein prints, he felt like getting up and cheering - another item of cultural heritage saved for the next generation. It was the metaphorical equivalent of hitting the ball out of the park during a home game. He looked at Kristina. She was happy, he could tell, as she whispered excitedly to the trustee next to her, pleased with her acquisitions.

Today's agenda didn't include any of the really hard issues that faced museums today - there were no discussions of cultural patrimony. The curator of ancient art did not have to undergo the third degree about objects that had entered the collection before he was born. These issues were being quietly dealt with by systematically going through the object records for every item in the ancient art collection. The provenance of each item was being reviewed, including issues of previous ownership and any other irregularities or perceived irregularities that might appear under closer scrutiny. Joe's contemporary in the ancient art department, had told him they were trying to be ready when, not if, the governments of Italy or Greece decided to come after the museum.

Joe didn't envy the current crop of antiquities curators. He had enough concerns of his own, although at least he had been able to assure himself and the museum's attorneys that none of the works in the collection came to the museum as a result of the Nazi devastation of great collections in the years preceding and during World War II. Some of his paintings might not be real, but at least he was convinced that the museum and any previous donors had acquired them honestly.

131

Joe looked down at the agenda - Bradley Boehm was next up. Boehm got up and started towards the front of the room. He hesitated, when he noticed the Director rise to his feet. The Director smiled at the group, pulled a gold pocket watch out of his pocket, looked at it briefly, and then nodded toward Boehm. "Mr. Boehm, I'm so sorry, but I'm afraid we are running behind schedule and, as much as it pains me to do so, I'm afraid we are going to have to table the consideration of your gifts and acquisitions until the next meeting of this committee."

Joe glanced quickly at Boehm, who was clearly shocked and affronted, and then towards PFM, who also looked surprised. He wondered what was up. It appeared for a moment as if Boehm was going to object or, perhaps, throw one of his temper tantrums. Joe suddenly remembered how joyful and secretive Boehm had been in PFM's office the day before. Joe felt sorry for the man. He had few friends in the room other than PFM. Though talented, Boehm alienated others with his air of superiority, and the Director had clearly decided to make a point of snubbing the man in front of the trustees today. The action was punitive and unnecessary; the committee often ran long and, despite special meetings planned for the afternoon, the group wasn't that far off schedule.

Joe saw PFM shake her head at Boehm. He managed to gather himself together and, with quiet dignity and very little of his normal flamboyance, Boehm addressed the Director. "I quite understand." Joe didn't like Bradley Boehm much, but felt in this case and in front of this audience the little man had shown himself to be the bigger man. Boehm returned to his seat. The only sign of his distress was his heightened color.

The Director addressed the group. "I'm going to depart from our normal routine for this last gift." He smiled rather unctuously at all of them. "I'd like to offer the floor to the President of our Board of Trustees, Rita Avi." There was some polite clapping.

Oh no, here it comes. Joe felt sick.

Chapter Twenty-Four

Rita stood and flashed the Director a brilliant smile. The registrar signaled to two of the art handlers, who stood waiting by the door just in case the trustees wanted to take a look at anything once more. The two art handlers moved noiselessly into the outer room.

"As you all are very much aware, on Saturday evening we will be celebrating this museum's centennial - 100 years of superlative service to the public as well as the scholarly communities here at home and around the globe. I'm looking forward to seeing all of you at the gala, which, I can tell you without giving too much away, is shaping up to be a stellar event." With this, she gave what she probably imagined as a silvery laugh. "In my role as president of the board at this significant time in the history of the institution, I felt I wanted to do something special for the museum and for the man behind the museum." She turned and smiled at the Director.

Joe barely managed not rolling his eyes. Her statement received an enthusiastic response from the trustees. Staff response, however, was a little less enthusiastic. *Of course none of the trustees are at-will employees.*

Joe saw the door to the hall open and one of the art handlers duck his head in and nod to Fanny. Fanny in turn nodded to Rita and the Director, who had been, less obviously, watching for her sign. "I'd like to tell a little story," Rita began, and she proceeded to tell the story, with colorful embellishments, of how she and PFM had 'discovered' the work she was about to present to the board of trustees. Rita was a good raconteur and PFM was looking gratified and proud to be included as a part of the story.

At the completion of the story, she dramatically announced to the room, "And now, ladies and gentlemen, may I present the 'Centenarian Virgin.'" Joe suppressed a chuckle. He heard one of the trustees mutter "not much chance of losing her virginity at that age."

The two art handlers brought the painting in and placed it on the easel that had been left empty for just this purpose. Rita allowed the crowd a moment or two to admire the work, and when the oohs and ahhs had died down, she turned the podium back to the great, great man and said modestly, "I'll let the Director make his remarks now."

Joe sometimes forgot that one didn't become the director of a major museum without people skills and some knowledge of art. The Director stepped over to the panel and gave a succinct and accurate, as far as it went, visual analysis of the finer points of the painting and the meaning behind the symbols - the roses, the European Goldfinch, the rather intense look shared between mother and child, and the ledge, which so obviously separated the viewer from the holy pair. The Director or someone, probably PFM, had clearly done his prep work. He closed his remarks saying, "The museum is both inordinately pleased and grateful to the overwhelming generosity of Rita Avi in the presentation of this gift. And, I humbly accept this extraordinary painting into the museum's collection."

There was another round of applause, and Rita and the Director beamed at each other and at the group. Then Joe, probably at the same moment as the Director, noticed that one of the trustees had his hand raised. It was the trustee whose family had given several Renaissance paintings to the museum. The man had a terrific connoisseur's eye. *Oh, this isn't going to be good.*

"This is a very generous gift, Rita, and so like you. I confess I'm a little concerned that this is the first the accessions committee has heard about this painting. I looked through our notes while the Director was speaking and I can't seem to find any supporting documents for this work, and I admit, I'd like to hear what the European curators, Prudence and Joe, have to say about this painting," glancing towards the two of them as he spoke. Joe could see a couple of the other committee members nodding their heads in agreement. Joe looked at the Director, but failed to make eye contact. Joe wasn't about to speak up first. PFM was the senior curator - he would follow the instructions he had been given unless asked a direct question. He'd decided in the early morning hours, just before falling into bed, that he would not lie if asked a direct question.

PFM stood up. She smiled a big smile and looked at Joe directly for a moment, perhaps trying to convey a message. There were altogether too many smiles in this meeting, Joe decided.

PFM began, "I am in complete agreement with the director about the importance of this gift."

Uh-oh, PFM has doubts now, too, and she's not going to lie because she doesn't know what's going to happen. She continued, "The painting seems to be everything the museum could hope for in a half-length portrait of the '*Virgin and Child*'."

The trustee who asked the original question was a stickler for detail. "What do you mean, Prue, when you say 'the painting *seems* to be everything?' Aren't you sure about the painting?" PFM was a little taken aback. She wasn't used to trustees questioning her word choice.

The Director stood up. "What Prudence means to say is this painting fills an obvious hole in our collection. She isn't uncertain about the painting at all, are you, Prudence?"

Put on the spot like that, PFM's response was immediate. She wasn't going to risk angering both the Director and the president of the board of trustees. "No, no of course not," and again, probably without realizing it, she darted a glance at Joe. Her action reminded the trustee of his original question, and he turned in his seat to regard Joe. "What about it, Cocktail? What's your opinion of the painting?"

For a brief moment, the world stopped and Joe was frozen. He noted, almost as if in slow motion, that the Director, who had been standing, had seated himself again, tipping back in his chair to make a comment to Mabel. She, as usual, was sitting directly behind him taking notes.

Joe had only seconds to decide how to handle this question. Did he destroy his career

138

here, or compromise his sense of ethics? Joe knew the Director was looking at him, and Joe met his glance calmly before addressing the trustee who had asked the question. "Well, Peter," he said addressing the trustee, "we've only known about the painting for a couple of weeks. It's an exciting find," he found he couldn't stop himself, " and I confess I'd be more comfortable if we'd had a little more time to research the work, but it's not my call." He broke off abruptly and sat down. The trustee, he noted, looked unsatisfied with Joe's response. He'd kept a smile on his face throughout his statement. He hoped he had sounded appropriately conciliatory as well as concerned.

The Director jumped in at this point and added, "As Mr. Cocktail says, this one is not his call and I, for one, am pleased to have an energetic, young, if slightly conservative, curator on the staff. He will learn as he moves forward in his career that sometimes quick decisions are required to get the finer pieces into a collection." Rita, sitting down next to the Director, seemed unsure about what had just happened, and PFM appeared worried.

Joe flushed. The Director had, as usual, contrived to make him look insignificant and inexperienced. The trustee looked like he was about to say something more, but officially the work had already been accepted into the collection. Peter could object to how the gift had been handled, but it was ultimately the Director who had the right, in special cases, to accept a gift at his own discretion.

"And with that, ladies and gentlemen, this meeting is adjourned. I know many of you will want to get a look at our new acquisition. Please feel free to come closer." People stood and began talking. Peter, who had been seated next to Kristina, looked at Joe and then turned to ask Kristina a question. Joe knew Peter would want to continue this discussion and wondered how he could avoid a direct confrontation right now. With interest, and without surprise, he noticed Mabel heading towards him through the group.

"Joe, the Director would like you to return to your office immediately."

He looked up at the Director who'd caught Joe's eye and indicated, with a nearly imperceptible jerk of his head, the direction of the door. He nodded in reply.

"You are not to discuss this acquisition with any of the trustees." Mabel looked apologetic.

"Yes, of course." Joe grabbed his computer bag and headed for the door. He heard, or thought he heard, Peter call his name. But Joe didn't stop, just turned around and waved. Peter seemed to understand. Joe made the universal phone signal bringing his hand to his ear, indicating he would call Peter. Peter nodded. Joe left the room feeling like a coward.

Chapter Twenty-Five

There was no doubt he was in some significant hot water now. The only question was how much hot water. *I had to answer a direct question from a trustee in a meeting. Not to do so would have been unthinkable.* As it was, he just felt like coward. He hadn't completely followed through on the Director's express instructions, nor had he taken the high road in an ethical sense. The whole brief episode left him feeling a bit queasy. Perhaps this was just the lack of sleep, and too much coffee, catching up with him. Whatever it was he didn't like it.

My problem is, he mused as he arrived at his office, *I'm not happy here and I'm in danger of becoming like the three witches if I stay here much longer. How to resolve the problem is the question. At least I have a job.* Any number of Joe's classmates from graduate school had moved on to do something out of the field. Two had become attorneys, one the head mistress of a prep school, one a business consultant, and one - the black sheep and the most successful of the group - had actually become a mystery writer. He'd never really wanted to do anything but work with objects. *I'm not going to be driven out of the curatorial field just because of the bullying of a few people above me.*

On the practical side, it's not that easy to just up and find a new job. The museum world is relatively small. A huge misstep here could cost me in the future. He wished there was something positive he could do that would make him feel better, and then, as he pulled his laptop out he happened to notice, once again, the *Chronicle of Higher Education,* centrally placed on his desk. *There is something I can do; I can finish my response to this strange advertisement. It may not result in a job, but it will be more interesting than trying to update my resume while I wait for the Director's phone call.*

He sat down at his desk and pulled the notebook he'd been scribbling on out of his bag. He took note of the instructions in the article; all correspondence was to be addressed to Sophia Bakerhurst. *Okay Sophia, I'm putting all my eggs in your basket this afternoon.* He opened a blank document and started typing his responses to the questions he had written down earlier, making minor changes and edits to the language as he went along. He'd finished drafts of all but the last two questions prior to the accessions committee meeting, and he focused on those now.

•Describe a favorite holiday memory
•Describe an object of material culture, something that had belonged to someone, that captured your fancy.

This really is the strangest job application I've ever read. It doesn't indicate where or what kind of museum this is, or who is in charge of picking the final candidates. He supposed there was some psychology to the questions and logic to their order, but he was darned if he could figure it out. A favorite holiday memory, hmmm. He let his mind wander for a few minutes and then began typing.

"I hope you don't mind if my favorite holiday memory is not actually my own. This isn't because I don't have happy holiday memories, I certainly do. Growing up I came from a pretty normal family, or at least it seemed normal to me. We weren't hugely dysfunctional, just slightly quirky, but I won't go into that here."

There, he thought, two can play at being mysterious with comments.

"I am a Christmas person. I love almost everything about the holidays and think this must be due, in large part, to my early familiarity with the movie White Christmas. In the days before VCR-DVD players - and hot and cold running Internet – we were at the mercy of *TV Guide*. When White Christmas was on we watched it - whether it started at 8:00 a.m. on a Sunday morning, or 10:00 p.m. on a Tuesday night. Mom would make hot cocoa and ham and biscuits if it were a Sunday morning, or holiday punch and popcorn if the movie was being shown in the evening. The family - my parents, my brother, and I - would hunker down with pillows and blankets to enjoy every single scene, from the opening number in the WWII battlefield to the final snow scene at the Inn in Pinetree, Vermont. And, while that was surely a Christmas memory, it's not my favorite memory - so you're actually getting two.

"My favorite holiday memory I share with Ebenezer Scrooge. My favorite scene from 'A Christmas Carol' is when Scrooge is taken to the warehouse of his old employer, Fezziwig, and reminded of a good Christmas in the past. I cannot tell you why Scrooge's past experience as an apprentice is my favorite holiday memory, it just is. Fezziwig's warehouse and the joyful relationship between Fezziwig and his two young apprentices is my fondest holiday memory."

Joe looked at what he had written. He felt deeply satisfied with the truth of what he was typing. *How strange that I should feel so strongly about a fictional character's memories.*

And, now for the final essay. *Describe an art object that captured your fancy.* He paused for a moment, deep in thought, and then smiled suddenly. He had a vision of himself as a young intern at a California museum. The paintings hadn't been terrific and his work for the European curator had been mostly routine, but on several occasions the registrar had made a point of taking Joe into the vaults and, under strict supervision, allowed him to browse through storage - opening drawers, pulling out screens, and poking into nooks and crannies. This particular registrar, curmudgeon that he was, believed that young curators-in-training should get as much hands-on experience as possible with objects, and he'd taught Joe vast amounts about art handling and the care of objects. He also told him innumerable stories about courier trips and demanding owners. It had been fun. When was the last time he'd really felt that work at a museum was fun, the way it had been back then? He started writing.

"When I was doing graduate work, I had an internship one summer at a small museum in California."

He went on to write about the registrar there and what he had learned, as well as the joyful feeling of exploration and discovery he was afforded.

"I can still remember, as clearly as if it were yesterday, spending a morning opening a series of small, deep drawers that contained the museum's rather random collection of sterling silver objects. Most of the stuff was pretty routine - Victorian service pieces, mango picks, pickle forks, sugar tongs, toast racks, and other luxury items that reflected the wealth and status of a class continually distinguishing itself from others by the specialization of eating utensils. What eventually caught my eye, however, was a much earlier piece, a sterling silver walnut. Of what possible use was a sterling silver walnut to anyone, I wondered. I called the registrar over and he laughed and encouraged me to pick up the piece and see what I thought it was. There was a small button at the edge of the walnut, and as I pressed it, it opened into two halves, hinged at the larger end of the walnut. Inside, one half of the walnut was open; a screen, perforated at regular intervals with jagged holes, covered the other half. I looked at the object and I was still clueless. The registrar walked me through the following narrative to help me understand the object I was holding.

'Okay, Joe, let's say you're a wealthy Englishmen toward the end of the 18th century. You aren't in business, of course, but you do have an interest in business and the goings-on of the government and the ships-at-sea. Where would you go to get information?'

I guessed, 'Parliament? My club? A nice ale house?'

145

The registrar shook his head at all these suggestions. 'Let's try looking at this object another way. When you want to find out about what's going on in this museum, what do you do?'

'I go grab a coffee with someone.'

'Exactly, and that's what the Englishman who owned this little item did. He would wander off to one of London's many coffee shops, perhaps even a little place called Lloyd's, for a cup of coffee, and being a rather superior sort, he liked his coffee spiced.'

'Spiced?' Of course, spiced. That was the clue. All of a sudden, standing in the vault at that California museum, I had a vision of my mother at her stove. One of the items that sat on the shelf just above the stove was her nutmeg grater, an elongated cylinder of tin with sharp-edged perforations, and at the top of the cylinder, a small, lidded space to hold the nutmeg. 'It's a nutmeg grater,' I said wonderingly.

'Exactly, well done Joe.'

I don't think I'd ever had quite that experience at a museum before - the experience of these objects as belonging to people and as part of their lives. It was a revelation for me, and I feel very warmly about that little nutmeg grater and the gentlemen who owned it. And, I confess, I feel sort of sorry for it sitting alone in its drawer, not being able to fulfill its raison d'être any longer - I know it sounds fanciful, but it feels like it's been sent to a kind of rest home for unwanted objects. An item that will never go on display and is marooned, if you will, in the museum version of the Island of Misfit Toys visited by Rudolph the Red-Nosed Reindeer and his friends."

Joe reread what he had just written, and as with the previous answer, he felt deeply

146

satisfied in a way he didn't really feel he could articulate. *Is it just because I'm feeling nostalgic for past times? Were they actually better times?* Perhaps the difference was that all of these memories involved works of art and people whom he either loved or respected for the talents. This included his family, Irving Berlin and Charles Dickens and their characters who were so much like old friends, the unknown artist of the silver walnut, and his old friend, the registrar in California.

Joe pushed the print button and stepped away from his desk to retrieve the papers. He spent the next few minutes re-reading all of his answers, again noting minor changes in the text, clarifying his ideas here and there. He made the necessary corrections to the document, and then in a rush of bravado, he wrote a cover email to the name provided in the advertisement, Sophia Bakerhurst. He attached the document he'd written, took a deep breath, and pushed the send button. Immediately, he felt a little shiver of excitement. *Who knows? Maybe I've just taken an important step toward a new career.*

Chapter Twenty-Six

The phone rang on his desk and he laughed out loud, fancying for a brief moment that Sophia Bakerhurst might be on the other end of the line, ready to offer him a job. The person on the other end of the line definitely wasn't the mysterious Sophia Bakerhurst. In fact, it was Mabel calling him to a brief senior staff meeting. He was relieved that it was a senior staff meeting and not a summoning to the Director's office. Back in the boardroom a few minutes later, Joe was chatting in a low voice with Al. Everyone was there and the mood in the room could at best be called subdued, if not grim. There was a small knot of people who were scared, really scared. There was no escaping the fact that the Director's earlier remarks had indicated changes, big changes, and as always in the museum world, people were afraid for their jobs. Joe noted that most of the staff had found seats around the periphery of the room, almost as if the bomb had gone off and scattered its survivors in a wide circle around the main table. The few seats at the main table that were occupied Joe probably could have predicted. Sitting together whispering were the heads of education, the library, and the registrar's office.

Boehm, too, despite recent events, and perhaps because of them, had taken a seat at the main table; he liked everyone to see him and he liked to talk at meetings. Boehm was looking rather defiant.

This is just wrong. Joe looked around at the members of the senior staff. *How many of these people had worked and would be working overtime with additional tasks made necessary by the gala? What goal was going to be served by making the entire senior staff anxious just before a big event?*

Once again the Director made his entrance and, once again, he was accompanied by PFM and the Dragon-Lady; both women were as unhappy as they had been earlier in the afternoon. A small portable podium had been placed in readiness at the Director's place at the main table. He looked around and noticed the lack of staff members near him. His eyes narrowed slightly but he said nothing. Staff had sided against him. PFM and Lori took places at the table.

"I'd like to thank you all for taking the time to attend this meeting." *No thanks necessary, you ordered us to attend this meeting.* Joe's inner voice supplied the response for everyone in the room. *Perhaps the Director is being purposefully ironic.*

"Before we proceed to the main business of the day, I'd like to hear updates from those of you involved in the gala."

He is going to make us wait for whatever news he had.

"Event planning?"

Scott snapped to attention. He'd clearly recovered from the excesses of the previous evening and was at his most professional, though

Joe noted the dark circles under his eyes. "Everything is on schedule, sir. The additional tables, chairs, dining service, and linens will be delivered tomorrow afternoon. Equipment will all be kept in the temporary exhibition storage. I'd like to thank Fanny and her staff for their help with this. Food deliveries will begin early Saturday morning. At 2:00 pm on Saturday we will begin closing off galleries and areas that are going to be used for service, cocktails, and dining and we will begin setting up at 3:00 pm. Invited staff are requested to be in attendance by 6:00 pm - as a reminder, dress for this event is black tie, please." He looked around the room and then at the Director. "I think that's everything."

"Thank you. Registrars?"

"The galleries are all in tip-top shape for the event. My staff," Fanny noted, "has spent the past week going through each and every department, making sure everything is in order."

"The new accessions will be in place?" The Director made the statement a question.

"The key objects, as you requested, will be on display in a side gallery during the cocktail hour prior to the formal dinner. When the guests move into dinner, they will be removed to object storage. The other new acquisitions have all been allocated places in the appropriate galleries, and we will be working with the curators and art handlers tomorrow to get those installed."

"Good." The Director smiled, clearly satisfied. He rubbed his hands together like a villain in a melodrama who had successfully tied the heroine to the train tracks, viewing the smoke from a distant locomotive.

"Performing arts?" The Director seldom, if ever, referred to his staff by their given names in large meetings. Staff members were tools to be used as needed.

We aren't individuals. Like medieval workmen, we are only known by our crafts - Joe the Curator, Charlie the IT guy, Katherine the head of Performing Arts.

Katherine stood up in the back of the room. She looked tired and tense and there were violet circles under her eyes as well. "We are working to a very tight deadline and have a lot to get done over the next 48 hours. It would be helpful if everyone who isn't directly involved with the..." and here she hesitated, glancing briefly at the Director, "...the performance would stay out of the atrium and the surrounding work areas - particularly the second story hallways overlooking the atrium, the sound booth, and the spaces we are using as temporary staging areas on the first and second floors. The only way we can be done with our jobs and out of the way for Scott and Fanny by Saturday afternoon," Katherine's eyes were again fixed on the Director, "is if we are allowed to get on with our work without constant changes and interruptions." Finished with her report, Katherine sank gracefully into her chair with a look of relief.

"Now," said the Director. "Tomorrow, as many of you already know, a special meeting of the Board of Trustees has been called by the Executive Committee." This, Joe knew, was the Director's way of indicating to his senior staff that whatever event or events he was planning to set in motion were already a done deal, and whatever the staff was going to feel or say about today's meetings, their opinions would have no real impact.

"I've never really been satisfied with the strategic planning exercises of my predecessors, and the museum sits today at a crossroads. I believe what this institution needs to survive and succeed in the coming five years, ten years, fifteen years, is an energetic staff fully engaged in a fresh strategic planning initiative. We need to look more closely at our mission and our goal and need to closely scrutinize every individual position at the museum. Every job, every department, every program, every initiative will be considered. In short - we must look at what needs to happen to the - let's call it the 'body' of the museum, to make it healthy. We may have to feed certain areas with more funding and more employees, and other areas may need to be amputated." He paused and scanned the room, looking at all of them in turn.

"Today, the Executive Committee has agreed to hire an outside consulting firm to come in and review and evaluate everything that goes on at this museum - from the volunteers to the trustees, no one will be exempt from this process. You will all be under scrutiny."

Ah-hah, Joe thought. *He said 'you' are all under scrutiny; he is apparently not to be scrutinized. It's good to be the king.*

"Tomorrow at noon, I'd like job descriptions for everyone employed in your various departments on my desk. From Human Resources I will need" - and here he looked at the head of HR – "a spreadsheet of all salaried employees, full- and part-time, along with attendance records, vacation privileges and salaries, as well as the duration of employment." He glanced at his watch. "I would like to stay and answer any questions, but I am late for a meeting

153

with several trustees. The heads of communications and HR will be happy to record your names and questions for later response. Thank you for your time. Good night." And with that he left the room, which was quiet for a moment and then erupted as people began talking all at once.

"Another strategic planning process, that's terrific." "What does he mean by amputated?" "Why does he need to see our salaries, doesn't he know our salaries?" "I wonder if he's already decided who he is going to eliminate?" "Of course he has." Joe heard a dozen or so voices asking questions of one another, not of Human Resources, in the same vein.

The relentlessly cheerful head of Human Resources, Linda, called the room to order. "You've all heard the Director, does anyone have any questions?" And with that, she placed a legal pad and a pencil in front of her. The room went quiet.

Joe heard someone near him mutter: "If I did have a question I wouldn't ask you." That seemed to be the prevailing sentiment. Finally, the associate registrar, part of the senior staff by virtue of her position in charge of the collections database, raised her hand tentatively and earned a sharp glance from Fanny, who seemed to take this question as a sign of disloyalty on the part of her staff. The young woman, though visibly frightened by her supervisor's glance, asked her question: "Doesn't HR have copies of all our job descriptions?"

Joe almost shouted *brava* at her question. You can always count on a registrar to get to the nitty-gritty about where information can be found. He saw several people around the room nodding their heads.

Linda frowned, seeing more work for her, then remembered her role as the jolly representative and answered, "We do, of course, have job descriptions for each of you, but it is our sense that people frequently do more than their original job descriptions indicate, and this gives you an opportunity to make a case for each and every one of your employees." She smiled brightly at the staff gathered in the room, obviously waiting for a sign of approval.

"By noon tomorrow?" someone at the back of the room asked in a slightly sarcastic voice. Joe couldn't tell who had asked the question.

"Well, of course, we assume that the managers of individual departments keep up-to-date job descriptions for each of their employees, so it shouldn't be a real problem. Are there any further questions?"

"What firm has been hired to do the consulting?" Joe asked. He figured he had little to lose, given his current situation.

Linda looked at him. "I'm not at liberty to give you that information." She made a note on her pad.

Charlie got into the spirit with him. "How was the firm chosen? Are they big enough to be able to analyze all the specialized tasks in a major museum? Will there be a final written report?"

Linda, who didn't care for Charlie at the best of times, looked narrowly at him and replied, "I'm not at liberty to give you the answers to those questions, but I'm sure the Director will be happy to answer them all in due time." She made another note on her pad.

Al, the conservator, cleared his throat and said, "Well, Linda, if you aren't at liberty to answer any of our questions, and if nobody has any further questions, I'd like to suggest that we end this meeting. It's been a long day and I for one would like to go home to my wife and dinner."

And with that the meeting adjourned.

Chapter Twenty-Seven

Joe and Charlie walked back to their offices together. "What are you going to do about the job descriptions?" Joe asked his friend.

Charlie looked at him and laughed. "Are you kidding?"

"What?"

"I run the IT Department here. First of all, there aren't many people here at the museum that have any idea about what my staff does on a daily basis. Second, my people are handpicked professionals. Their job descriptions aren't determined by the museum, Joe, they are determined by the market - a programmer is a programmer, a systems analyst is a systems analyst, a network supervisor is a network supervisor. The required documents will be on the way to the Director's desk before I leave the museum tonight. It will take me about 15 minutes to put them together. Bring on the consultants. I run a tight ship in Information Technology."

"I guess I never really looked at it from your point of view before. I don't suppose it will actually take me too much longer than that to revise my job description. I just need to add the database stuff and, I suppose, the work that will need to be done on the files after yesterday's incident."

They arrived at the turnoff to IT; Joe said goodbye to his friend and walked on to his own office. There was a sticky note on the door with a brief message for Joe. *Be in my office first thing tomorrow morning. -PFM*

He removed the note from the door as he opened it. He stuck it to the top of his desk so he wouldn't forget it and decided to check his email one last time before he left work. There were only a few emails in his in-box, one an invitation to an annual meeting of a Renaissance literary society he belonged to, one an announcement that he was the recipient of an $18 million prize (if only), and the third...for a minute he didn't recognize the name.

The third email was from Sophia Bakerhurst. His heart started thumping in his chest. He'd sent his email to her - he looked at his watch - just over an hour ago. She hadn't really had time to even read his answers. Maybe they'd already filled the position and this was just a polite thanks-but-no-thanks note. Maybe it wasn't a personal note at all, maybe she was on vacation and it was an out-of-the-office reply. *Well,* he thought. mentally preparing himself, *there is only one way to find out.* He opened the email and read:

Dear Dr. Cocktail:
I was pleased to receive your email this afternoon. I wonder if you would be available for a short telephone conversation sometime tomorrow morning or afternoon? If you are available simply reply to this email with a time and a number you

158

can be reached. I look forward to speaking with you.

> *Yours sincerely,*
> *Sophia Bakerhurst*
> *President, The Bakerhurst Foundation*

Chapter Twenty-Eight

Joe woke up the next morning after a long and restful night's sleep. He felt better than he'd felt in months. He sang in the bathroom as he showered. He sang in the kitchen as he prepared his breakfast. And he cranked up the radio in his car and sang on the way to work. He hadn't realized how miserable he'd been feeling about his position at the museum. *Maybe I've been over-doing it in recent months, or maybe I've just let himself get sucked into the idea that all museums were dysfunctional and that museum work and art history weren't going to be as much fun as I thought they were going to be.*

Whatever the realities of the situation, he found himself looking forward to this day's work, and, he had to admit, to the gala, and spending some time with Katherine. But of course what he was most excited about was the chance to talk to the mysterious Sophia Bakerhurst. *She's probably just very efficient.* He had to admit, though, there was just a tiny part of his imagination that already had him off on a new adventure at a new institution.

I need to be careful. Just because things are bad here, I need to be wary of jumping from the frying pan into the fire. A new situation may not be any better. Although, I don't know how a new job could be any worse than my current situation. And with that thought, he parked his car and headed into the museum.

He arrived a little earlier than usual so he could have his job description ready to hand to PFM at their morning meeting. He suspected he was going to have to answer for his actions at yesterday's accessions committee meeting, but hoped any immediate anger would have died down a bit. He needed a drama-free day.

He cheerfully bade the security folk at the staff entrance a good morning, picked up his keys, and headed down to his office. He liked to arrive early. He liked the quiet of the hallways and galleries before the day got started. Once in his office, he opened his laptop and quickly found the most recent copy of his curriculum vitae and job description. He spent the next quarter hour revising his job description so that it more closely reflected his actual activities and responsibilities. Then he added a couple of recent papers and some professional activities to his curriculum vitae. He printed a hard copy of each document and placed them in a folder to take with him to his meeting. A brief glance assured him he still had a good half hour before he was expected in PFM's office, so he decided to head up to his galleries.

He completed a regular circuit through each of his galleries at least two or three times a week, just to make sure everything was in order. He also walked the galleries, because he found looking at art was a reminder of why he was in the business. It wasn't any good sitting in an office or library all day. He needed objects, and always felt reinvigorated after he'd spent time in the galleries. The more he looked at the objects, the more questions he had. Examining objects raised questions about the context in which they were created, the methods and materials used to create them, and the intent of the artist. Many times, their sometimes simple, sometimes complex, stories could be told through placement, story labels, contextual photographs, and other means of interpretations. And sometimes not.

For Joe, each object was a doorway into another world. A world that could be explored, described, and shared with others who were interested enough to take the time and make the journey.

Today he chose the stairs instead of taking the elevator to the galleries. He hadn't had much exercise in the past few days and needed to get his blood flowing. He always felt better when he got a morning run in, and that hadn't been a part of the schedule recently. He sprinted up the four flights of stairs and arrived breathless on the main floor of the museum.

The museum hadn't opened yet, so the information desk wasn't manned and there were no security guards to be found. As he entered and began to cross the atrium to the grand staircase, he suddenly slipped. His left foot went out from under him, and he landed on the hard marble floor with a thud. Luckily, he'd been able to break his fall with his hands, but he hadn't been able to avoid the expletive that came out of his mouth as he fell. He was glad there was no one around to see or hear him. He got up and peered closely at the floor. He identified a small pool of what looked like water as the agent of his fall, and he noticed several others - tiny perfect circles of water. He looked up to see where the water was coming from. He didn't think the drops were coming from the roof - particularly since scaffolding was currently obscuring the atrium roof. Perhaps someone had spilled something on the scaffolding. He'd mention the problem to Katherine or security. He took a handkerchief out of his pocket and wiped up the spills he could see.

Back aching, he marched up the grand staircase to the balcony overlooking the atrium that led to the wing housing his galleries. He and PFM shared responsibility for the galleries containing medieval art and European paintings and sculpture before 1800. He was responsible for anything created before 1500 C.E., she for anything later.

At the top of the stairs, he wasn't surprised to find that temporary enclosures had been set up all around the balcony - this presumably was to allow the contractors and Katherine's people to get their work done. He wondered if the plywood panels would be removed before the gala, or if they were a part of this mysterious performance to which everyone kept referring. He heard sounds from the other side of the enclosures - people working - and he stopped to listen for a minute, hoping he would hear something to give him a clue as to what was going on. Joe heard only curses from a worker who had dropped a piece of equipment that rang with a metallic clang against the marble floor of the balcony. The sound made Joe wince.

A temporary door had been installed, closing off the entrance to the galleries on the right, where the construction equipment was being stored. He considered knocking on the makeshift door and telling someone about the water spots, in case there was something leaking, but decided instead to tell the first guard he saw about the problem. Joe turned to the left and entered the first of the medieval galleries, passing quickly through the main gallery, and through a doorway that led to the next gallery. This gallery had two small bijoux galleries, one on either side. The bijoux room to his left was his destination. Sometimes his trips to the galleries were like this. He came not really knowing what he was looking for, but by the time he reached the entrance his subconscious had determined a specific destination.

This particular gallery contained a number of objects from the seventh and eighth centuries, and Joe headed for a small case set against one of the walls. It held a series of disc brooches, probably made in France, sometime between 650 and 700. These large brooches were not uncommon, made of bronze and decorated with gold and semi-precious stones. More than thirteen centuries ago, perhaps on a December morning like this, a Frankish goldsmith had carefully twisted threads of gold into sinuous shapes and applied them to the surface of the brooch. Perhaps the brooch was intended as a New Year's gift. Perhaps it was a reward for services rendered, or, perhaps, this form of "portable wealth" had been made as part of a cache for burial.

The brooch had originally belonged to someone, and that someone, like Joe, had been made of flesh and bone, had been a baby, a child, and then an adult, and had laughed, cried, and hoped. Joe came to the galleries to remind himself that, even though these objects were now considered works of art and might have been even when they were created, they were objects that spoke to the humanity of man. And, sometimes, they even spoke of the inhumanities mankind inflicted upon each other.

He looked closer at the little s-shapes and curves and squiggles of the filigree decoration. Most scholars agreed that the little symbols were purely decorative, a holdover from types of decoration known in Rome and transferred through a variety of sources, probably via Byzantine examples, to a Frankish goldsmith of long ago. Joe sometimes imagined the designs looked more like a form of cryptic writing than a now indecipherable coded language. *I bet someone like Dan Brown would have a field day with finding lost messages in these 7th century disks.*

He became suddenly aware of the time. He'd spent more time in the little gallery than he had planned, and if he didn't hustle, he'd be late for his meeting with PFM. He fled back the way he had come and took the main staircase two steps at a time, stopping only when he noticed the two female volunteers at the information desk watching him with broad smiles on their faces.

One of the women spoke to him. "Morning, Joe. Slow down on the staircase, please. I wouldn't want to see you fall." The gentle admonishment came from Mrs. Winterbottom, the head of the information desk volunteers. She was an energetic grey panther with snowy-white hair; she was, as always, impeccably coiffed and dressed.

"You are too right, Mrs. Winterbottom, I've already fallen once today." She looked concerned and started to say something; he held up a hand to forestall her. "It wasn't my fault, I promise, I wasn't running. Would you mind calling security and telling them I found little spots of water here on the main floor of the atrium this morning? They can call me if they want more information."

"Of course, Joe. Are you hurt?" Mrs. Winterbottom asked. The other woman, possibly a new recruit as Joe didn't recognize her, was looking at Joe as if expecting to see blood or broken bones.

"I'm fine but there could be something wrong, or a piece of equipment leaking up above." They all glanced at the floor and then up at the improvised ceiling hiding whatever was being built above.

"Do you think we need to close the atrium to traffic today?"

"No, no. They were just small spots, but it's probably best to find out what is causing them. Security and operations will take care of it. Don't you worry about it, Mrs. Winterbottom. I'd love to stay and chat but, like the white rabbit, I'm late, late, late" - and Joe hurried off to retrieve his folder and meet with his boss.

Chapter Twenty-Nine

PFM's door was partially open but he knocked anyway. "Come in," she said. PFM was alone in the room, working at her desk making notes on some index cards. She looked up at him as he walked into the office and indicated with a nod of her head that he should sit. She wasn't smiling at him and she wasn't frowning at him. "We have a problem," she began.

Joe said nothing, but waited for PFM to continue. It seemed like the best approach to take.

"In fact, Joe, we have a number of problems, but let's start with the largest among them." She opened a folder in front of her and looked down at the papers it contained and continued to speak, "After your outburst at the accessions meeting yesterday..."

Joe must have made some movement or sound that indicated his objection to the way she had phrased her sentence, because she looked up at him and made a motion to indicate that he should remain silent. "As I was saying, after your outburst at the meeting yesterday, a number of events have transpired behind the scenes." She looked down at the folder again. "At least two of the trustees on the committee spoke or left messages for the Director and the president of the Board of Trustees expressing concern about Rita Avi's gift. As a result, he has decided not to announce the gift at the gala on Saturday night."

"This, as you must certainly realize, means that there IS no big gift for presentation to the museum at the 100th Anniversary Gala - and, more to the point, there is no large magnanimous gift from the president of the board of trustees to the Director in honor of his leadership." PFM looked up and directly into his eyes. "The president of the board of trustees is unhappy, I am unhappy, and the Director is very, very unhappy, Joe." Up until now her voice had been quite calm, but her next sentence revealed the level of her anger with him. "Was it your intention with this maverick move to ruin the 100th Anniversary Gala, or was that just a side benefit of your superior curatorial knowledge?"

He hesitated for a moment, his mind whirling. *How do I answer without making the situation worse?* When he did speak it was with a quiet firmness. "I apologize, I did not intend to cause problems. I was surprised last week." He had started to say 'you surprised me last week' but didn't want to dig himself in any deeper by appearing to push the blame on to her. "I was very surprised last week when you called me up to conservation. I've seen pastiches like that one before."

"It's not a pastiche," she said.

Joe continued as if he hadn't heard her objection. "I'd seen works like that before. There are several diagnostic tests that can be done to determine authenticity, and I assumed the museum would be doing them before the painting was seriously considered for acquisition. I was further surprised this week when I learned, from you, that this painting was on a fast track for acceptance. I attempted to raise my concerns with both you and the Director, and, until a trustee asked me a direct question in the accessions meeting, I kept my mouth shut as instructed. I was resigned, if not happy, to remain silent, but I won't lie to a trustee and, in fact, all I did was to express a desire to do further study on the piece." He finished his comments as quietly as he had started them. He hadn't raised his voice, hadn't gotten angry.

His comments cut no ice with his supervisor and she didn't respond to them. "You've proven to your superiors that you cannot be trusted to be diplomatic in meetings that involve trustees, so, for the foreseeable future, until you can be discreet, you will no longer be attending accessions committee meetings. From now on, all your observations and concerns about purchases and gifts will be conveyed to me in written form two weeks prior to the actual meeting. The Director and I will review your reports and make any necessary changes prior to their distribution to the board of trustees. This administrative action and the reasons for the action will be reflected in your work record. As you can imagine, this will impact your end of the year review."

Joe began once again to object, but she held up her hand, forestalling his comments.

"I have spoken with the Director about whether or not he would like you present at Saturday's gala. He and I both feel it is necessary for you to be present, but we strongly encourage you to avoid discussing recent events with any of

171

the trustees in attendance. We cannot keep certain trustees from making inquiries, but hope that you will restrain yourself and not make an already bad situation worse. Failure to comply in this area, Joe, will have serious consequences." She paused and consulted the papers on her desk once again. "I've confirmed with Human Resources that you have some vacation time coming. The Director has strongly suggested that you take a few days off next week and think about your future employment."

She looked at him for some further response, but Joe again declined to speak. His mind was busy with her last comment. *Do her words mean I'm going to be let go as soon as the gala is over, or that I need to contemplate my future here at this museum?* There wasn't much point in trying to argue in his own defense - PFM's mind was made up and nothing he could say at this moment would change it. He'd just been banned from accessions committee meetings, his reports were going to be censored, he'd been put on notice, and the museum's director had sent a message for him to get out of his sight for a time. There wasn't much to add to that. Again, he said nothing.

PFM realized he wasn't going to make a comment. "Moving on, then. I understand from security that there was some kind of incident in your office late Wednesday or early Thursday morning. Would you care to tell me your side of the story and also explain why I have not yet had a report from you on the incident?"

I'm an idiot. Joe hit his forehead with the heel of his hand. "PFM, that was an oversight on my part. I didn't think. I apologize. I wasn't thinking straight. I should have been in here first thing yesterday morning with an explanation, but I'd gotten so little sleep the night before and got involved in other tasks. I don't have an explanation. I screwed up." He couldn't help but realize how bad this looked, given the other events of the past few days.

Joe went on to explain what he thought had happened, and how he and Al had dealt with the problem. By the time he had finished his story, PFM's earlier anger had dissipated, and now her concern, like his, was for the curatorial records of the museum. "Al thinks the prognosis is good for the few documents that were badly damaged. The folders were so tightly packed together that the bulk of the papers weren't damaged."

"Any ideas about how this accident might have happened, Joe?"

"Well, that's just it, PFM. It can't have been an accident."

"What do you mean not an accident? It says here that apparently a bottle of cleaning solution was left on top of the file cabinet and accidentally spilled, soaking the drawers and the papers within." She was reading from the security report.

"PFM, think about it. If the file cabinet drawers were all closed, as they were when I left that day, and the bottle of solvent had been on top of the file cabinet, then tipped over, and accidentally spilled, it wouldn't have seeped into the files themselves but down the sides of the file cabinet. The guard who discovered the situation noticed an unidentified puddle of fluid at the foot of the file cabinet and traces of the liquid coming from all of the drawers - which were shut. I might have, in a great hurry, left one drawer open, but it is impossible to leave all three of the drawers open, extended their full lengths and not notice it. Someone did this on purpose."

PFM was really concerned, now. "What about the security cameras?"

"All the security cameras in that area were disabled just after the museum closed on Wednesday, and the problem wasn't discovered until later in the evening. Someone planned this, and I can't think of any earthly reason why. Security is looking into the issue. My guess is that Sgt. Pat has identified this as an accident in the formal report until he has determined how it could have happened and who might be involved."

PFM nodded. He had to hand it to PFM - though she might be upset with him about the mess with the *Virgin*, she had given the better part of her professional life to this museum and this collection, and she wasn't any happier than he was about the sabotage of his file cabinets. His collection included some of the earliest gifts and purchases in the museum, and the destruction of those files would have been a tragedy for the institution.

Now PFM looked sternly at him again and said, resigned, "I assume you've been so busy with events," and she stressed the word events, "over the past couple of days that you won't have all the European works finished."

Joe wasn't sure whether she was asking him a question or not, but he answered anyway. "We did discuss this earlier in the week. I should be finished by mid-December."

"I suppose that will have to do, particularly since you will be taking some time off next week.

That's all. I'll see you tomorrow evening, if not before."

He agreed and left his supervisor's office considerably relieved. It could have been worse. There could have been more of a confrontation about the painting of the *Virgin and Child.* He could well imagine the Director's anger, Rita's too. After all, the museum had just accepted the gift of a painting that was probably going to turn out to be not what they expected, and Rita had probably had to pay a pretty penny for a magnanimous gesture that she was now, due to his interference, unable to make. He tried to tell himself that he wasn't to blame, but he knew he was.

He just couldn't see how he could have better handled any of the run-ins this week. *I should have taken PFM aside last week and told her exactly what I thought.* Water under a bridge now; he couldn't change the situation by worrying. *All I have to do is get through today and tomorrow night, and then at least I'll have a few days off to think about things.* Maybe he'd call his brother and plan a surprise trip home to see the family. *That would please Mom, and I could use a few home cooked meals.*

The tentative plans cheered him up and he walked towards his office whistling "Deck the Halls" under his breath. *I have another thing to be cheerful about. My upcoming phone call with the mysterious Sophia Bakerhurst.* He'd arranged to speak with her right after lunch. He'd have to miss his regular Friday lunch with Katherine and Charlie. *I'll grab a sandwich at the café and do a little research on the Bakerhurst Museum before the call.* And with his plans in place, he headed off to his office to get some work done.

175

Chapter Thirty

During a late morning coffee break, Joe called his favorite reference librarian and asked if the museum library had any information on the Bakerhurst Museum and Historic House. Joe swung by the library on his way to the museum café and picked up a small, slender volume that had been pulled from the stacks, along with print-outs of two newspaper articles. He checked these out to his office, dropped them into an inter-office mail envelope, and tucked the envelope under his arm before wandering down to the café.

He didn't eat in the café very often. It was expensive, priced for the patrons not the employees, and even with the staff discount it wasn't a bargain. The food was good, but the variety wasn't all that great. He often envied his colleagues at the Metropolitan Museum of Art and the J. Paul Getty Museum. They had access to large cafeterias and restaurants offering what seemed to Joe an endless variety of interesting options. He longed for a time in the distant past, when museum cafeterias had been places for staff to get a good meal in the middle of long workdays.

Today, however, he picked up a pre-packaged sandwich, a bag of potato chips, and balanced an apple and a soda on top of the pile. He chatted for a moment with the employee at the register and dropped a tip in her plastic cup - he seldom forgot that no matter how underpaid he felt, the wait staff in museum cafeterias primarily worked for minimum wage and dealt daily with the outrageous demands of patrons and staff alike. Demands that went far beyond "Do you have any Grey Poupon?"

Soon he was back at his desk and munching happily away as he flipped through the small book that gave a brief history and the highlights of the Bakerhurst Museum. The property, he discovered, wasn't just a museum - it was actually the estate of a prominent 19th century mid-western industrialist and included a number of buildings, as well as formal and informal gardens, and was a working farm. Reading on, he discovered Samuel A. Bakerhurst was far more than an industrialist. He had also been a quirky collector, who had developed a passion for collecting fine arts and antiquities.

The slim guidebook implied there was some mystery surrounding Samuel Bakerhurst's personal history, but failed to provide further details. Joe turned to the two articles the reference librarian had found; one had been written in the early years of the 20th century and told the following story: After an industrious youth and having amassed a considerable fortune while still only in his late twenties, Samuel had taken a self-imposed leave of absence from his business interests in order to find a spouse.

His pre-nuptial travels took him to the East Coast, and then to Europe, and then back to the East Coast. He eventually found and married a young paragon of virtue and breeding, Ruth Roland Coleman, in 1859. Together they produced three sons: Nicholas, Arthur, and Eric. In 1870, Samuel packed up his family and off they went to explore the world. For more than a decade, the family traveled and collected in Europe, the Mediterranean, Egypt, and some of the more accessible parts of Asia. In 1880, Samuel brought his family, which now included three-year-old Alexandria, born in Egypt, home to the estate his own father had built in the first half of the century. Awaiting the family's return was an entire storage barn full of unopened crates and packages sent from destinations around the world - the material record of their decade as transients ready to decorate every surface of their home, as befitting a good Victorian family.

From the article, Joe further learned that when Samuel died in 1901, his collection numbered less than 25,000 objects total, but Samuel had gone for quality, not quantity. On the walls of the Bakerhurst home, genre scenes by 17th century Dutch painters vied for space with gloriously exotic paintings of the places and people they'd visited on their travels.

The museum housed a large collection of small-scale Etruscan, Roman, and Renaissance bronzes from Italy, jewelry of all sorts, as well as Egyptian artifacts and the usual hodgepodge of decorative arts, furniture, and Victoriana found in any collection established in the latter part of the 19th century. What differentiated the Bakerhursts from other collectors of the period, as far as Joe could tell, was their unerring good taste - the Bakerhurst collection was a cut above other private family collections, according to the article.

Joe realized that he was vaguely familiar with some of the items from the collection, though he'd never visited the museum. It was situated in a small town of some prominence in the 19th century, now a sleepy historic community. Joe realized, rather after the fact, that Sophia, whoever she was, must be of some relation to Samuel and Ruth Roland. Or, perhaps, she had married into the family and the Bakerhurst Museum was probably still a family-held museum. That might be good or bad. The whole situation thus far had an element of fantasy about it, and he looked forward to speaking with her and finding out a little more about the mysterious Samuel for himself. He hoped that however Samuel had made his money, it wasn't in some nefarious way, since he realized he'd already started feeling kindly towards the industrialist.

Well, I'm as ready as I can be to speak with Ms. Bakerhurst. He set the documents aside to finish his lunch and flip through a journal or two. He got so involved that when the phone rang a short time later, he found he'd forgotten the upcoming interview. "Early European art, Joe Cocktail speaking," he answered.

"Mr. Cocktail, this is Sophia Bakerhurst of the Bakerhurst Museum - I believe you were expecting my call?"

Thirty minutes later, Joe said his goodbyes to Sophia, completely, as the song said, 'bewitched and bewildered,' but not bothered. If Samuel had been anything like his descendent, Joe could understand how he'd managed to amass his collection. Sophia was a force of nature. He could tell that even over the phone. This rich-voiced woman had sailed into his life and, in less than a half hour, turned it completely upside down. She had asked him about his education and his interests. She had asked him to describe his most recent research. He'd had little time to get in any questions of his own. She told him she was intrigued by his application. She knew it was the holiday season, but could he possibly take a few days to come and see the museum and ask any and all of his questions at that time. They would take care of all the details and expenses. He had a few days this coming week. Good. That was perfect. Her secretary would be in touch with him to make the travel arrangements, and she looked forward to meeting him on Monday. With that, Sophia rang off.

Joe felt like dancing around his office, but contented himself with a rather loud whoop. *I can't believe it. In less than twenty-four hours, I've gone from worrying about this job to, just possibly, being offered a new job -and a rather exciting new job at that.* Clearly the phone interview had gone well - well enough for them to want to see him, and soon. Well, the Director had indicated that he wanted Joe to take a few days off to think about his future. Joe would do just that. He needed to tell someone. He wondered if Charlie would want to grab a beer after work tonight or if he'd be too busy with the gala. He dialed his friend. "Charlie. It's Friday."

"And you think I didn't know that?" his friend joked.

"If you don't have gala duties, let's grab a beer after work."

"Can't do it just after work, got to get stuff finished here. Why don't I give you a call when I'm through and we can meet?"

"Good enough."

Joe rang off and quite happily turned to the work on his desk. He put the brochure about the Bakerhurst to one side for further review, and the two photocopied articles in his laptop bag, and, with a renewed burst of energy, turned to see if he could make a dent in the necessary work for PFM.

Chapter Thirty-One

On the morning of the long-awaited gala, Joe got up early and drove down to a local park to meet some friends for a trail run. As he stretched and warmed up, he cursed the fact that he hadn't gotten out more during the week. *I'm going to feel this workout.* There was snow on the ground, but the trails were mostly clear and it was cold enough that the ground was hard and not all slush and mud. Joe focused on thinking about nothing but running and enjoyed being outside. He liked to run in cold weather and always felt it must be a throwback to his northern European roots, ancestral memories of chasing reindeer across vast ice fields.

When he arrived back at his apartment, he found a note from Mrs. Watson taped to his door, asking for some assistance in the thrift shop if he had some time during the morning. People often delivered items that were just too heavy or bulky for the Watsons - who were in their early seventies - to move. Joe helped out when they needed him. He liked the Watsons, and certainly Mrs. Watson was always doing little favors for her bachelor neighbor. He thought of the tuxedo hanging in his closet, ready for the gala this evening. That had been a find of Mrs. Watson's after she had learned that his job often required him to attend formal occasions and she discovered he had been renting formal wear. The tuxedo fit him well, and for his last birthday, the Watsons had presented him with a handsome set of gold wingback cufflinks, decorated with the profile portraits of Antinous, the young lover of Emperor Hadrian who'd drowned in the Nile. He'd objected about the value of the gift, but Mrs. Watson had just smiled. They'd been her father's, and both she and Mr. Watson wanted Joe to have them. She'd even cleared it with her two sons, both of whom lived in California, had families of their own, and expressed no interest in the cufflinks or Antinous.

He quickly showered. I'll shave later, he decided, rubbing his chin thoughtfully. Dressed in an old pair of jeans and a Kalamazoo College sweatshirt, he headed down to the thrift shop. The Watsons were glad to see him. They swapped news as Joe moved boxes and helped organize some over-sized chairs that had come in as part of the week's donations. Joe didn't mention the job opportunity at the Bakerhurst; he didn't want Mrs. Watson worrying about him or about having to find a new neighbor. But he did mention his upcoming trip.

"Tonight's the big gala, isn't it?" Mrs. Watson asked.

"Not only is tonight the gala, but it's a long weekend for me. The director told me I could take a few days off next week." *That's putting a positive spin on the actual events.* "I'm off to visit the Bakerhurst Historic Home and Estate."

"Well, that's just fine, Joe. You deserve a little vacation. You've been working long hours.

We'll keep an eye on the apartment while you're gone; come over tomorrow morning for coffee and muffins, we want to hear all about the gala, don't we, Pop?" Mrs. Watson's last remark was addressed to Mr. Watson, who nodded enthusiastically, but said little. *Talking is Mrs. Watson's forte; Mr. Watson is one of the world's patient listeners.*

All three worked companionably until lunchtime. Joe ran out and brought back corned-beef sandwiches and potato salad from a popular local deli for them all - his treat as a belated thank you for the tuxedo, he explained. Mrs. Watson made iced tea and brought out a plate of cookies, and they ate at a table in back of the store, because it wouldn't do to leave the store unattended on a Saturday, which was one of their busiest days. They took turns waiting on various customers who came in to make purchases or to just browse. After lunch, Joe took his leave of the couple.

Joe suddenly realized he'd completely forgotten about ordering Katherine's flowers for the evening. *Idiot, you remember to ask the color of the dress and then don't follow through.* He ran back downstairs calling for Mrs. Watson. She, as usual, knew someone who had a friend with a daughter who ran a local floral shop. Two quick phone calls and Joe was on the phone having a friendly discussion with the daughter. He explained what he wanted, and she assured him she could provide what he required. "I'll swing by to pick them up just before 4:00 pm. Thanks." Joe hung up the phone, picked Mrs. Watson up and swung her around, gave her a big kiss on the cheek, and headed back up to his apartment.

What now? Two hours to kill. Shave, laundry, and read, though not necessarily in that order. Just after 3:00 pm, laundry done and freshly shaved, Joe grabbed the suit bag that held his tuxedo, double-checked that he also had shoes, shirt, studs, cufflinks, and his tie, and set off for the floral shop.

The daughter had done Joe proud. Nestled in the box was a strikingly simple and elegant corsage - a single green cymbidium orchid with pale ribbons of lapis and green. Joe effusively thanked the pretty blond for doing such a great job with his last-minute order. "I'd promise you all my future business, but there isn't likely to be much." *She has a fantastic smile and she's pretty too. I wonder if she's single? Mrs. Watson will know.* Before he let himself get too optimistic, the rational part of his brain joined in the conversation. It's probably not the best time to think about starting a new relationship, Joe. Meanwhile, the woman walked him to the door of the shop and in a minute he was back in his car and on his way to Katherine's apartment.

Chapter Thirty-Two

The trip didn't take him long. Katherine lived in an area of high-density housing close to the local university. He rang the bell for her apartment and she buzzed him in. Her apartment was on the fourth floor and, as usual, the elevators were out of order. He couldn't remember ever seeing them in order, and Katherine always insisted she preferred them not working as an enforced daily exercise regimen. Joe didn't care for the building, or for some of the characters that he'd seen in the hallways or hanging around outside, but he knew that Katherine probably didn't make a huge salary at the museum. *This building is probably the best she can afford right now.*

   She stuck her head out of the door as he came around the final bend in the staircase. "Come on in, Joe, I'm just gathering up my glad rags. I've been on the phone most of the afternoon putting out fires - some jerk dumped bleach all over a set of costumes that were needed for tonight. I've finally found replacements; the choir robes at St. Peter's should do the trick. Do you mind if we pick them up on our way to the museum?"

"Of course, no problem. What happened? What did you say about bleach?"

"Yes, one of those huge bottles from custodial supplies. Someone opened up a closed wardrobe and doused the costumes in bleach. If I get my hands on the person who did this, I will personally choke the life out of them. This, I swear." She finished melodramatically with one hand lifted into the air palm turned outward. "On the positive side, something always goes wrong at the last minute. Let's hope the bleach incident was that last minute thing, because frankly I'm nervous as a cat."

When she said the word cat, Katherine's big tabby, Copyright, for the large white "c"-shaped mark on his forehead, lifted his head, looked at the two, and meowed. Katherine laughed. "Well I'm more nervous than you are, Copy. Which reminds me, I need to fill his bowl or he'll order expensive takeout while I'm gone this evening." She ducked into her small kitchen. Soon Joe and the cat heard the shake of a cat food box. Copyright looked towards Joe at the sound, and Joe thought it only polite to respond.

"It's your food, Copyright. I'm not interested." Copyright gazed at him, apparently considering his reply. The cat got up, stretched, arched his back, and jumped neatly off the couch and padded off to the kitchen.

Joe decided not to mention his own recent troubles with cleaning solvent, but resolved to ask Sgt. Pat about what happened to Katherine's costumes. *There's got to be a connection.*

"Right, I'm ready," Katherine reappeared and disappeared again immediately. She ducked into what Joe assumed was the bedroom and came back with a dress bag and handed it to Joe.

188

"Hold this a minute while I find my coat and keys." Items found, they headed off to the car. Joe opened the door to the passenger seat for Katherine and then moved to the back of the car to place her dress bag on top of his own in the trunk. When he opened his door and got in, she was holding the flower box, looking at it with amazement.

"Oh, the orchid is for you, but you probably already figured that out."

"Joe, it's beautiful." She was beaming. "I can't remember the last time anyone gave me a corsage - and wait until you see it with my dress - it's absolutely perfect."

"Good, I'm glad - a girl deserves flowers for a gala. Particularly after all you've been through this week." On that cheerful note, they drove off to the museum. The emergency stop at the church to pick up the necessary choir robes didn't take long. Joe managed to get the robes into his small trunk, without crushing either the robes or their formal clothes. At the museum, Joe helped Katherine carry the robes into the green room near the performing arts area.

"I'll meet you here just before events get started. I can't wait," Katherine said. "Soon I will hand over responsibility for this fiasco - sorry, performance - to my superior from NYC and I'm free to simply enjoy the show." She grimaced and then smiled. "I've gotta fly, Joe - see you in a little while."

He wandered down to his office, wishing they'd gotten a cup of coffee as planned. It was too late to try the museum's café, as they'd have closed early and would all be engaged in setting up for the gala. He decided to take a chance that there might be some in the registrar's office. He found he was in luck. One of the junior members of the department was holding down the fort. She welcomed Joe and got him a cup of coffee.

"Where are all your fellow office mates?"

"Oh, they're off in the galleries, most of them, making sure everything is ready. I'm here waiting for Dr. Boehm to deliver the diadem. He wanted Conservation to have one more look at it to make some adjustments before..." Her words trailed off and she suddenly looked a little frightened. "I'm not supposed to tell."

"Don't worry. Don't worry. You didn't tell me anything." He smiled. "I promise I'll even clean my fingerprints off the coffee mug when I return it so no one will know..." and here, he dropped his voice to a whisper, "that we've even had this conversation." He winked at the girl and she giggled. Coffee in hand, he headed back to his office.

Chapter Thirty-Three

Joe had planned to work, but decided instead to turn on the space heater, sit back, put his feet up, and think about what had been going on at the museum. *First, cleaning solvent on my files, now bleach on Katherine's costumes; what do my curatorial records and Katherine's costumes have in common? Nothing. Is this just someone practicing random acts of vandalism, or is there a larger plan? What do Katherine and I have in common? We both work at the museum. We are friends and we are both friends of Charlie. The cameras had been turned off the day the vandalism to my files occurred. Could Charlie get in trouble for that?*

Joe just couldn't see a link and it puzzled him. *Cleaning solvent probably wouldn't damage fabric in the same way it had the papers, so whoever was doing this had chosen bleach. Perhaps someone was just trying to make life harder for his or her chosen victims. How and where did the perpetrator, if it was just one person, get the solvent and bleach? Where were the bottles kept in the museum? Probably near the washers and dryers the janitorial staff used to clean rags and towels. The area containing the machines was really more of a hallway than an actual enclosed room, so I suppose it would be relatively easy for someone to pick up a bottle. But wouldn't it look strange if it were someone other than a member of the janitorial staff? Could it be someone on the janitorial staff?* Joe dismissed that thought as beneath him. To suspect a member of the hard working janitorial staff was like a wealthy socialite who accuses the maid of thieving when the mistress has mislaid a piece of jewelry.

No, this was someone with a definite plan or plans in mind, and Joe didn't like it. The damage to Katherine's costumes may have been a copycat incident, but he didn't think so. Joe didn't think Sgt. Pat had widely circulated what had happened in his office. Certainly, the Director and PFM had gotten word of the incident, but Joe thought it wouldn't have been widely discussed among the staff, particularly since Sgt. Pat had labeled it an accident for the time being. Joe finished off his coffee. *It's monkey suit time.* He picked up the suit bag and headed for the closest men's restroom. *Time to forget my worries and just enjoy the party. This should be a night to remember.*

Chapter Thirty-Four

Getting into his tuxedo took Joe rather longer than he had anticipated. He liked to tie his own bow tie, but had been frustrated in his efforts, and it had taken him several tries to get it right in the dim light of the men's room. He gave himself a final look in the mirror before gathering up his discarded clothes and stuffing them into his suit bag. Task completed, he headed back to his office.

The message light on his phone was flashing, but it was already past time to meet Katherine. *Whatever it is can wait. Probably just Katherine looking for me.*

He nearly slipped and fell as he left his office, but just managed to right himself by grabbing the wall. This was getting to be a habit with him. He looked on the floor for water, didn't see any, and decided the culprit in this case was his darned new shoes. He rushed back to the desk, slipped off the shoes, and scored some marks on the bottom with his scissors, and then slipped them back on. A little firmer in his footing, he headed off to find Katherine. As he started up the staircase closest to the green room, he thought he spotted the back end of Boehm, heading for the second floor.

The green room was packed with a local madrigal group wearing the deep purple robes that Katherine and Joe had borrowed. The choristers milled around the room talking and helping each other put silver lamé stoles over their heads and tugging them into place. They looked like a large, but mobile, field of eggplants with racing stripes.

The Dragon-Lady was standing by the door, looking furious. "Have you seen Boehm?" she asked Joe. "He was supposed to have delivered that blasted diadem to me here twenty minutes ago."

"Everyone seems to be looking for him. I saw him headed up to the second floor just a minute ago. Perhaps he thinks he's supposed to deliver it to you there."

"Drat that little man. He's been nothing but a pain in the rear over this. If the Director doesn't have that diadem in the next few minutes we will all be in trouble." The woman turned suddenly pale and shuddered. Joe caught her arm.

"Are you all right, Lori?"

"I'm fine. I'm fine, just anxious and nervous about this event." She pulled her arm away from Joe's hand and seemed to pull herself together. "If Boehm does show up here, will you tell him to meet me upstairs as soon as possible?" Joe nodded and she hurried away, nervous, anxious, and very angry.

Joe scanned the room for Katherine and eventually saw her weaving her way towards him through the throng. At first, he could only see her head – the dark brown hair free now of the ubiquitous ponytail, floating around her shoulders. She broke through the crowd and Joe caught his breath slightly. Katherine cleaned up pretty well. She was tall and sinewy and her dark blue gown fit her perfectly, flaring just below the knee and flowing gracefully as she moved. Pale green orchids were embroidered down one side of the gown and crossed the front just where the skirt flared out. She had a diaphanous wrap tossed nonchalantly, but elegantly, around her bare shoulders. Joe could see why Katherine had looked surprised in the car when she had seen his floral tribute - it seemed to have been made to go with this dress. Instead of pinned to her dress, she wore it on her right wrist.

"Katherine, you look fantastic."

"Well, don't say it as if you're surprised, Joe." He flushed and she laughed at his embarrassment. "Oh, come on, we don't want to be late and miss all the excitement." As she spoke the choirmaster called his eggplants to attention and led them out the door to perform whatever role had been assigned to them.

Katherine grabbed his hand. She was clearly looking forward to whatever was going to happen next. They wound their way through some back passageways and came out through a fire exit just inside the front doors of the museum. There, they joined a group of trustees and staff that had just arrived and were headed towards the darkened atrium. The lights were low, and it took a few moments for Joe's eyes to adjust. Here and there in front of him, he recognized the figures of people he knew. The museum's grand front hall emptied out into the atrium and Joe looked around, completely amazed. The atrium had been transformed and he couldn't decide where to look - the special events team, led by the soon-to-be-unemployed Scott, had outdone themselves.

The most remarkable part of the whole scenario was that the second floor of the museum and the vaulted ceiling of the atrium seemed to have vanished completely. Suspended at various levels in midair, thousands of candles seemed to dancing. Joe was reminded of the opening banquet scene in the first Harry Potter book. He looked down at Katherine, who was watching him. "How did you do it?" he questioned wonderingly.

"You don't really want to know - just suspend your disbelief for a while and let it be magic. The truth is so prosaic."

"Okay, but you'll tell me later, right? Can I get this effect in my living room?"

"Yes, if your living room can accommodate a two-ton flying stage and elements that revolve around multiple axes." She smiled at him, clearly enjoying herself.

"Oh." There wasn't much to say about that. "Probably not, then."

She laughed again. "Let's explore Scott's creation. I've seen the plans and bits and pieces of the set, but the finished product is always so much more glamorous."

The entire effect, Joe supposed, was designed to be vaguely medieval. Gilded cocktail tables were placed around the atrium, and elegantly dressed museum patrons sipped their drinks from what appeared to be crystal, silver, or gold-plated goblets. Pedestals, shaped and painted to resemble twisted and gnarled tree trunks wound with ivy, held fantastic glass vases filled with clear floral marbles in which Scott and his team had arranged green and purple orchids. He looked at Katherine again and she saw his look.

"Did you know about the orchids?" she asked him.

"No," he said, "but clearly you did."

"That's why your choice of flower was so surprising." She glanced at the elegant flower on her wrist.

Enormous sterling silver candelabra with narrow beeswax tapers were scattered throughout the rotunda on more pedestals. Joe noticed thankfully that someone had thought to put velvet-roped stanchions around each of the pedestals, reducing the likelihood that a tipsy patron might stumble into one and risk setting fellow patrons ablaze. Pockets of light glittered here and there as the candlelight reflected off the jeweled necks and sequined bodices of the partygoers.

Tables bearing silver platters of elegant tiny appetizers were covered with rich purple or pale green table linens. In the center of the atrium, there were two long tables covered in purple and each held an elegant, multi-tiered sterling silver champagne fountain, including a fantastic arrangement of green orchids set in great glass orbs filled with more marbles. The two tables angled out from a central table that held an exceptionally large and beautiful 19th century Cantonese punchbowl filled with mulled red wine. People were laughing and holding their glasses beneath the fountains, or filling their goblets with the red scented wine.

Katherine explained, "The Director wanted one fountain to contain mead, until he tasted it, and Scott convinced him that what he'd have is a whole load of leftover mead when the party was over." Joe sympathized with the Director. He had tried mead once in college when he'd gone reluctantly with some friends to a Renaissance faire, and he had found it quite distasteful.

"Is champagne my lady's choice?" he asked and bowed to his date.

"Gallant sir, champagne is in sooth my choice, and if you prefer a beer you will notice tasteful medieval taverns set up in the darkened corners of the room where you can get whatever your heart desires - including the finest of Belgian ales in honor of this evening."

"Champagne isn't really a medieval drink, m'lady."

"I know, but I like the bubbles. How sad that there was no champagne in the dark ages. Poor King Arthur. Poor Guinevere."

"Champagne it is then, no more sad thoughts this evening." He offered her his arm and, laughing, they joined the other guests also filling their goblets at the table.

Katherine drank and then switched her champagne glass to her left hand and looked at her wrist. "Darn, this orchid doesn't tell the correct time. I left my watch in the dressing room - what time is it, Joe?"

He looked at his own watch, "7:35, what time does whatever is going to happen, happen?"

She looked up at the ceiling, slightly worried. "7:45 – time enough for all but the latest attendees to arrive, and then the spectacle begins. Nothing I can do now, everything will be fine, I'm going to enjoy myself - and look." She pointed across the atrium and called out. "Charlie." He saw them and walked to join them, a bottle of Belgian ale in his hand.

"Where's your goblet, chum?" Joe asked his friend.

"I'm not going to drink beer out of a pseudo-medieval goblet. The metal makes the ale taste funny."

"Don't let the Director see you with a bottle," Katherine said, "We're all supposed to be in theme."

"In our medieval tuxedos and evening gowns?" Charlie asked cynically.

All three laughed, and Joe went to fetch Katherine and himself more champagne. He made a mental note to slow down on the alcohol; just because it was running free didn't mean he needed to drink it all. He returned to his friends and they continued chatting about the party and the folk around them.

Katherine glanced over Joe's shoulder. "Oh my, looks like we are about to witness a little unplanned drama just before the big show. Aren't these people supposed to have keepers? Who let them arrive at the same time?"

Chapter Thirty-Five

Joe and Charlie turned to see that the Director's wife, Elizabeth, and Rita had arrived at exactly the same time. Elizabeth was looking positively medieval in a long purple velvet gown with tight fitting sleeves that covered her hands and came to a point over her fingertips. The gown was open in the front and inset with silvery-white brocade. The edges of the velvet skirt and the low, low, low neckline were trimmed with what Joe hoped was faux ermine. Her hair was down and she was wearing an elegant silver diadem. Clearly, Elizabeth planned to play her part as the elegant young queen in this evening's festivities to the hilt. She was a Pre-Raphaelite princess lovely enough to inflame any man. Joe could hardly take his eyes off Elizabeth. When he glanced at Charlie it was to see that his friend was equally as entranced.

Elizabeth was looking down her superior nose at the president of the board of trustees, who was wearing, Joe could hardly believe his eyes, a simple white satin gown that looked suspiciously like a wedding dress. Rita was older than Elizabeth - a lot older - still a good-looking woman, but she was a far cry from a young debutante or blushing bride.

The two women looked for a moment as if there might be a face-off, but each smiled, nodded, and spoke briefly to the other, before walking in opposite directions around the atrium. Rita melded into a group of the trustees, and Elizabeth stopped to speak to Scott, who was hovering nearby. He immediately moved off towards the champagne table, presumably under orders to fetch her majesty a drink.

"Wow, that was close." Katherine spoke, breaking the silence. Joe said nothing but noticed Charlie's eyes following the Director's wife, and he felt something resembling concern for his friend. *Oh no, that would not be good.*

Party chatter rose to a feverish pitch as patrons discussed when and how the Director might arrive. Rumor had it that tonight's grand entrance was going to be spectacular and something surely never to be forgotten - it was a closely guarded secret known only to a few staff members.

Joe thumped Charlie on the back to get his attention. "So, you two know anything about the mysterious arrival? Where should we be standing for the best viewing of whatever's going to happen?" Charlie and Katherine smiled at one another.

Katherine offered, "Here's just about as good as anywhere, don't you think, Charlie?" He just grinned and nodded.

The crowd suddenly grew a little quieter. The choral group had gathered and begun to sing. Katherine came closer, leaned against him, and whispered, "They will be performing Thomas

202

Morely's 'The Triumphes of Oriana' in its entirety tonight."

"The whats of who? Tell me about it."

"Twenty-five madrigals in honor of Queen Elizabeth the First. Now, listen to the words, they are important. The Director picked the piece himself." And the chorus sang:

> Hence stars! Too dim of light,
> you dazzle but the sight,
> you teach to grope by night.
> See here the shepherd's star
> excelling you so far...

And then Joe stopped listening to the words being sung, as his eyes and everyone else's were drawn to the dancing candles above the atrium floor. One by one they began to wink out, now slightly faster, and then in groups. The musicians continued to sing, and for a brief moment, the rotunda was plunged into complete darkness, except for the candlelight offered by the candelabras placed around the room. Suddenly, a shaft of light from a spotlight revealed a vision above the heads of the gala guests.

"You've got to be kidding?" Joe bent slightly to whisper in Katherine's ear. He could feel her shaking with repressed laughter.

High above the crowd, descending apparently to earth from the starry heavens on a silvery cloud came the Director. In a reverse apotheosis, the Director began his descent from the atrium ceiling, standing comfortably on his personal cloud. He was clothed as a Renaissance princeling in a silver brocade tunic and purple tights. A tall man, he formed a striking vertical axis between the silver of the cloud and his full head of almost silver hair. The staff and guests alike saw the Director's smile widen in triumph at their obvious surprise - in his element, he raised his hands in a grandiose gesture of benediction. "Good evening and welcome." The acoustics in the atrium were such that he had no need of a microphone.

His silver hair seemed to gleam and sparkle. Then Joe realized, he should have known, the Director was wearing the *Helt Diadem*. Something was wrong, though. Even from the floor Joe could tell there were little streaks of red running down the Director's face - like blood, as if the diadem was a crown of thorns and not a hero's crown of golden laurel. And just at that moment, the Director threw his head up and back like a woman tossing her hair over her shoulder, in a triumphant gesture. To Joe, it appeared at first as if the Director was about to speak again; his mouth opened wide, but the voices of the madrigal singers were raised once again in a crescendo of sound and the Director's words were lost. Joe saw the man's upper body jerk once more and then the Director seemed to lose his balance, and he fell.

Time stopped. The entire assembly watched as the Director reeled back, grasping at but missing the suspension cables that Joe knew must be supporting the cloud stage prop. The Director plunged thirty feet straight down into the Cantonese punchbowl. Hot mulled wine and shards of porcelain with images of peony blossoms, butterflies, and precious objects flew into the crowd.

Looking back at the event later it seemed to Joe as if the pandemonium that erupted happened in slow motion. Rita Avi and a number of other patrons had been standing near the table with the punchbowl, watching the Director's unplanned descent. They were now drenched with hot wine and several had small cuts and lacerations from the chips of porcelain. Rita's white gown was stained a patchy red. Her face was bleeding. Bowls of peeled, cooked shrimp were overturned, their contents, along with the ice that kept them chilled, lay distributed across the floor, alternatively sticky and slippery, both equally as hazardous.

Joe scanned the crowd in search of the Director's wife. He located her just in time to see her begin to fall as well. She tried to keep herself upright by holding on to one of the decorated pedestals, but fainted, toppling the pedestal as she fell. The tall glass vase atop the pedestal crashed to the floor, freeing a flood of floral marbles onto the atrium floor. The fast-traveling marbles caused a succession of startled men and women to lose their balance, crashing into one another as they rushed to her aid.

Katherine had grabbed his arm at the moment of the accident and was keening, "Oh my god, oh my god, oh my god. I tried to get him to wear a harness. Oh my god, Joe, is he hurt badly? I can't look."

The entire episode had lasted no more than twenty or thirty seconds, and then the crowd erupted - women screamed, men swore, and the museum's security staff fought through the crowd to get to the Director. Through a brief opening in the crowd, Joe saw where the man had fallen - his elegant torso bent at an impossible angle, the silver-coiffed head shattered. Security didn't need to hurry - the Director was dead.

Chapter Thirty-Six

It was just shy of 11:00 pm. Joe and Katherine were seated together on a couch in the green room. Joe had his arm around Katherine and she was dozing on his shoulder, snoring slightly in a very quiet and ladylike manner. The police had arrived within minutes of the accident and, with the help of museum security, had efficiently moved all the guests from the atrium to the galleries, where they sat benumbed at elegant tables set for the festive dinner.

Eventually, a police officer arrived and spoke briefly to the assembled guests, apologizing for keeping them, and explaining that he needed to keep them a while longer. Because of this, he continued, the wait staff had been directed to serve the planned dinner in a reduced form. Joe, slightly nauseous at the turn of events, had been surprised to see the variety of responses to this announcement. Several people looked pale at the mention of food. Others wolfed down the food when it eventually arrived as if whatever was on their plate might be their last meal. Some left food untouched, but drained their wine glasses, or water glasses, or coffee cups, as if quantities of liquid might wash away the evening's earlier events.

Joe noticed that someone, probably Scott or PFM, had taken charge of the Director's wife and had spirited her away to someplace more private, away from curious or prying eyes. Rita had not had the same attention paid to her distress. She sat frozen in place, at the head table, raised on a dais at the front of the room. There was a large bandage on her head and someone had tried ineffectively to scrub the wine from the white gown. She sat huddled in one of the thrones that faced out towards the crowd. The seat next to her, which was slightly elevated, had been intended for the Director; it was empty. She ate nothing. She drank nothing. A close friend crouched at her side, occasionally offering quiet, supportive comments to which she made no response.

After the abbreviated dinner had been served, a bevy of blue-uniformed police officers carrying clipboards had entered the room with the officer in charge. "I'd like to thank everyone for your patience. We are going to let all of you except senior staff and key museum personnel go home now. These officers have copies of the guest list for this evening. I'd appreciate it if you will confirm or provide a number where you can be reached. Those of you who are senior staff," and at this the officer-in-charge looked at the crowd as if the senior staff members were marked in some way, "we'd like you to gather in the," and here he looked at a paper in his hand, "the green room. We'd like to speak with senior staff members individually and we'll try to get through these interviews as quickly and efficiently as possible so you all can go home and get to bed."

Although the information had been presented politely enough, Joe didn't think senior staff members really had any option but to proceed to the green room.

And so, Joe and Katherine sat together on a couch waiting their turns. The atmosphere in the room had a rather surreal quality - like an audition or a job interview. The room had started out full of shocked museum employees, and gradually, one-by-one, staff members had been ushered out the door and into, Joe presumed, another office. Those who left the room did not return. Conversation among those who remained was quiet and unusually stilted. A uniformed guard stationed at the door had asked them to refrain from speaking of the events of earlier in the evening. Most staff members seemed glad to follow his advice.

Eventually an officer came to the door and called Katherine's name. She awoke with a start. "I feel like I've walked into some television drama."

"Don't worry," Joe encouraged her. "All they want is to get a sense of what happened this evening. I don't know how long it will be before I'm called; do you want to wait for me to finish or shall I ask the nice policemen to arrange a ride home for you?"

"Ever the gentleman, aren't you Joe?" She smiled. "I'll wait for you in my office, get some paperwork done if I can concentrate. That is, I will if they aren't using my office for their interviews."

Katherine's office was very near the green room, and Joe realized that it would have been a convenient space for the police to appropriate for their brief interviews with the party guests.

Joe took his keys out of his pocket and started to hand them to her, saying, "If they are in your office, why don't you go to mine?"

She waved the keys away. "That's a plan, but I'll use the cleaning code if I need to get into your office."

"Does everyone know about this cleaning code BUT me?"

"Pretty much. See you soon I hope, Joe." Joe sat back down on the couch and closed his eyes, not really wanting to engage in conversation with any of his colleagues at the moment.

Chapter Thirty-Seven

"Cocktail, is there a Cocktail here?" The voice faltered for a moment and Joe, opening his eyes, saw one of the policemen, whose face betrayed the familiar smirk. Joe didn't even react; he was too used to people finding his name funny and waited for the inevitable gratuitous comment. The policeman couldn't help himself. "I wish I had one, a cocktail, I mean," he commented to Joe as Joe approached him. Joe smiled tiredly in response.

"Must have been a drag growing up with that for a last name. Is it real?"

"Yes to both questions."

"Ms. Harding told me you were together, so the boss said to bring you in next."

"Thanks, I appreciate it."

The policeman led the way into a small rehearsal room, in the opposite direction from Katherine's office, and opened the door, standing aside to let Joe pass into the room, shutting the door behind him.

A tall man, a little older than Joe, stood up from behind a small table and leaned over to shake hands with him as he approached. "Dr. Cocktail, I'm Detective Weber. Sorry to keep you so late. Have a seat. I just need to ask you a few routine questions and then you can take Ms. Harding home."

Joe sat.

"What is your position here at the museum?"

"I'm Associate Curator of European Art."

"Did you know the deceased well?"

"He was the Director of the museum and I'm a junior curator. I didn't know him well. He was the big boss. We weren't chums and we didn't hang out together, if that's what you're asking?"

"I understand you were in some trouble here recently?"

Joe looked at the man across from him. Joe had no interest in airing the museum's dirty laundry to the police, especially under the circumstances, but apparently one of his co-workers had. He considered his next words carefully. He wanted to clarify his position in as few words as possible.

"Earlier this week, I expressed a difference of opinion with the Director and my immediate supervisor."

"That would be," and here the officer looked down at some notes, "Dr. Prudence Fenn-Martin?"

"Yes. They took exception to a recommendation I made and suggested I take a few days off."

"Can you tell me what the difference of opinion was about?"

"Of course I can, but is this information relevant?"

"Dr. Cocktail, we aren't sure yet what information is going to be relevant in this case, but anything you can tell us will give us a better picture of the situation here at the museum."

"Am I in some kind of trouble?"

Detective Weber sighed and rubbed his temple with a large thumb and forefinger. "No, Dr. Cocktail, you aren't in trouble. Let's just say that it has come to my attention over the past couple of hours that the Director was not terribly popular with his staff."

Joe laughed and said, "That's putting it mildly." He felt instant remorse and Detective Weber seemed to understand.

"Don't feel bad, Dr. Cocktail. With a few exceptions, everyone I've talked to tonight seems to have disliked the man, but many of your colleagues are quick to point out that there are others with as much reason to dislike him."

"You think his fall tonight wasn't an accident?" Joe asked and realized how much more terrible that made the night's events.

"I didn't say that, Dr. Cocktail. I'm just trying to get the picture clear here in my head. I don't have any reason to believe that what happened tonight wasn't simply a tragic accident, but I wouldn't be doing my job if I didn't look into the issue a little more closely. Now, would you explain your troubles with the Director to me?"

Joe recapped the events of the week. Detective Weber stopped him at times and made him go over details, and he made several notes on a legal pad that he kept in front of him, occasionally nodding his head when something Joe said seemed to tally with something he'd already written. He seemed particularly interested in the vandalism of the curatorial files.

"Okay Dr. Cocktail, I think I understand what you've told me about the past week. Now I'd like you to walk me through everything you did and saw this evening. Just go through the events that immediately preceded the accident. We are having everyone do this to see if we get any new information." Joe took a moment to recall what he'd seen.

"You understand, Detective Weber, that the entire evening was unusual. It's been a busy week here and the demands of putting on an event of this magnitude have taken their toll on everyone. Katherine," Weber looked up and Joe sought to clarify his comments. "Ms. Harding, Charlie Miller, and I are good friends, but the Director's need for secrecy meant that while they both knew approximately what was going to happen tonight,", He quickly edited himself, "I mean, of course, they knew what the spectacle was supposed to look like, but not about the accident."

The detective simply nodded and continued to watch Joe and listen to his story.

"As I said, the whole thing was simply over the top. I mean, really, appearing from the heavens on a cloud?" Joe made the comment come out like a question. "No disrespect intended towards the dead, but that takes some real balls. I was dumbstruck watching the show unfold." He stopped a second as something tugged on his memory, and he remembered.

"There was blood on his face before he fell," Joe blurted out.

Detective Weber seemed to understand his comment, but shook his head. "No, not real blood, but it probably looked like blood."

Joe raised his eyebrows, but said nothing, hoping the detective would explain.

"I'll explain in a minute, you just continue to tell me what you saw."

"I looked up at him and noted that he was wearing the *Helt Diadem*."

The detective nodded his head.

"And then, I noticed streaks of red running down his face, like he was wearing a crown of thorns. So was it just a trick of the lights?" Joe asked hopefully.

"Oh no. You saw something that looked like blood all right. It seems that one of your colleagues," and at this he glanced down again to look at his notes, "a Mr. Bradley Boehm," he looked up for acknowledgement of the name from Joe, who nodded his head, "It seems that Mr. Boehm had a grudge against the deceased for a number of reasons, not the least of which was the deceased's decision to wear the," he looked back at his notes, "the *Helt Diadem* during tonight's event. Mr. Boehm felt that the deceased was exercising his authority in an inappropriate manner and took steps meant to humiliate him in front of the crowd of party-goers."

Joe found himself transfixed by the detective's words. He realized his jaw had dropped open and he closed his mouth, swallowed, but found he couldn't stop himself from asking, "Geez. What did he do?"

"You understand, I have not seen the *Diadem* yet myself, Mr. Cocktail, but there is apparently a kind of narrow band of soft fabric and pillowing material inside the diadem which, as I understand the situation, allows the object to be safely displayed on a mount in a showcase. Earlier today Mr. Boehm undid the stitching in several places and inserted small pillows containing fake blood inside the lining that were designed to burst when the crown was pulled into place on the forehead. Mr. Boehm then held onto the diadem until just before the deceased was due to put the item on his head and, hmm, descend from the clouds. Boehm apparently delivered it with just moments to spare, and the deceased, in a hurry and angry, something Mr. Boehm had counted on, pulled the diadem down sharply onto his head, releasing the slow flow of the fake blood. It would have taken a moment or two for the liquid to seep through the fabric and begin to run down his face, and by that time, he was already above the crowd and in the spotlight. Mr. Boehm seemed quite pleased at what he'd achieved."

"I'm speechless."

"I confess, I was too. Mr. Boehm is going to be in some serious trouble, but not with the police, unless we discover that his little stunt had anything to do with the accident. There wasn't any fake blood on the deceased's hands..."

Joe grimaced, but the detective continued... "so he doesn't seem to have lost control because he believed he was bleeding."

There was quiet in the room for a moment as the detective let Joe come to terms with Boehm's behavior. Then the detective spoke again.

"Is there anything else you remember or you can think of that might be helpful to us, Dr. Cocktail?"

Joe gave the matter some serious consideration. He could add to the confusion and talk more about events he had seen or overheard during the past week but, according to Detective Weber, some of his chattier colleagues had already covered that ground.

216

"I guess not. He, the Director I mean, seemed confident, even jubilant, as he addressed the crowd from his position on high. It wasn't until he looked surprised and started to fall that any of us realized something might be wrong, and at that point, events moved far too quickly and," he stopped before continuing, "and at the same time in slow motion. Do you know what I mean?"

The detective nodded.

"It just happened and then he was there on the floor and the place was in an uproar."

"Thank you, Dr. Cocktail. I appreciate your thoughtful, relatively unemotional approach to the events of this evening."

"Well, I am trained to look at pictures and this evening's events do seem to have left an indelible impression on me. I'm afraid I haven't been much help."

"Oh well, I wouldn't worry about that. It all adds up and, more than likely, this has just been a tragic accident that has been complicated by the fact that no one inside the museum much liked the fellow."

"There is that. So I'm free to go?" Joe questioned the policeman.

"Yes, of course. Make sure the sergeant outside has your up-to-date information so we know how to get hold of you if we need to."

Joe had a thought. "I was planning on taking a brief trip this Monday and Tuesday, is it okay for me to leave town?"

The detective looked at him and laughed. "This isn't a locked-room mystery, Dr. Cocktail. As I said, just make sure we know how to find you if we need to ask you any more questions."

"Right. Will do. Goodnight, Detective Weber. I won't say it's been nice to meet you." Joe trailed off uncertainly.

"Not to worry, Dr. Cocktail, detectives are like dentists, we know we are needed but don't expect to be met with open arms. Oh, and would you ask the sergeant to bring the next staff member to me? Goodnight, Dr. Cocktail." And with that the detective turned his eyes once again to his notes.

Chapter Thirty-Eight

After speaking with the sergeant, Joe walked down the short hallway to Katherine's office. She was seated at her desk, illuminated only by the light of a small banker's lamp. Like the detective he had just left, she was looking at a document and chewing on the end of a pencil. "Knock, knock," he announced softly.

She looked up at him and gave a small sigh, "I'm so tired."

"Let's go home then." She gathered up her belongings and followed him to his office so he could grab his coat, clothes, and laptop bag. They maneuvered their way out of the building, past exhausted-looking museum guards and several alert policemen who'd probably just come on duty. Both turned in their keys and said their goodnights to the guard at the desk. Neither of them spoke as they walked to Joe's car. He opened the door for Katherine and made sure she was comfortable before closing the door. He opened the trunk of the car, took off his coat and folded it, and put it down before placing his laptop bag on top. Then he continued to the driver's side.

It wasn't until he'd started the car and glanced over at his passenger that he realized she was crying. In the fluorescent lights of the garage he could see the tear marks on her cheek. "Katherine, are you okay?" he asked.

She turned and looked at him, her eyes filling with tears. "I hated him, but I didn't want him to die."

"What are you talking about?"

"Joe, I'm the person responsible for the performances here at the museum. If something was wrong with that equipment or if there was some kind of liquid or oil or, I don't know, something on that platform, then I killed him." The last part of her statement came out as an anguished sob.

"Katherine," he spoke sharply to get her attention and she looked at him. He knew enough, or he thought he knew enough, not to be overly sympathetic at this moment or his friend might break down completely. "Katherine," he continued, using a softer tone, "It was an accident. You didn't cause this to happen. You've spent the past two weeks worrying over the tiniest details related to the gala performances - it's not your fault." He spoke the last four words precisely and clearly, looking into her eyes the whole time.

Katherine shuddered and then made a visible effort to get herself together. She opened her small evening bag, rummaging inside but failing to find a handkerchief or tissue. Joe pulled out his silk pocket square and handed it to her. If the waterworks really got started it wouldn't be much good, but for now it was better than nothing.

"Thank you, Joe. I'm awfully sorry. I'm so tired I don't know what I'm saying."

"Don't worry about it so much, Katherine. Let's put some distance between the museum and us. I'll have you in bed in no time." He stopped and sputtered, "I didn't mean, I mean, I don't mean I want to go to bed with you, but I don't mean I don't want to not go to..." he trailed off, thinking that anything he said would make this moment even more awkward. When he looked at Katherine he saw her enjoying his confusion, and then there was something else in her eyes and Joe felt a stab of excitement.

Joe held his breath, willing to let Katherine take the next step. Her voice was only slightly huskier when she finally spoke, "How 'bout I let you come up and we discuss this over a much-needed nightcap?"

"Agreed." A sudden surge of adrenaline made him feel alive and overly aware of his companion. The adrenaline rush didn't last long for either of them. The ride back to Katherine's apartment was accomplished mostly in silence. Joe parked the car and they walked up the sidewalk to the apartment house side by side.

Once in, they took the stairs up to her apartment still in silence. On the way up they passed small groups of teenagers, mostly boys, hanging out in the stairwell. The kids ignored the two of them, but Joe saw one or two of the boys give Katherine the once-over in a manner with which he wasn't entirely comfortable. He wanted to say something. He'd never thought much about how and where Katherine lived. Given her position at the museum, it was highly likely that she often came home late in the evening, after performances were over, and if she walked up these stairs alone she was putting herself in danger. He didn't much like the thought, but imagined now wasn't the best time to bring the issue up.

They arrived at the apartment and Copyright was there to meet them, complaining loudly about the lack of food and attention. Katherine turned and asked him if he'd like a glass of wine or a beer - Joe could see she was exhausted. "Listen, Katherine, it's been a long evening. How about I take a rain check on the drink tonight?" Here he stopped and smiled at her. "You get a good night's rest and I'll take you out somewhere nice for lunch or brunch tomorrow, if you don't already have plans?"

"Okay. It's a deal." She gave a great yawn and brought both hands up to cover her face, rubbing her eyes as she completed the gesture. "I'm so tired I can't see or think straight right now. Brunch is a much better plan than a nightcap. Give me a call in the morning, the late morning, in fact the bit of the late morning that is almost noon."

"Will do." He pulled her close and hugged her, dropping a brotherly kiss on her forehead.

She looked at him and smiled. "Not quite the evening either of us expected, was it?"

"Not by a long shot. Okay, I'm leaving now. Lock the door behind me."

"Yes, Joe."

He left the apartment and hesitated in the hall to make sure she bolted the door. He heard the bolt slam home and headed for the stairs, his car, his apartment, and his bed, in that order.

Chapter Thirty-Nine

It was late Sunday morning when Joe finally came to, untangling himself from his down comforter and mound of pillows. Every morning it was the same - he didn't so much sleep in his bed as unconsciously struggle with his bedclothes all night long. The process never stopped him from getting a good night's sleep - in fact, just the opposite - having vanquished pillows, comforter, and sheets he woke up ready to face the day, but realized this morning was different.

What is it? The Director. The gala. Oh, and I promised Katherine I'd take her to brunch this morning. Joe looked at the clock - a little after 9:00 am; that meant he had time for a run before doing anything else. He grabbed running tights and a turtle-neck running shirt, pulled them on, pulled a pair of running shorts over the tights, grabbed socks and shoes and headed for the living room.

A few minutes later, suitably dressed with his muscles stretched, he headed down the stairs for his run. Though there was still snow on the ground, the sun was shining and the air felt more like autumn than winter. The brisk air cleared his head and for the first 15 minutes he concentrated on running, not letting himself think about events of the night before. There were quite a few runners out this morning, taking advantage of the sunshine. He nodded to those he knew, but didn't fall in with anyone – today, he needed to be by himself.

A lot had happened in the past week - the death of the Director was just the latest - and admittedly the worst of the events. Joe's office had been vandalized. The Director and PFM had come down on him like a ton of bricks about the painting of the *Virgin and Child* and suggested his leave of absence and, coincidentally, right at the same moment, the Bakerhurst opportunity had presented itself to him - and even more remarkable, he'd gotten an interview.

Should I call Sophia Bakerhurst and try to reschedule this interview? The more he thought about that the more he disliked the idea. Admittedly, the senior staff and administration of the museum were going to have their hands full this week, but he couldn't see how any decisions would require his input. PFM, as chief curator, would likely be put in charge in the interim - and boy would she love that. In the end, he convinced himself to go ahead with the interview. *It's the right thing to do.*

I should probably call Mom and Dad, too. If the news of the Director's death makes the national news, Mom will already be imagining that I'm next. He decided he'd call as soon as he got home. He turned a corner into the last lap of his regular run, and for the final mile, he ran for the sheer joy of running, arriving home breathless and invigorated.

Walking in large circles around the back yard of the building to cool down, he didn't see Mrs. Watson come out of the back door from her apartment until she began talking to him. "Well Joe, it sounds as if your gala evening had a rough end last night. I can't help but feel sorry for that poor man and his family. It's all over the front page of the newspaper. Listen," and here Mrs. Watson switched conversational horses in midstream, "I've got a batch of sour cherry and pecan muffins due to come out of the oven in about 10 minutes and Mr. Watson's just brewing his second pot of Sunday morning coffee. That should give you plenty of time for a quick shower. You just come right over after you are done and tell us everything."

He smiled up at her. "Yes, Mrs. Watson. I'll be right over. But not too many muffins - I've got a brunch date."

"Well, you can just tell us all about that too, young man. Brrr...it's cold even if it is sunshiny out here. I'm going inside now. I'll leave the inside door open." She stepped back through the door into her tiny kitchen and Joe ran upstairs to his own apartment to shower, but was already anticipating the warm muffins and coffee he didn't have to make himself.

"And that's how the evening ended, with all the senior staff invited to have a seat in the Green Room prior to a private conversation with one Detective Weber." He finished his story a short while later and rewarded himself with another bite of warm muffin, savoring the textures of the plumped sour cherries, crunchy pecans, and warm sweet cake.

"Detective Weber. Tall boy. Slightly older than you, Joe?" asked Mrs. Watson.

He nodded.

"Then he would be Bill and Margaret Weber's boy. What was his name? Let me think. Ted perhaps. He stole a pie from me once and now he's a detective. I should call Margaret this week."

"He was a nice kid, and a heck of a shortstop when he was in high school. I think he played in college, too," Mr. Watson added his own contribution to the conversation.

Joe had long since stopped being surprised at the number of people known to the Watsons. It only made sense they'd have some connection with a police detective who Joe would probably meet only once in his life. Well, if they ever did meet again Joe could ask him about his college ball career. Let Detective Weber think there was a little bit of the detective in Joe, too. He didn't need to tell the police officer that he was a member of the privileged inner circle of the amazing Watsons.

"Anyway, I told Detective Weber what I've just told you and then he sent us off, so you can see I don't really know a whole lot more about events than you do from this morning's paper. The Director appeared above us in the clouds, raised his hands to say something to us, and then he just plummeted." Joe shivered as he recalled the events of the previous evening. "I didn't like him and we had had some serious problems with one another in the past week, but I never wished him dead."

"What kind of problems, Joe?" Mrs. Watson asked.

"Nothing to be worried about, particularly now and particularly not for you to worry about, Oh Marvelous Maker of Muffins. Oh, I meant to tell you. If there's any heavy lifting you need done in the store in the next few days, let me know and I can make some time this afternoon. I'm headed out of town tomorrow and won't be back until late Tuesday or Wednesday."

Mr. Watson thought about it for a minute. "I think we got most everything done we needed to do yesterday morning, Joe. You just go off and have a nice long luncheon with your young lady. We'll pick up the mail and the papers for you and set 'em inside the door on the dining table. What's that place called you are headed off to this time?"

"It's a small historic estate called the Bakerhurst Collection. Ever heard of it?"

"Can't say I have, but you know that doesn't mean much, I never was one for art museums. Mrs. Watson will confirm that."

"It's true. He wanted to drag me to Civil War battlefields and I wanted to drag him to museums, so mostly we just compromised by antiquing and going to car shows. Marriage, it's about compromise."

"And cooking, m'dear, never forget cooking. Compromise and cooking."

Joe pushed his chair back from the table, gathered up his plate and coffee mug, walked into the tiny kitchen, and rinsed both before leaving the dishes in the drain pan. "I've told you before, Joe, just leave the dishes on the table."

"And I've told you before, Mrs. Watson, my mother raised us to be responsible for our own dishes and I'm darn well going to be responsible." It was a running joke they both enjoyed. She reached into the cabinet and pulled out a stack of paper coffee cups she kept just for such occasions and poured him a to-go cup. He thanked her and affectionately ruffled her hair -

in return she gave him a swat as he headed for the door.

"If we don't see you again before you leave, travel safely Joe."

"Will do, Mrs. W. Bye, Mr. W."

He returned to his apartment. Called Katherine and arranged to pick her up just after noon. He then called one of his favorite local restaurants and was luckily able to secure a last minute brunch reservation. He thought about calling Charlie and inviting him and decided against it.

Then Joe called his parents. His mom picked up on the second ring - she called his father and put Joe on the speakerphone. He took his cup of coffee and settled down in his comfy chair to rehash the week's events with his parents. His mom was appropriately angry, horrified, and pleased as he recounted the events of his week: his fight with the Director, the events of the previous evening, and his impending interview. His father, as usual, said little but Joe knew he liked hearing from his son. His mom was a compulsive worrier and, luckily, Joe thought there was enough to worry her about his current job that she seemed pleased about this new opportunity. Joe eventually rang off, satisfied that he'd honored all his family and neighborly commitments, and went to pick up Katherine for brunch as promised.

Chapter Forty

The waiter seated them at a window table, overlooking a bit of the park; the early frost meant that some of the trees still bore vestiges of their leaves - now frozen and blackened, but overall the view was lovely. They watched small clusters of cross-country skiers out taking advantage of the sunny weather and sipped mimosas as they waited for brunch. Joe felt they both wanted to talk about the events of last night, but neither could quite bring up the subject, so they talked about how odd the weather had been lately. Finally, Katherine mustered the necessary courage and said, "What do you think will happen at work tomorrow?"

"There must be some process for what happens when a director dies or leaves. My guess is, if Rita has recovered, she will have called the other trustees and they will name an interim director, probably PFM. I didn't check my email this morning; has there been any kind of announcement?"

"Not so far. I don't think Linda was at the event last night. She or someone in the HR office produces those horrible, 'We are saddened to inform you...' emails. There will probably be an All Staff meeting tomorrow, won't there?"

"I guess so. I won't be there."

"Why won't you be there?"

"Remember, the Director and PFM suggested I take a few days off."

"But surely now that... I mean with events..." Katherine seemed unsure how to phrase what she was trying to say.

"I've already made arrangements to be out of town tomorrow. Detective Weber said it was okay." He realized he was talking to himself more than Katherine.

"Out of town where?" She looked at him curiously. He realized he was being evasive and decided to open up.

"I've got a job interview."

She appeared stunned. "You're leaving the museum? Now? When all this is going on? Things might get better now that the Director is..," she hesitated, and finished lamely, "gone."

"Katherine, I'm not leaving my job yet. This was just a shot-in-the-dark that turned into an interview faster than I imagined." He told her the story of the odd application questions and the call from Sophia. "And when she called and wanted to see me this coming week, it seemed like an ideal chance to get away and let the Director and PFM cool down a little bit."

Katherine looked unconvinced, but said nothing.

"So tomorrow I'm going to catch a short flight and see if there's really an opportunity for me at the Bakerhurst. I'll tell you one thing. From where I was sitting last week, taking this chance is a whole lot better than doing nothing and letting PFM and the Director steamroll me."

"I know it's been tough for you - tough for all of us the past couple of weeks. The idea of you leaving just came as a shock this morning on top of last night's shock. Oh Joe, if you leave, who will take your place at the Fox? Charlie and I have only just broken you in." She gave a mock sigh and threw up her hands and complained, "The good ones always get jobs somewhere else."

"If I'm one of the good ones, Katherine, I really think you need to start setting the bar a little higher."

Just then, the waitress appeared with Western omelets, fresh tortillas, bacon, sausage, and hash browns and they turned their attention to their meals. A few minutes later, hunger sated for the moment, Joe sat back in his chair and took another sip of coffee. "It was weird last night - everything about the evening was so surreal."

"I know. I fell right asleep last night, but when I woke up this morning for a minute I couldn't remember why I felt as if something terrible had happened, and then it all came rushing back to me. I'll never ever forget seeing him in the spotlight and then falling, slowly falling, but it wasn't really slow at all."

"Did you notice his face - before he fell? The streaks on his face."

"The blood streaks you mean?" She paled and set her fork down. "I thought I'd imagined them or that it was a trick of the light. You saw them, too?"

"No, you didn't imagine them, but the good news is it wasn't actually blood. Bradley Boehm rigged the *Helt Diadem* with fake blood capsules - so as soon as the Director put the diadem firmly in place, the capsules released their goo."

"Is he insane? What in the world was he trying to do?"

"According to Detective Weber, he had hoped to embarrass the Director."

"He'd have been out of a job the next day."

"That wouldn't matter to Boehm. He doesn't actually need the money - he comes from money - but he loves his collection. I think the Director had just piled so much on him in the past week that he felt he needed to take dramatic and public action. My guess is, knowing Boehm, he's terrified that his little prank had some sort of role in the Director's fall. He probably didn't get much sleep last night."

"I just don't understand how he fell, Joe. That rigging was solid - meant to bear the weight of someone much heavier than the Director. Even if he felt the trickles of fake blood running down his face, wouldn't he just have thought it was sweat? It wouldn't have been enough to make him lose his balance. I double-checked all the equipment during the dress rehearsal on Friday evening. What happened? Why did he fall? Excitement? Adrenaline? You don't think he did it on purpose, do you?" Her face turned even whiter. "Suicide?"

"Absolutely not. Now who's acting crazy? He was on top of the world - literally and figuratively. He had all of us just exactly where he wanted us, looking up in worshipful adoration. I'd bet money the police didn't find any evidence of a sudden terminal illness that made him choose to end his life in such a spectacular fashion. And speaking of spectacular falls, how about the chaos that resulted when Elizabeth fainted?"

Katherine looked at him closely for a moment and said in a flat voice, "I don't believe

Beth fainted any more than you believe the Director committed suicide."

"Oh, come on Katherine, I know you don't like her, but she had just seen her husband fall to his death."

"She couldn't have known it was to his death and, besides, this doesn't have anything to do with me liking or not liking her, Joe. I've known Beth since we were children. I told you guys the other night - she grew up around all these brothers. I don't have any reason to believe there was sexual abuse, but there was certainly physical abuse - the kind that siblings perpetrate on one another. You know what I mean? The abuse ranged from spitballs to physical beatings and was meted out whenever one of her brothers would go into a rage. Beth learned how to take it and dish it out and was a formidable mean girl in school. She may appear frail, but she is skilled at non-physical revenge, and she is always in complete command of herself. I don't believe for a minute that she fainted. My guess is she thought her husband's fall was less serious than it was and wanted to grab some attention and, as you say, cause a little chaos of her own."

"Okay, okay, sorry I brought it up. I'll take your word about Elizabeth. I haven't been around her enough to see that side of her. You've got to admit the aftermath of the fall was something straight out of a Stephen King movie - did you see Rita Avi?"

"Oh my gosh, yes, in her red-wine soaked vintage wedding dress, blood on her face from the shards of the punchbowl."

"The punchbowl." He stopped, stunned.
"What?"

"I've just realized that I feel a lot more emotion about the loss of that beautiful Cantonese punchbowl than I do about the Director's loss of life. That's sad and makes me feel like a pretty crappy person."

"Joe," Katherine reached across and took his hand, "It's okay. We are all still in shock. You aren't a bad person. It's not like you and the Director were best buds or even had much in common, and you'd been at loggerheads with one another all week. Just because he's dead doesn't make him automatically a nice guy. He wasn't a nice guy. He liked his power and he liked to belittle his employees. Making us feel small made him feel big. I'm not glad he's dead, but I can't honestly say his death makes me sad. Empty, a little frightened for the future, and concerned about whether the equipment I was in charge of played a role in his death, but not sad. Maybe it's a good thing that you have the next couple of days away from the museum to focus on this opportunity. Let's change the subject. Tell me what you know about the Bakerhurst. What kind of collections do they have?"

And as easily as that, the conversation shifted and Joe found himself happily discussing what he knew and loved best, museums and collections. After lunch they tromped through the snow in the park, and Joe encouraged Katherine to tell him how she had ended up in the field of performing arts.

The entire afternoon was perfectly convivial, and Joe found himself glad that the two of them hadn't actually complicated their relationship by falling into bed with one another the previous evening - he didn't bring the subject up, nor did Katherine, but he was pretty sure she felt the same way. Now, with an interview ahead of him and potentially a move to a new job, it wasn't an ideal time to start a new relationship - but he did feel like he and Katherine had taken their personal friendship to another deeper, and more satisfying, level.

When he got back to his apartment, the light on his phone was blinking. He pushed the message button and heard Sophia Bakerhurst's rich voice. "Mr. Cocktail, this is Sophia Bakerhurst. I just heard the tragic news about your Director's death and wanted to extend my sympathy to you. I will of course understand if you feel you need to reschedule your interview for another time, but I hope - we hope - that you'll come as scheduled. I think you will find the visit to the Bakerhurst just the respite you need during a trying time. Do please call and let me know if we can still expect you tomorrow."

Joe smiled to himself. *She's concerned for my welfare and is offering me an out, but encouraging me to come anyway. That's a good sign.* His mind made up, Joe picked up the phone to confirm his plans. *Tomorrow, the Bakerhurst!* And with that thought, Joe headed off to pack his bag for the trip.

Chapter Forty-One

The next morning, shortly after 9:00 a.m., Joe ducked his head to avoid connecting with the doorframe and headed down the steps of the small commuter plane that had brought him to the regional airport closest to the Bakerhurst and the nearest town of any size, Leighton. The day was snowy and gray; big puffy flakes fell heavily to the ground and had evidently been falling for a while as, except for the cleared runway, everything else was covered with snow.

Joe had been one of only a handful of travelers on the plane. Most of his fellow travelers seemed to be businessmen who had quickly wrapped themselves in large black or camel-colored coats and hurried off the plane towards a row of black commercial limousines waiting just outside the chain link fence enclosing the landing field and runways. Joe didn't know what kind of businesses were in the neighborhood, but these men appeared prosperous.

There was one car and one individual left waiting when Joe came off the plane. Lounging against a vintage Bentley, seemingly impervious to the snow, stood a large, impish-looking, bearded older man wearing gray flannel pants, a fisherman's sweater, and an over-sized leather bomber jacket. He stood up when he saw Joe and gave him a little salute - even at this distance, Joe could recognize a faint twinkle in the man's eyes. Joe grabbed his bag off the cart and headed towards the gap in the fence. He smiled at the man, but couldn't take his eyes off the Bentley.

"Mr. Cocktail, I presume?"

"Yes, sir."

"No sir necessary. I'm Ambrose Bakerhurst."

"Pleased to meet you, Mr. Bakerhurst." The two men shook hands and Joe's eyes strayed once again to the automobile.

"You like the car?"

"Quite a bit. Early 1960s?"

"Spot on, young man. It is, to be precise, a 1964 Bentley Silver Cloud III."

"I've read about them, seen one or two zipping by in London, but this is the first time I've ever seen one up close and personal." Joe wanted to run his hands down the bonnet, but managed to control himself. The two men walked around to the back of the car, and Ambrose pointed out some features before opening the trunk and indicating to Joe that he should place his small bag inside.

"What do you drive, son?"

"Nothing like this. A 1985 Alfa Romeo Spider."

Ambrose nodded his head appreciatively. "What color?"

"Cherry red, a legacy from an uncle."

"Well, this is a positive start for your interview, Mr. Cocktail. You like cars."

"Has the interview started already? And please, call me Joe." Joe thought he must have looked a little concerned.

"Well, no, the interview won't really start until you meet with my niece Sophia. The Bakerhurst is a family concern and we all take a special interest in new employees. We're small enough that we can afford to do so. Don't worry, though. Sophia is an excellent judge of character, and if you've gotten this far, I shouldn't worry much about comments like mine impacting the outcome one way or another. Shall we head home? Would you like to drive her?"

Joe considered the question, looked at the snowfall, and the level of snow already on the ground, and shook his head. "Don't think me a coward, but I'd hate to start this whole process by running a beautiful car into a ditch or worse because I'm nervous. Maybe on the way back to the airport?"

"A wise decision. Let's head off then." Joe ogled the immaculate interior with its burled walnut veneers and stunning orange-red leather seats. The two men discussed the features of the dashboard and the interior for another couple of minutes as the car warmed up.

"She's a beauty, isn't she?" Ambrose was clearly fond of the machine.

"Where'd you find her, if you don't mind my asking?"

"Didn't have to find her; she belongs to the family. One of my favorite models, and I love to watch the reactions of people as I drive by. I'm not a looker myself, but this little beauty sure is. She makes people smile, and when I drive her downtown or somewhere new on an errand, I always try to leave myself enough time on the front and back ends to let people tell me their car stories. You know everyone has them."

Joe nodded, intuitively understanding what the older man was saying. "They want to tell you about Bentleys they've seen, or their first car, or about falling in love with someone who had a nice car. You mean your Bentley brings out the good side in car people. It's the same with art in a museum."

"Exactly right. Now, enough about this Bentley, how was your trip? Not too bumpy, I hope?"

"No turbulence to speak of. Those little propeller jets are a real treat as far as I'm concerned. It really feels as if you're going somewhere when you fly. Even though there is more legroom on big commercial planes, there is something kind of impersonal and institutional about a 747."

"Yes indeed," was Ambrose Bakerhurst's only reply and so Joe allowed himself to continue following his line of thought.

"In the big planes you file in, find your seat, the doors close, and sometimes the whole process - the take-off, the ride, and the landing - is so smooth you aren't really sure you've gone anywhere. And it's particularly disconcerting when it's a multi-legged flight. All the airports look more or less the same, and sometimes I walk out into a taxi queue and have to look at my ticket to remind me where I am," Joe finished with fake distress.

Ambrose laughed and the two men went on to discuss more mundane matters. The countryside on either side of them was mostly farmland. Soon, houses began appearing with greater regularity; a sure sign of an approaching town. Blocks of fairly well-preserved 19th century row houses lined both sides of the street, which was bordered on either side by railroad tracks. It appeared the city of Leighton had once been a significant destination during the great age of railroads.

The row houses gave way to Victorian gingerbread houses, and they passed through a small downtown area with a wide main avenue. Joe saw people - mostly older women, or women with small children, and a few men - moving from storefront to storefront, bundled up in scarves, gloves, and hats busily going to and fro. Ambrose, serving as tour guide, took great delight in honking the Bentley's horn in response to a child's wave. The town, like many in the Midwest, had its share of monumental bank buildings and soaring churches, complete with a Neo-classical town hall and requisite town square. Before Joe knew it, they had passed through the small town. "It's like a miniature Bedford Falls from 'It's a Wonderful Life'."

"There's something to that. We've got a lot of Bedford Falls about us."

They passed through an elegant, old-fashioned residential area with larger Victorian houses adorned with copious amounts of gingerbread decoration; the further they drove, the larger the lots and the spaces between the huge old houses became.

"The holly hedge there is ours," Ambrose pointed through the windshield toward the left; the snow was falling more heavily now - it looked as if it might turn into a full-on blizzard. Joe peered through the flakes as they crossed an intersection and noted a tall, snow-covered, but finely pruned hedge of American Holly that seemed to stretch as far as he could see in both directions. Above the hedge, he could see the tops of trees - black in the grey and white of the snow. Ambrose continued to drive and then Joe, alerted to a new event by the sound of the turn signal, saw the break in the holly hedge and the huge, ornamental, wrought iron gates that marked the entry to the property. They were open.

"Here we are," Ambrose announced, "Home Sweet Home."

Chapter Forty-Two

The wrought iron fence was superb and unlike anything Joe had ever seen. Ambrose, noticing his interest, slowed down and stopped the car so Joe could get a closer look. The gate, at first glance, appeared to be an elaborate stand of ivy responsible for obscuring the property from view. Joe thought there was something slightly post-prick Sleeping Beauty about it when the gates were closed. But on second glance, small grinning figures, wee beasties, and grotesque creatures appeared gazing out from between the vines and leaves - each wearing a hat or cape of snow. Joe turned to Ambrose, delighted. "It's like a manuscript illumination in wrought iron. Where did it come from? Who made it?"

"Samuel Bakerhurst hired local craftsmen when he could and brought workmen and their families from all over the world when he started building the estate proper. The fence was a labor of love for everyone in the family - you'll find all of their favorite characters from The Brothers Grimm peeking out at you. In the summer when the weather is nice, we run a story-time project here at the gates - we must move on, though, or

Sophia will think that I've kidnapped you. One more quick stop before the main house."

They drove just inside the gate and stopped at the gatehouse. It wasn't just a gatehouse, but a real-thatched cottage - built of stone, two stories high, with a tall red brick chimney, sending forth a plume of smoke. There were four small-paned windows on the front of the building - two up, two down, and a thatch-covered portico over the little door. Ambrose lowered the window on the driver's side just as the top half of the divided front door opened and a man in a security uniform leaned out and called "Good morning, Mr. Ambrose."

"Good morning, Terry. Will you kindly call Sophia and tell her I've got Mr. Cocktail and will be dropping him off at the front door."

"Yes sir, I'll let her know." The man gave a little wave and closed the door, presumably headed for a phone.

Ambrose turned to Joe. "No need for you to begin your visit in the garage. That was Terry Ryan head of security staff. He lives in a small apartment on the second story of the gatehouse. The lower floor is an all-purpose lounge and office for the guards. No doubt Sophia or someone will take you on the grand tour and you can see for yourself later today or tomorrow."

"How many guards are there?"

"I'm not really certain; you'll need to ask Sophia about that. It changes, slightly, depending upon the season. We all have our roles to play. Mine is avuncular black sheep of the family, although not too black. In terms of the estate I mostly make sure that the cars are taken care of; oh, and I grow roses and simples." Ambrose looked over at Joe.

"Medicinal plants, like they did in the Middle Ages and Renaissance."

"Right on target again; I like you, boy." And he continued, "The culinary herbs, fruits, and vegetables are taken care of by the garden staff - supervised by Chef." Here he stopped again to let Joe ask the question.

"Chef?"

"We are a busy establishment. There's a local college and we try to work with them as closely as possible. Several years ago they hired a food historian interested in 19th century American foods and in the preservation and teaching of early American cooking techniques and recipes. We started working with the college, because this house has the ideal 19th century test kitchen - at least in terms of facilities for an upper-class family. And there are a couple of other structures on the property that allow students to explore log cabin cooking and open air cooking. We hired a chef a few years ago to provide students with supervised practicum experience, and since then he's developed a fairly rigorous program that has been modeled by institutions around the world. The bonus is the chef and the students run a small museum restaurant and do all the catering for us. If you are at all interested in food," he glanced at Joe, and Joe nodded enthusiastically, "this is a good place to be."

"That's fascinating. Do you grow all your own food here?"

"We grow a fair amount of vegetables and native fruits in the kitchen garden, greenhouses, and at the home farms. What we don't grow ourselves we try to purchase from local farmers.

Now, how did I get off on a tangent about the chef?"

"You were telling me about your interests."

"That's right, that's right. So cars, and roses, and simples, and I dabble with snuff boxes and smaller decorative arts objects in the collection - that is, when Wilton lets me."

"Who is Wilton? The director?"

"Oh, no, no. Wilton is the house curator - furniture and objets d'art - as opposed to paintings. He's also the official and unofficial historian for the place. He's been here forever and knows pretty much everything there is to know about the collection and the family. He's a bit of a curmudgeon, but in a good way. Hercules Bakerhurst, Duncan and Sophia's eldest, is the director, but you shouldn't let that bother you."

Joe was just about to ask why Hercules being director of the museum should bother him when the avenue of trees they had been driving through made a turn, and suddenly the house was before them. Joe had seen photographs of the Bakerhurst Museum, when he'd done his research, yet he wasn't quite prepared for the actuality of the structure. Because the trees leading up to the actual house obscured it from view, Joe had been unable to get a feel for the size of it or for the fact that it seemed to sprawl and soar at the same time. The wide three-story frontage - Joe had little idea from this vantage point about the depth of the house - was surmounted in the front by a variety of gables and turrets. From the covered portico, two stairways curved up to the front of the house.

"It is something, isn't it?" said Ambrose proudly.

"Fantastic."

"Ah, there's Sophia now," and Ambrose inclined his head towards the front of the house.

A spare, elegant figure wrapped in a large soft coat was coming down the staircase nearest the automobile.

"I'll just hand you over to Sophia. Is there anything you need from your bag?"

"No. Thank you for the ride, Mr. Bakerhurst. This was quite a treat." Joe gave the soft leather of the seat a last caress as he exited the car.

"I'll see you at dinner. Enjoy your interview." And with a wave of his hand, Ambrose Bakerhurst drove away.

Chapter Forty-Three

Joe turned to greet Sophia Bakerhurst. She held out her hand.

"Mr. Cocktail. Welcome to the Bakerhurst. I'm so glad you could come. It's good to meet you in person. You are very like your writing, you know. I trust Uncle Ambrose treated you well and didn't talk your ear off on the way here - he's so inclined to give away all our secrets." She smiled confidently.

"I've never been inside a Silver Cloud before. It was an unexpected and wonderful way to begin the day."

"I'm glad to hear it. It was a belated birthday gift from my husband's father to Uncle Ambrose. He loved to give people presents, but often waited for several weeks or months after an event for his gifts to really be a surprise. I've always thought it had something to do with the way time seems to warp around the Bakerhurst. We are never quite sure if we are living in the past, present, or future - that's what makes it such fun. Do you have a sense of humor, Mr. Cocktail?"

Joe had been watching Sophia and listening intently to what she'd been telling him, so her question surprised him. "I hope I do, Mrs. Bakerhurst. There's not much point in going through life without one. If my choice is to laugh or to cry, I would just as soon laugh."

"I'm glad to hear it. I don't like to list 'sense of humor required' in the job description. A sense of humor is useful in a quirky old house filled with unusual things and people, and it is positively a requirement in some situations. Let's go inside and rid ourselves of these coats so we can talk."

She approached the front door, which seemed to open automatically. This surprised Joe, until he realized a guard had been waiting at the ready to provide the service. "Thank you, Frank. Frank, this is Mr. Cocktail, he's come to interview for the research curator position. If you could let Terry know that I, or someone, will be bringing him down to the gatehouse later this afternoon, I would appreciate it. Let's play it by ear, but probably around 4:00 p.m., if you don't mind an extra person for afternoon coffee?"

"I'll let Terry know, ma'am, and welcome to the Bakerhurst, Mr. Cocktail."

"Thank you, Frank. How long have you worked here?"

"I'm a third generation Bakerhurst employee, Mr. Cocktail. My grandfather was a stableman for Mr. Sam II; my father was an auto-mechanic responsible for keeping cars like the Silver Cloud in tip-top shape; and I do a little bit of everything here - but mostly security on Mondays when the museum is closed to the public."

"Don't let Frank kid you, Mr. Cocktail, he does a little bit of everything here right now because he's studying for the bar exam - he zoomed through law school and was president of his class and editor of the law review. As soon as he passes the bar I fear we'll lose him to some high-powered firm on one of the coasts."

Frank blushed but looked pleased at the praise from his employer. "Aww, Mrs. Sophia, you know this will always be my home."

"That's right, it always will. Come on, Mr. Cocktail, we've got places to go and things to do."

"Nice to meet you, Frank," Joe said, and they moved into the house proper.

Stepping through the large enclosed foyer that separated the steps outside from the main part of the house, the two emerged into a magnificent two-story space dominated by an imposing mahogany staircase on the left, and a row of arched windows at the far end. The space was bathed with the diffuse grey light of the snowy day.

Though large enough to accommodate an extraordinary number of people, there was something intimate about the space. The marble floors were covered with soft Turkish carpets - worn in places, but still rich with color. A smattering of chairs and settees were placed in convenient spots; all of them looked as if they were meant for use, not for show, and Joe saw no sign of the red velvet stanchions with the red velvet ropes so commonly found in historic houses.

There was a palpable sense that this was a lived-in space, not a show space. Joe wondered if any of the family still lived in the house. Perhaps Ambrose, so he could be close to the automobiles and the gardens? Joe could easily imagine a group of Gilded Age beauties coming in from outside, closing their parasols, and chattering to one another as they removed their shawls; or, the man of the house, just in from riding, accompanied by one or two of his dogs or children with balls and hoops. It was because of this lived-in feeling that Joe realized neither he nor Sophia Bakerhurst looked out of place in their modern clothes. This was a home - bigger and finer than any place he had ever called home - but a home nonetheless.

"This is the main reception room; the ballroom is above us on the second floor. You'll forgive me if I move you along, Joe. I won't begin with a guided tour. I've asked Wilton, our house curator, to do that after luncheon, if you don't mind?" Joe nodded his ascent to her plan.

She continued, "Wilton and some of the other staff will join us for lunch, but I thought it would be nice if we could get to know a little bit more about one another first." She headed across the reception room past the enormous staircase and turned left, stopping in front of a small door that deceptively opened into an enormous walk-in closet with shelves and pegs for coats at three different levels. Most of one side was empty. "That's for the school groups," Sophia explained. The far end of the closet held coats, cloaks, a box with hats and gloves, and a variety of walking boots in all sizes.

She held her hand out for Joe's coat, and he took it off and gave it to her. "We'll just hang our coats here and Ambrose will make sure your bag joins your coat. This is where we put (and find) almost everything. In fact, I'm reasonably sure at this point that the closet simply supplies items we need on its own." She chuckled, enjoying a secret joke.

Sophia pointed out the necessities. One wall had two doors - one marked Men, one marked Women - not cutesy signs, Joe was glad to see. "As you can imagine, these aren't original to the house, but quite a necessary and useful addition for visitors, particularly schoolchildren. When you're ready, go out the door, take a right, cross the reception room, and keep heading towards the back of the house until you can smell the coffee. Give a shout if you get lost. Take whatever time you need." She headed off through the door she'd indicated and he watched her turn right and disappear from view.

A few minutes later, he was following what he assumed was her path. It was kind of Sophia, he thought, to give him some time alone. Although he wasn't taking the time to stop and look at everything, something he was itching to do, he was able to walk through and absorb some of the atmosphere on his own. After crossing the reception room, he had entered what was clearly the formal dining room - a long room with a massive fireplace and elevated oval area at the far end with enormous windows looking out on to another pristine expanse of snowy property.

As Sophia had suggested, he was following his nose, which drew him through a swinging doorway and into a smaller private dining room. He continued on and found himself in an enormous butler's pantry. He stopped for a minute to gaze at the glass-fronted cabinets filled with dishes of every variety, plates of all sizes, service dishes, punch bowls, and glassware. He bent down and was delighted to find the butler's original ice box.

At the end of this room was a serving window, and through it Joe could see into the kitchen. From his vantage point he was unable to gauge the size of what is typically one of the most important rooms in any home. He started to duck his head in and say hello but stopped at the last moment, thinking that might not be the thing for a prospective employee to do. He followed the butler's pantry around to the left and then took two quick turns to the right and found himself inside the large terra cotta tiled kitchen, bustling with activity.

Chapter Forty-Four

The kitchen was quite a different space from the rest of the house, and Joe, who had spent a lot of his time doing research in small towns and villages in Tuscany, felt as if he'd been transported back in time. This was no ultra-modern stainless steel kitchen, nor did it remind him of the dated, white-tiled kitchens often found in historic houses of the past; this was an authentic Tuscan farm kitchen, down to the heavy beams on the ceiling. A large stone fireplace and a brick, wood-burning oven were the defining features of the far wall of the room into which Joe had just walked. The defining features of the room consisted of a large stone fireplace and a brick, wood-burning oven.

Sophia sat at a huge scrubbed wooden table with a cup of coffee in front of her, talking to a man in chef whites. Several small clusters of what Joe assumed were students, also in whites, were busy working at various tasks in the kitchen. Two of the students were discussing the contents of a large steaming pot on the stove. One was chopping vegetables next to another, up to his elbows, kneading what must assuredly be bread dough, and three students, sitting on benches around a kitchen fireplace, were occupied doing something with large baskets of onions.

Sophia looked at him and clapped her hands. "You made it."

"I followed my nose just like you said, but I had to walk with my eyes closed, because I wanted to stop and look at everything."

The man in chef whites stood up and turned to Joe. Big, tall, and heavily bearded, he moved quickly and efficiently despite his bulk.

"Chef, this is Cocktail, come to interview for the chief curator's position. Mr. Cocktail, this is Clark Nelson, but everyone calls him 'Chef'."

Joe found his hand enveloped in a big calloused hand. "Nice to meet you. Welcome to the kitchen. Would you like a cup of coffee, Mr. Cocktail?"

"Yes please, if it's no trouble."

"One cup of coffee coming up - cream or sugar?"

"Black, please."

The man didn't move and he made no request, but one of the students by the fireplace, a young man, had gotten up as the question had been asked, moved to an enormous urn, and, taking a large majolica mug from a tray next to it, poured a cup of coffee and brought it over to Joe.

"Thanks. What are you and your friends doing with the onions?"

"It's not onions, but garlic, sir. It's the last of the three harvests of the year, and today we're taking turns braiding the garlic for storage." He pointed out a few braids already hanging near the stove.

"Oh, I see," he said. "I should have realized. I've seen garlic braids before, but I've never seen anyone actually braiding the garlic heads. Is it difficult to do?"

"Not at all, particularly for those of us who have sisters." Assuring himself that Joe seemed to have no further questions, he returned to his work and friends by the fireplace.

"Sit down, sit down, Joe. If you are interested in the kitchen and historic food program, I'd be happy to show you around sometime, perhaps tomorrow?" Chef directed his observation to both Sophia and Joe and left it open-ended. "But now there are things to be done if you all want to eat lunch as scheduled. Who wants to go down to the root cellar with me?" He addressed his comment to his crew. The students braiding and kneading chose to stay with their tasks, but the young man chopping vegetables and one of two watching the stock wiped their hands on their aprons and followed Chef out of the kitchen, smiling and talking as they went.

Joe took a sip of his coffee and looked around the warm kitchen. "Is it always like this at the Bakerhurst? Coffee and camaraderie all the time?"

"Of course not, Mr. Cocktail. Let me assure you this is not the Stepford House and Museum. We are just like any other institution or family. We have our good days and our bad days, and of course everyone is on their best behavior today because you are visiting. The holidays are fast approaching and the house is very busy at the holidays. We are in this tiny post-Thanksgiving lull of activity that allows us to be our best selves a little more frequently."

Sophia tactfully switched gears. "I must admit the kitchen is one of my favorite places in the house - it's quite an anomaly in houses of this period - Ruth Roland Bakerhurst was definitely not one of those frail and hypochondriacal women so common in the late 19th century. She was quite taken with some of the large kitchens of the country estates they visited in Italy and was determined to have a Tuscan kitchen of her own. She was as perfectly happy in here baking and cooking as she was dancing in the ballroom upstairs. The tile, the majolica ware for kitchen use, and indeed the entire fireplace and oven were shipped here from Italy." Sophia looked around the room fondly, as if she were watching the original owner and his wife about their daily business in the kitchen.

They sat in companionable silence for a few more moments, both enjoying the dark rich brew. The sounds of the student chefs going about their work washing dishes, stirring, and sautéing made for pleasant background noise. Joe, who was already feeling relaxed in Sophia's presence, had ceased, for the time being, to worry about the fact that he was on an interview. Sophia broke the silence after taking another sip of her coffee.

"Well, Mr. Cocktail. You've had a sad and exciting week. Are you comfortable sitting here, or would you prefer to move to an office?"

"I'm quite happy right here.

"Good." Sophia patted a plain manila folder resting on the table in front of her that was labeled with his name. "It's time then for me to find out more about you."

Chapter Forty-Five

Joe gave Sophia the short version of his life story, including school, college, graduate school, his excitement at being offered the position of associate curator at a large museum, and the subsequent joys and disappointments of working at a large institution. He found himself telling Sophia about his controversial meeting with the Director, and his subsequent interview with his own supervisor. Sophia listened to him, asked questions, and allowed him to tell the story at his own pace. He finished by saying, "I guess, Mrs. Bakerhurst, when I discovered the advertisement for this position it felt like the antidote to what I was currently experiencing. Your application process, or should I say, your essay questions, forced me to reevaluate my work and rediscover what I loved about museums in the first place."

She nodded thoughtfully, but made no immediate reply. Instead she pulled a heavy sheet of cream-colored paper out of the folder and handed it to him. "Here's a tentative agenda for the next day and a half. We don't want to overwhelm you." She went briefly over the outline. "You and I will be with one another until lunch. After we finish our coffee, we'll walk downstairs and I'll show you the office areas and introduce you to the staff. Wilton, the curator of the home; Jennifer, the registrar; Miranda, the CFO; and Ellen, the head of education and programming will join us for lunch. They are the full-time professional staff of the museum at this point - excluding the security staff, two contract conservators working on special projects, and the adjunct staff from the college and craftspeople that work in the various workshops and historical areas."

She looked thoughtful for a moment and then added, "I should say they make up the full-time staff who aren't family members. I realize that coming from a large museum this will seem like a rather strange set-up to you, but, from the perspective of the entire staff, the Bakerhurst is as much an intellectual center and a research institution as it is an historic property and museum. Samuel and Ruth Roland Bakerhurst were both polymaths - interested in everything and inspired successive generations of the family to develop our specialties - even those of us who are only associated to the family by marriage or employment.

"You've already met Uncle Ambrose. He probably let you know that his responsibilities include the rose and simple gardens, as well as oversight of the cars, other vehicles, and garages. My younger son Roland is a Byzantinist. Samuel's wife Ruth was particularly interested in Byzantine art and icons, and our son seems to have inherited her interests and has immersed himself in the collection. I'm a librarian by training and a bookbinder by avocation. I generally care for the books in the collection and oversee the administration of the small research

260

library and a press - my husband, Duncan, who is otherwise occupied teaching today, is a classicist and a map aficionado. Our eldest son, Hercules, is the director of the museum; you'll meet Hercules and his wife this evening at dinner." She gave Joe a curious look and paused for a moment as if waiting for him to ask something, but he stayed silent. She nodded her head and went on.

"Duncan and I have two daughters, Isolde and Helena. Isolde's a bit of a lost soul at the moment and hasn't really found her niche. She's very good with animals and currently takes care of the small contingent of animals here on the estate (dogs, chickens, a litter of pigs). There are stables here, but we no longer keep horses on the property. My daughter Helena is an art historian, currently finishing her dissertation on the development of American museums, travel, and collecting practices of the mid to late 19th century. She is currently on an extended research tour in Europe.

"Other than family and the full-time staff, we have a dedicated corps of excellent volunteers from the community who lead tours of the home and work with school children. You've already seen that we work with various departments at the college and provide workshop space for teachers and practical experience for students in all aspects of 19th century life. We are an unusual living history museum--our goal is for visitors to discover for themselves the types of objects, events, and experiences that engaged Samuel and Ruth and their family. And when I say living history, I mean living history, Mr. Cocktail. We try to teach conservation and care along with use. Things here are meant to be used – the rugs are made to be walked on and the chairs and chaise lounges are for sitting and lounging on. Drawers are meant to be opened and their contents explored. Certainly, the items that are particularly fragile will be found under glass or behind plexiglass, but this was and is a home and you won't find velvet ropes and plexiglass panels in front of paintings, except in a very few cases. Samuel and Ruth meant for the items they brought home from their travels to be used and appreciated, and we continue to facilitate their wishes. Samuel's last will and testament included directions to his son that this house was not to become a mausoleum, frozen in time, but was to be kept a vibrant and active home filled with people and ideas for as long as the family's wealth was able to provide those experiences. His exact words to his children were 'by residing in this house, do not fail to live in it as a home, and make it a place of welcome and exploration, and learning, and laughter for the Leighton community.' "

Joe found himself listening intently to this woman and getting excited about the possibilities of working in such an environment. She had stopped talking, so he asked the question that was uppermost in his mind, "Why me?" He realized as he asked the question that it sounded pompous and self-centered. "I don't mean, why did you pick me for the job - I realize you must be interviewing a number of people." He stammered slightly in his rush to apologize and clarify his question for her, "I mean, what do you want this new person to do?"

"That's a very good question, Joe. The staff here has a commitment to this family, this house, this estate, and this community - pretty much in that order. We are like thousands of other historic properties in the United States, but with one very important exception: we have always had the luxury of financial independence, which has allowed us to establish programs as needed to support our mission. A month or so ago, we all sat down around a table, and, when I say we all sat down, I mean we all sat down. The whole staff gathered and we discussed what we wanted to do next and decided to focus on curated content. We decided to hire someone new, and fresh, and energetic, and to invite them to come and immerse themselves in the collection, and see what turns up. We thought about endowing an artist-in-residence program or a series of scholarly fellowships, but in the end we decided what we needed was another staff person, dedicated completely to collections. We determined it would be best to bring in someone from outside the community and the family, someone who can see the collection as part of a bigger picture.

"You have to understand, Joe. This institution is financially secure. We don't anticipate ever having to have a capital campaign. The property - the grounds, the buildings, the physical plant, and the technology infrastructure - is sufficient for our current needs and our future needs can be met as part of our operational budget.

"Miranda, the CFO and de facto head of operations here at the museum, makes sure everything works the way it is supposed to. Perhaps that makes a complex job sound rather simple, but Miranda is a special individual and we were quite lucky to find someone with her talents.

"Now we are looking for someone who, once we've told that person our story, can't think of any place they'd rather spend the next five or ten years. I think the right person will discover there is so much to do and there are so many avenues for exploration and new research that they'll settle down and become a part of our extended family. We aren't looking for a young Turk associate curator who wants to jump up a level by moving to a smaller institution and taking the curator job with plans to move on in a few years," she looked at him shrewdly. "We've found over the years that we're pretty good at weeding out the folks who don't know what they want. Over the next 24 hours it will become clear, to you and to us, whether the Bakerhurst is someplace that captures your imagination. I don't mean that in a smug way. With some people, the job feels too big and the small town life too confining; for others, this just isn't the right time in their life and career to make this commitment, or they might have family who don't feel connected to collections and research.

"We want someone who can come here and be excited by the work at hand, and not someone who is looking for fame or fortune. We aren't looking to hire the museum professional motivated by ideas that life at a museum is going to be one high-rolling glamorous experience after another."

"I can't say that glamour and high living has played much of a part in my museum work recently," he acknowledged cheerfully and a little ruefully.

Sophia looked at the kitchen clock and said, "We have about a half-hour before lunch;

let's stretch our legs and take a walk down to the offices. We can talk while we walk."

Joe finished the last of his coffee and without thinking walked over to the main sink and rinsed his mug. The student chopping vegetables by the drain board looked up, smiled, and said, "Just leave it in the sink, I'll take care of it."

"Thanks," Joe said.

Sophia had watched him the whole time, and in response to her gaze, he shrugged his shoulders. "Old habits die hard; my mother is a stickler for rinsing dishes and we were taught to be responsible for our own stuff. Doesn't matter how many miles away she is, some inborn mother warning system would tell her I hadn't rinsed a mug properly and I'd hear about it the next time I talked to her."

"Kudos to your mother."

As they left the kitchen, they heard, and then saw, Chef and his students coming back from the root cellar, their arms laden with potatoes, beets, leeks, and some type of large squash or gourd Joe didn't recognize.

"Lunch in half an hour," Chef reminded them.

"We'll be ready, don't worry," Sophia responded.

Chapter Forty-Six

They walked back through the butler's pantry and into the small dining room, where Sophia stopped and turned on the lights so Joe could get a better look. He couldn't stop himself, but whistled slowly as he turned in the small room that was decked out with alternating green and turquoise panels, gleaming gold trim, and exquisite images of phoenix and peonies. He turned to look at Sophia, "Is it Whistler?"

"Good guess, it's very like the dining room he painted for Frederick Leyland, and probably inspired by it, but the designs - we think - are taken from ones found in Ruth's sketchbook and were probably all done by craftsmen gathered by Samuel to complete the house. Of course, Ruth Roland may have seen the designs somewhere on one of their trips, we just aren't quite sure. I think Wilton has been doing some work on this recently; you should ask him about it."

They moved quickly through the dining room and, instead of moving out into the reception area, walked through a set of lovely double doors into a drawing room furnished with Neo-Rococo furniture. The overwhelming impression was brilliant crimson - carpet, heavy curtains, upholstery, and table-coverings all in crimson, with an occasional chair done in crimson and white stripes. Large gilt-framed mirrors separated the windows looking out onto the front of the house, and through another set of doors Joe could see what looked like an old-fashioned conservatory. On impulse, he reached out to touch the fabric covering a high back settee and then stopped himself.

"It's all right, Mr. Cocktail. Really, you can touch the fabric and you can even sit on the settee, although I don't think those in this room are terribly comfortable." He looked around in amazement. The room looked as if it had been furnished yesterday - there was some wear on the carpet, and the drapery might be slightly faded, but the chairs and settees were in pristine condition. Joe didn't know a whole lot about textiles, but the upholstery fabric didn't look like reproduction fabric.

"Do you keep the upholstered pieces covered? These pieces are beautiful."

"Ah, that's Ruth Roland again. Remind me to have Wilton take you upstairs to the Bolthole. When Ruth Roland found a fabric, a style of carpet, or table linens she liked, her rule was to buy three to four times more than she thought she would need. She was rich and thrifty and knew what she liked and didn't have modern ideas about swapping furniture, wall-coverings, and rugs every three or four years to "freshen up" the place. The furniture in this room was all custom-upholstered, of course, and we have enough extra fabric in storage to re-cover every piece in here at least twice over. The piece you are currently sitting on was re-covered some time in the past few years, I don't exactly remember when."

They walked back into the grand reception area and crossed over to a hidden area, where a staircase descended into the basement. "This wasn't part of the original plan," Sophia explained, "but it's a more direct way to reach the general office spaces. I think you'll be surprised at how comfortable the office space is, despite the basement location."

Joe felt he ought to have been less surprised at the beautiful vaulted basement ceilings - he had, after all, mounted steps to get into the house, so it made perfect sense that they weren't headed into a dark, dank crawl space or a wood-paneled rumpus room type of environment. The red brick piers and the floor of this part of the basement had been laid out in a herringbone pattern, but other than that the area was surprisingly modern. The offices were pocketed between the piers on each side, and in the center of the large space was a large double-wide conference table stacked with papers, objects, and all the ephemera that finds its way into back office spaces at museums. The entire area was well lit and comfortably warm.

The offices had been created by suspending large panels of some kind of frosted glass or plexiglass from the barrel vaults above. The offices had doors and most of them were open. *The doors are all open. That's a change from my current place of employment - physically and metaphorically.*

Sophia stopped at each of the doors in turn, and if the office was occupied, Joe was introduced. A couple of the offices were empty, including that of Wilton Dieptiech, the primary curator for the property. Wilton was always out and about, Sophia explained, and they'd see him at lunch. Sophia ducked into a small office and came back with a large bronze key ring clattering noisily with old-fashioned keys. They walked through a doorway into another part of the basement. The ceiling was still vaulted, just not as high, and Joe was reminded of a trip to France as a graduate student and a surprisingly exciting tour of the wine caves beneath the Burgundian city of Beaune. And in fact it wasn't long before Sophia showed Joe some of the storage spaces - including a refrigerated space for photographs that was located adjacent to the house's wine cellar. Sophia pointed to an open recess a little way down on the right, indicating the stairs the Chef and his team had descended to get to the food storage areas, which were further on in the basement. Sophia referred to it as the root cellar, but to Joe that seemed a poor term for spaces that seemed monumentally medieval in feel.

They retraced their steps to the offices and were joined by Miranda and Jennifer, who were also headed up to lunch. Miranda, Head of Operations, was a long-legged blond and didn't look a bit like any museum head of operations Joe had ever seen. She joined Sophia to answer a few questions about a current work project somewhere external to the house, and Joe fell into step beside Jennifer, the Manager of Collections. As they talked, Joe discovered they had a few mutual acquaintances and the discovery made for some pleasant conversation as they made their way up the stairs.

Sophia turned to Joe at the top of the staircase. "I hope you don't mind going back to the kitchen for lunch? There will only be six of us

- with Wilton and Roland. Ellen is off giving a presentation at the high school today. If we eat in the kitchen it actually makes it easier for the kitchen staff to serve and clean up after us, and it's slightly friendlier than sitting in one of the dining rooms."

"Wilton will be disappointed. He won't get a chance to show off the fine china," noted Miranda.

"Well, yes, that's true, but I've promised him Joe for most of the afternoon, so he agreed to the change in luncheon venue."

Chapter Forty-Seven

The atmosphere in the kitchen had changed a bit from the casual bustle of the morning. The large table had been covered with a crisp white linen tablecloth and set with more of the large majolica dishes, including large pitchers of water. "It's the well water," Jennifer explained, "and it's fantastic - you'll be surprised at how great it tastes. We all are at first. Chef serves it with all the meals, even when there's wine or beer, because he thinks it makes the food taste better."

Two men entered the room, and Joe was introduced to Sophia's son (he couldn't be anyone else, he looked so much like his mother), Roland, and the much-mentioned Wilton, who was small and a little chubby, with a shock of white hair standing straight on end. Sophia placed them at the table with herself at one end, and Joe at the other. The two women were seated on either side of Joe, the two men at either side of Sophia.

After taking their seats, three of the students, now suitably togged as wait staff, moved into action, placing plated salads in front of the six. One of the students, a young woman, had clearly been designated as head of the wait staff for the day. As they served, she informed the table in a quiet voice, "Our starter for today is roasted heirloom beet salad with goat cheese and pear vinaigrette." Two of the students returned to place baskets of sliced, crusty, warm-from-the-oven bread on either end of the table, and two small dishes, each with a square of butter that had been stamped with a decorative sheaf of wheat. Joe expressed interest in the design, and one of the students brought him the wooden butter stamp to examine, while Wilton explained this particular stamp was often found on butter and was emblematic of wealth and abundant crops. "We also have stamps with pomegranates, pineapples, thistles, and double-thistles in the collection."

Joe couldn't have been any happier. Good food and conversation about objects. He looked around the table and then at his plate. Beautifully sliced purple and gold beets sat in the center of a bed of curly lettuce with crumbled goat cheese on top. He thought to himself, not for the first time that day that even if he didn't get this job, the trip had been completely worth the effort. The young woman who had set his plate down in front of him addressed him by name, "Mr. Cocktail, Chef wants to know if you have allergies or if there is anything you don't like."

Joe hesitated for a moment, "No allergies. I don't like tripe, sea urchin, or sea cucumber."

"I'll tell him," she said and moved quietly away from the table.

There was a moment of silence and then Roland said, "I think you can be assured that none of those items are on today's menu. Chef does occasionally make tripe stew and I find reasons to avoid the kitchen and the restaurant on those occasions. Tripe is an acquired taste, certainly, and I don't like the way it smells."

"And, it's not a taste I intend to acquire," chimed in Wilton. The others at the table nodded in agreement, except for Jennifer who mentioned she'd spent time studying in Florence. Though she wasn't fond of tripe stew, she did like the tripe sandwiches available in the street markets of Florence, particularly with a chile-laced red sauce.

They dug into their salads, and the conversation moved on to more general issues related to the house and the museum. There seemed to be tacit agreement, thought Joe, to let him eat before starting any "grilling" of the potential new hire.

Soon the students were back to remove the salad plates and replenish the baskets of bread, which turned out to be the perfect complement for the rich chicken stew with dumplings that arrived in the lovely majolica bowls. Chicken stew was one of Joe's favorite meals, and he looked down at the bowl knowing that even if it didn't taste like his grandmother's, it would certainly still be delicious.

"Can we take it you like chicken stew, Joe?" Sophia queried the seemingly appreciative interviewee.

"Yes indeed. In almost all shapes and forms."

"Almost all?" Jennifer apparently sensed a story.

"Almost all. I was crazy about this woman in graduate school. She was beautiful and a lot of fun to be with, but she was a terrible cook. I happened to mention how much I loved my grandmother's chicken stew and my girlfriend

275

surprised me with her own version of the dish made with canned chicken, bouillon cubes that hadn't dissolved, and gloppy lumps of flour." He grimaced with distaste. "Even new love couldn't make that edible."

His anecdote seemed to break the ice in some way, because, as they ate, various members of the staff took turns talking about their roles in the museum. Wilton clearly had pride of place in this group as the individual with the most encyclopedic knowledge of the family and the collection, though Roland and Sophia both chimed in when they felt some point of history or story needed further clarification. Jennifer spoke about collections care and storage, as well as answering a few specific questions from Joe about how the collection was catalogued. Miranda addressed issues of sustainability and growth and told Joe more about the relationship - financial and administrative - between the museum and the college. By the time the last bites of stew and final bits of bread and butter had been consumed, Joe felt he had a pretty good picture of how Bakerhurst functioned, and he had to admit he liked what he heard and saw. He realized that everyone around the table, including himself, was on their best behavior, but really there was something so civilized about the whole lunch.

Everyone he'd met thus far had seemed wholly engaged in the success of the institution. *Perhaps if I join the staff here, I'll see evidence of gossip and staff rivalries, but on the whole these people seem to get along with one another remarkably well.* So far there had been no awkward silences or pregnant pauses; he hadn't seen anyone rolling their eyes when anyone else was speaking. All in all, the Bakerhurst looked to be a tolerably functional institution, although he had yet to meet Hercules Bakerhurst, the director of the museum.

Sophia had told him he would meet Hercules at dinner, but what seemed even more curious now that he thought about it, was that none of the people around the table had mentioned him in connection with anything they'd discussed - collections, finance, programs, exhibitions, events, or history. Well, no doubt he'd find out more this evening. He thought about what kind of question he could ask to elicit more information on the topic and decided that being straightforward was best.

At the next lull in conversation, as the dishes were being removed and replaced with smaller plates for cheese and fruit, Joe asked his question. "This is a small institution, what kind of interaction do you have with the director on a daily basis?" All eyes turned to Sophia, indicating that she should be the one to take this question.

Chapter Forty-Eight

"While I am wary of coloring your opinion of Hercules, you will see this evening that my eldest son is a born impresario. It's a shame that he was born in the 20th century instead of the 19th...," Sophia hesitated for a moment. Miranda and Jennifer nodded in agreement, while Wilton regarded Sophia with a slightly skeptical air, and Roland, when Joe glanced at him, winked and smiled. "Hercules could have given P.T. Barnum a run for his money, at least on the showman side of things.

"My son has always been interested in theater and story-telling. He's tall, handsome, a larger-than-life presence. To be honest, Joe, he's not very good at the day-to-day business of running the institution, so you might say," and here she hesitated again, choosing her words carefully, and then smiled as she made her choice, "...so you might say that Hercules is Oz the Great and Powerful, and those of us around the table are players behind the curtain. Hercules is the commercial face of the museum - he interacts with the press, opens functions and exhibitions, and gives entertaining talks about the museum all over the world. But, in general, you don't have to worry about Hercules interfering with the life of the museum." Wilton harrumphed at that, and Roland coughed into his hand in a manner that sounded suspiciously like laughter to Joe.

While Sophia was speaking one of the student waiters brought out a big bowl full of autumn fruits - apples, pears, plums, and enormous red grapes cut into convenient sections. A cheese board followed with more bread, a basket of water crackers, a small pot of honey, and one filled with fig preserves. Joe and the others silently passed items and filled their small plates, eating and listening.

"It's not that Hercules isn't important to the running of the museum, he is," Sophia continued. "It's just that those of us around the table, with Ellen and my husband Duncan, really are the core work group that keep everything moving and on schedule. So, for this first part of your visit we felt," and here she looked around the table at all the staff members present, "it was critical for us to understand you, and for you to understand us. Does that answer your question?"

Joe put down the cracker and large slice of white cheddar cheese he had been about to consume and considered his response; perhaps it was time to clarify his position here. "Yes, thank you. It's just, well, I'm in a rather awkward place right now where I currently work." Joe began relating a shortened version of recent events, and was surprised to find in doing so that he felt a little sick to his stomach; suddenly, it was all much more real than it had been Saturday evening or even yesterday. He quickly recounted the story and explained, "The problem is, he and I weren't on the best of terms when the accident occurred, and I'm free to be here today because he and my supervisor suggested that I take some time off to consider my future."

He explained about his research and concerns about the purchase/gift of what he was sure was a fake 15th century painting. "And the fact is, even with the Director gone, I'm no longer confident that my museum, or most big museums, are even interested in discovering the truth. I'm disheartened, and while I love working with objects at a large encyclopedic collection, the constant politicking really has me asking myself if I'm still in the right business. I think I'm a pretty easy-going guy, but I seem to be fighting an uphill battle to do what I believe is right, and I'm not sure I can compromise on intellectual honesty. I was willing, though not happy about it, when instructed, to keep my mouth shut, but decided that where I needed to draw the line in the sand was at being fundamentally dishonest. When asked a direct question by a trustee, I had to answer truthfully." He looked around at the table, "I'm not trying to make myself out to be a martyr. I just don't feel like where I am is a perfect fit for me right now."

Miranda looked around the table. "We all know how that feels, don't we? After I'd finished my MBA and taken the CPA exam, I landed a job at one of the big national accounting firms. I was right where I'd planned to be my entire life, and I was completely miserable - it was numbers for numbers sake 24/7 and I began to lose touch with anything resembling reality. I was young, paid too much money, and running with a crowd of people in exactly the same situation. When someone mistakenly tossed a professional newsletter on my desk with the Bakerhurst job opening in it, I felt like the universe had tossed me a lifeline."

The student-chefs arrived with mugs of coffee, cream and sugar, and put them down in front of each person at the table.

Jennifer chimed in, "I was working at a historical society on the east coast when I got the call," she smiled. "A decade or so before I arrived, someone had given them an important collection of weapons and firearms, spanning three centuries. The collection had never been researched or catalogued - although the collector had kept immaculate records about the date and prices he'd paid for items. He had all the knowledge in his head and never felt he needed to write the histories of things down in any fashion. When he died, his only son - a devout pacifist with small children - couldn't wait to get rid of the collection. I was hired as the research assistant for the collection - based on the fact that I was young, smart, and they didn't have to pay me very much."

Jennifer continued her story, "Word got out about the collection, and suddenly I was on the road two or three times a month as a courier - I did that for five years and had begun to feel like a gun runner. You can't imagine the hoops you have to go through at airports - nationally and internationally - to hand-carry guns on flights, even if they are boxed and crated! I found out about the Bakerhurst when Sophia and I were trapped in a hotel elevator for two hours at an ALA conference. By the time the doors opened, I'd agreed to come here for an interview. I'm blissfully happy being a homebody registrar here and letting other people do the courier runs."

After listening to their stories Joe said, "That's exactly how I felt last week - the advertisement was like a lifeline, and after I'd applied I thought to myself, even if I don't get an interview or I get an interview and don't get the job, the process has made me understand that I can't stay where I am. I guess for me it was less of a lifeline and more like a big kick in the seat of the pants."

They all laughed and Sophia took the linen napkin off her lap and folded it on the table, a signal that luncheon was at an end. "I'm leaving you in Wilton's hands for the next couple of hours. Wilton, could you make sure to deliver Mr. Cocktail to Roland by 3:45, and Roland, I'd like you to take him to the gatehouse for coffee with Terry and whoever else is there. After that, you can grab his bag and get him settled in at your place."

She addressed her next remark to Joe. "We can get you a room at the inn in town if you'd prefer, but I thought you might be more comfortable in Roland's guest room?" He nodded his willingness to be accommodated at her son's, and she continued. "As the two of you are not dissimilar in age, you can ask him all the questions you don't feel comfortable asking the rest of us." With the arrangements settled, the group dispersed, and the students moved in to clear the table.

Chapter Forty-Nine

Joe headed into the house with Wilton, and witnessed a transformation. Wilton changed from a small, crotchety older man into a vibrant and compelling storyteller. His voice was almost without an accent, although Sophia had told Joe that Wilton was originally from Belgium. The man spoke carefully and precisely, and Joe was captivated by the story of Samuel Bakerhurst, his wife, Ruth Roland, and their descendants.

At some level, Joe knew, Wilton was telling him the same anecdotes, incidents, and facts and figures he'd told to hundreds of others before today, but for both of them, it seemed that Wilton was recounting his stories for the very first time. As they moved from room to room, Joe began to feel that he was coming to know and understand the various personalities of family members, friends, and important figures of the 19th century -Abraham Lincoln, Mark Twain, Adelina Patti, Pope Pius IX, Thomas Nast - and its important events and places - the American Civil War, the Franco-Prussian War, the Risorgimento, the Milan Cathedral, the Paris Opera, Booth's Theater, and the St. Nicholas Hotel in NYC. All these people, places and events played a part in the story. As a curator, Joe knew that every object had a story, but here at the Bakerhurst, the old aphorism was true and real in a way that was somehow different than anything he had ever experienced before.

Here was a child's sewing basket that played music when it was opened, purchased for a daughter of the house on a trip to Switzerland in the early 1870s. There, a handsome gold ring inlaid with an amethyst profile portrait of a stern Roman patriarch had been a gift to a son, who had a love of all things Roman and Latin, on his fifteenth birthday. In the library, Joe spied a three-volume leather-bound set of the *Complete Works of William Shakespeare*, which turned out to be a gift from Ruth Roland to her husband on their wedding day. In the music room Wilton pointed out Samuel's wedding gift to Ruth Roland, a piano. All of her sheet music was still in the house, along with that of countless other Bakerhursts who had grown up learning to play the piano.

Joe and Wilton spent several minutes looking through the titles and commenting on the songs and cover illustrations. By this point Joe was so under Wilton's spell that when Wilton sat down at the instrument and began playing *Ta-Ra-Ra Boom-De-Ay!*, Joe found himself joining in on the chorus. There seemed to be no set plan for the tour; the two men wandered from room to room, looking at an object here, at a particularly fine view from a window there. When one of the many clocks in the house alerted the men, in a series of deep rhythmic bongs, that their time together was fast coming to a close, Wilton slowly began to bring Joe out of the past and into the future, talking about the more mundane aspects of working in a historic house. He discussed the need to balance the desires of the audience and to know and understand an object through touch and use, while still doing right by the object in terms of conservation and preservation.

"There's one last object I'd like to show you, Mr. Cocktail," and he walked over to a large contraption in the corner that Joe had been eyeballing while they sang. "Do you know what this is?"

"It's like nothing I've ever seen before."

"It's called a Megalethescope. Samuel had it imported from Venice in the 1870s. The device was designed by Carlo Ponti, who was a Swiss-born scientist, photographer, and optician who became the Royal Optician to Victor Emanuel II of Italy. Samuel had seen one in the house of a friend. You can think of it as an early attempt at a slide projector, or a giant View-master, with more bells and whistles. In these drawers," and he bent down and pointed to three drawers on the bottom of the framework, "are specially prepared albumen photographs of images from all over the world. Samuel, Ruth Roland, and the children were very keen collectors of tourist photographs, and although I don't in my heart think that Samuel and Ruth Roland were the kind of people who would invite friends over and bore them to tears with their travel stories, we do know that people liked to look at travel photographs.

"The photographs are backlit using an oil or kerosene lantern as an internal light source. Samuel, or Ruth Roland, or one of the older children, perhaps, would choose an image that was colored, or translucent, or even pierced for dramatic effect, and by manipulating the light source they could manipulate the scene." Wilton followed all the steps he had just outlined, and in a moment Joe found himself transported to the Colosseum by night.

"Here's a case, Mr. Cocktail, where we had to decide the importance of this object, and, more importantly, the use of this object in the life of this museum. It's a technology that most people in the modern world have never seen displayed before, but it is one that resonates with many people. They can immediately grasp the importance of this tool in the Bakerhurst life, because they understand how important visual media (television, movies) are in their own lives. This is a case where it simply is not good enough to be told how the Megalethescope works; an audience wants to see the device in action. We found ourselves faced with a set of options to evaluate. We could simply display the machine as is and not attempt to show people how it works. We could use it as seldom as possible, or we could use it as often as the situation calls for, acknowledging that the inevitable wear and tear on the object and its component parts will lead inevitably to its destruction. Or," and here he grinned, "we can make a facsimile of the tool and its component parts."

"Non-use was not a viable option. It doesn't align with our mission here at the museum. If the Megalethescope had been a unique object, we might have had to consider non-use a choice, but it's not. There are others still in existence at museums and historic properties across the world. Our second choice was to use it sparingly. That's a difficult one for us here at the Bakerhurst as well, because we really don't believe in privileging one set of visitors over another. We hope, I hope, that every visitor leaves

288

the property with some joy, a spark, a connection that they'll remember. I don't mean that every visitor has to hear every story and look closely at every object. That would be impossible. We know, however, that this device somehow captures the spirit of the Bakerhurst and engages the imagination of the visitor, and so we really want everyone to have a chance to see it in action."

Joe felt like a kid and could hardly wait for the end of the story. "So what did you decide? What did you do?"

"We engaged the local community in our decision in a significant way and created a committee that included a mechanical engineer, two opticians, a tailor, three cabinet-makers/woodworkers, the owner of a screw-machine factory, and the print-making and photography instructors at the college, as well as the local high school art teachers. Then we told them exactly what I've told you today. A couple of summers ago we held a two-week-long retreat here at the property and invited the committee members to come and asked them to invite a second person in each of their fields of expertise to function as an apprentice.

"You haven't had an opportunity to visit the workshops yet, have you Joe?" Joe shook his head. "We've got workshop space here in abundance - a print shop, a machine shop, a foundry, and wood-working spaces. So we brought all these people together and used a little old-fashioned Yankee ingenuity, coupled with some ancient specification documents that Helena, that's Duncan and Sophia's youngest daughter, located in the records of collection in Venice. We took the whole thing apart and photographed every piece. We documented and diagramed how everything went together, and each of the groups, armed with the bits related to their craft, disappeared into the various workshops. About mid-way through the retreat we all came back together with the real bits and pieces and rebuilt the original. In the meantime, everyone was working furiously in their own groups, making replicas as close in material and technique to the original as possible, and doing a little - what is it that you young people call it - some out-of-the-box thinking, to see if any parts could be better made with some material that wasn't available in the late 19th century.

"By the end of the two weeks we had three complete working replicas - one as close as possible to the original, and a second and third, both a little sturdier, and, perhaps a little more durable, made with readily available synthetic materials. As a result of that work, we have the plans, the molds, and the casts to enable us to re-create the parts we need.

"So, how does this impact the house today? We still use the original machine. We tried using the closest replica for a while, but pretty much everyone involved in interpretation and tours here felt the need to be up front and honest with the visitor. We found that once we told the audience that they were looking at a working replica, the idea of the Megalethescope lost some of its magic. So we took the decision to use the actual object, and when something breaks or needs to be repaired, we can fix it with a replica piece. We've accepted the responsibility for shortening the lifespan of the object, and, of course, at any point if we change our minds, we have a working replica and one slightly more modern version that works perfectly fine as well.

We gave the second modern version as a gift to the collection in Venice that shared the plans with us."

Roland had come in to join them as Wilton finished his object lesson. "I know how difficult it is to disengage Wilton from a fellow historian when he gets on a roll, so I came to find you. We'd better get a move on, Mum wants us to stop at the gatehouse and talk with Terry for a few minutes."

Joe thanked Wilton for spending the afternoon with him and sharing his wealth of knowledge. "Well, you've heard about the family from an outsider's perspective; I hope we'll have a chance to speak again before you leave, Dr. Cocktail. I look forward to hearing your take on the family after spending the evening with them."

Roland chuckled and promised Wilton that he would do his best not to undo all of the good work accomplished that afternoon. "As long as Hercules and Heidi behave themselves and don't scare Dr. Cocktail away."

"Would you both please call me Joe?" Joe begged. "People don't really call me 'Dr.' anything unless they want money from me, or are displeased with me. I'm assuming neither of those is the case here?"

"Okay, Joe it is. And now we'd better go or we'll be late for the gatehouse."

Chapter Fifty

They said a final goodbye to Wilton, who headed back downstairs to his office. Joe and Roland went to the coatroom to grab their coats and Joe's bag. At the front door, Joe noticed the security guard, Frank, was still at his place, seated at a small desk, doing some reading. He stood up when he saw them coming and walked around the desk to open the door, and Joe noticed he also had his coat on.

"Hey Frank, you want to ride with us?"

"Thanks for the offer, Roland. I told Scott I'd wait for him. He's just checking the outbuildings in the golf cart. Could you tell Terry that we'll be along just as soon as Scott's finished his round?"

"Can do, Frank. Let's go, Joe. If you think the coffee is good in the kitchen, wait until you taste it at the Gatehouse. I think Chef provides them with some kind of high-test version that those of us here in the house don't get. I don't know about you, but right about this time in the afternoon I can use a nice big injection of caffeine."

They opened the door to the outside and were hit by a blast of cold air. Both men turned their collars up to give themselves a little bit of protection against the wind. A 1969 acid-green Bonneville stood in the driveway.

"Wow! That's the second great car I've seen today."

"This is my winter car. I bought it from my dad. The seats are the size of sofas, and that's what they're called in the original advertisements for the car. And it's got pile carpeting - can you imagine? I'm a huge fan of Bonnevilles in all shapes and forms. In the summer, when Gamby, that's Uncle Ambrose, allows it, I borrow one of the other Pontiacs, a sweet little turquoise Bonneville Special."

Roland, who'd been carrying Joe's bag despite Joe's protests, tossed the bag on the backseat of the car. Because of the size of the seats, it looked more like a briefcase than a full-size carry-on bag. The interior of the car was enormous.

Roland drove rather carefully. "Ambrose will give me one of his lectures about taking care of my possessions if he finds out I've been tearing down the driveway," Roland explained. "In any event, the gatehouse is so close it's not worth building up any speed."

"Do you mind if I ask you a question about the security on the estate, Roland?"

"Not at all, but I may not be able to answer it. Security isn't really part of my purview."

"Well, my question is really less about security and more about how you go about enforcing security in a museum that is also a house, and in many senses, still a home. I wasn't alone for long periods of time today, but your mother did allow me to find my way from the restrooms to the kitchen. There's lots of stuff around. No one searched me, or you for that matter, when we left."

"Did you take anything?" Roland looked at Joe mischievously. "Trying to test us?"

"No, of course not," Joe flushed with embarrassment and realized that his whole approach to the security issue probably sounded either suspicious or sanctimonious. "I just wondered how everything works."

"Well, it's people like Wilton, and Frank, Terry, and Scott, who you'll meet in a few minutes, and the rest of us to a lesser extent, who ensure that everything is exactly where it should be. Wilton walks the entire house three times a day, four or five if school groups or outside tour groups have been in the building. Wilton is a kind of idiot savant about the Bakerhurst estate, except that he's no idiot. He knows exactly where everything should be, and he walks the place, adjusting, moving things, returning chairs to their appropriate places, twitching the drapes, maneuvering the antimacassars, straightening the pictures. If something has gone astray, he'll know soon enough and, to be honest, we know the kinds of objects that go missing."

"On very rare occasions one of the security staff will have a quiet conversation with a teacher, who will in turn have a quiet conversation with a particular student, but more often than not it's an adult who just can't seem to resist the lure of something. In that situation, one of the security staff will have a special kind of conversation, which generally leads to the object mysteriously re-appearing in a designated box in the coatroom. The suggestion that searching is an option is usually enough; we seldom have to do an actual search. We've been able to ameliorate some of this by putting smaller, more valuable objects in specially designed showcases. We have some surveillance cameras on the property - in the vault storage areas downstairs and in the butler's pantry where the daily and display sterling are kept. We also have cameras aimed towards the showcases where jewelry is displayed – but we're aware even these measures won't deter a determined thief. After all, even the most sophisticated surveillance systems, cameras and all, can be disabled."

Joe thought sadly how much that statement resonated with him right now. Roland continued, "Every lowlife who has an interest in ransacking historic homes has taught himself how to pick locks, disable camera systems, and distract staff and volunteers. What helps protect us and our collections are our special circumstances, Joe.

"First," Roland held up the index finger of his right hand, "we have a relatively small staff, all of whom are thoroughly familiar with the items on display. Second," and another of his fingers went up, "all of the staff who work in the house itself, or in the workshops, or any of the outbuildings - Wilton, the paid security staff, and the volunteers - have been with the estate for a long time, so they recognize suspicious behaviors. Third, most of the year the house is open for tours only. If an individual wants to view the house and its contents, they have to make an appointment in advance. If they ask to see something very specific, or seem to have an unusual amount of knowledge about a part of the collection, and they aren't a recognized scholar or known collector, we make sure there is someone with them at all times. And, there are absolutely no briefcases or spacious handbags allowed. And finally, Leighton is a very small town. If a stranger appeared to be asking unusual questions about the estate or any of the buildings, we'd know about it soon enough. Knock wood, we've been pretty lucky to date."

They pulled up to the Gatehouse, and Frank, the man Joe had seen earlier upon his arrival, appeared and made a welcoming gesture, encouraging them to come in. Roland parked the car and the two men hurried from the car to the warmth of the gatehouse. Roland spoke first, "Joe meet Terry; Terry meet Joe."

"Welcome to the Gatehouse, Mr. Cocktail, I mean Joe." Inside, Joe glanced around, interested. There was something more than a little Snow-Whitish about the interior, as if the house expected the imminent return of a group of gem-mining dwarves. A fireplace at one end of the room featured comfy chairs on either side and, on a rug in front of a blazing fire, was an elderly Dalmatian. The dog opened weary eyes at the newcomers and, upon seeing Roland, thumped a tail and struggled arthritically to its feet. Roland strode quickly over and caressed the dog's head, speaking quietly, and the dog relaxed gratefully back down on the carpet with a satisfied sigh.

Terry walked Joe over to a long wooden farm table that had rustic benches on either side with heavy wooden armchairs at either end. The table appeared well-worn. The scratches, gouges, and alternate smooth patches were definite signs of continued use over a number of years. Two men were already seated at the table, engaged in a game of cribbage. "Special extended afternoon break today," Terry explained, "partially in your honor, but not completely; we always have a long break on Monday afternoons, mainly to talk over anything that needs to be resolved from last week, and go over anything coming up in the next week. Usually Sophia or Duncan or," and here he nodded at Roland, "one of the family is present. And sometimes the Director," he added almost as an afterthought.

Joe was starting to feel slightly nervous about the mysterious Hercules Bakerhurst, although he was honest enough with himself to admit that part of his fear was due to his track record with his now-deceased employer. The two men at the table made as if to put the cribbage board away. "Go ahead and finish your game, we are going to grab some coffee," Terry encouraged the men. "We need to wait for Frank and Scott to get here before we can start."

Roland joined them as they crossed the room to a small kitchen. He offered to sit in front of the fireplace with the dog if Joe wanted a private chat with the security staff. The day had been so enjoyable that Joe had forgotten he was sizing up the place, and being sized up in return. He considered Roland's offer, "I don't have any objection -unless there are deep dark family secrets I need to know about - skeletons, vampires, or, say, hidden treasure. Anything like that?"

"Well, if there was, Terry and his team would know about it. Nothing stays a secret for long around here."

"What about the secret of the disappearing Santa Claus drawings?" asked a voice from the door. Joe turned and saw Frank and another man, who was taller than all the rest and angular in a way that made Joe think of Ichabod Crane.

Chapter Fifty-One

"We do have an unsolved mystery here at the Bakerhust, Joe. Thanks for reminding us, Frank." Roland paused to introduce the newcomer and then picked up the story, "Samuel met Thomas Nast while on a trip to London when Nast was working there. There is a family legend that at least two of the earliest drawings of Santa Claus were done as gifts for the children. As the story goes, Nash sent the drawings along with instructions to Samuel in a letter, instructing they be hidden each year and then found as a kind of holiday game. We don't really know for certain if the drawings ever actually made it to the property, and if they did, what happened to them. I can tell you that Wilton's been through every scrap of paper and book in the house, looking for them over the years, but no sign of them or Nast's letter's to Samuel ever turned up. Of course, they may well have been destroyed - neither Samuel nor Nast had any reason to suspect the drawings and letter might be worth something someday. He probably forgot about them, and someone unknowingly chucked the whole lot into a fire one day."

Terry chortled, "Roland, when has anyone in the Bakerhurst family ever thrown anything away? There's enough stuff in that house to keep a dozen Wiltons busy for the next century. All that stuff we moved from the attic rooms into storage when we converted them into conservation spaces? I don't know what Wilton's plan is for those trunks and boxes, but I know Wilton and Jennifer haven't had a chance to do much more than a cursory register for what they found. Those papers, if they exist, could be anywhere in that house and you know it. I believe in Santa Claus and I believe those drawings are there somewhere, even if they don't crop up in my lifetime."

A natural lull in the conversation allowed Joe to ask a follow-up question to the conversation he and Roland had been having in the car. "How does it work with security in a private family museum? I don't quite understand. Do all of you live here?" This last question was addressed to Roland.

"Good lord, no. I can remember my grandparents living in their private suite of rooms, and visiting them as a child. The house and estate were already functioning as a museum, and I guess I grew up, until I went to school that is, thinking that everyone's grandparents lived in a museum. In a way they do, I suppose. All of the moms and dads, uncles and aunts, and cousins turned up for major holidays - Thanksgiving, Christmas, and Easter. Most of us spent time here in the summers. My parents built a rather lovely home on a piece of Bakerhurst property when they were first married, and as we kids came along they just kept adding onto the house. My brother also has a home on the property and so does my sister, Isolde. I teach at the college and keep an apartment in town so I can wake up late and make it in on time for lectures. My sister Helena, the world traveler, stays either with my parents or with me when she's in town. Like Mum said, you are welcome to stay with me tonight in my spare bedroom, unless you'd rather stay in a hotel? I'm not much of a cook in general, but I'm a good with breakfast, as long as you like things that are fried."

"I'm in."

"And I've once again run off at the mouth and haven't let you get your real question in, and I haven't let the guys talk at all. I'll shut up now."

"I'm really trying to get the situation straight in my head. So, the family doesn't live here, but it's a family-supported museum?"

"Completely," Roland chimed in and then clapped a hand over his mouth, took it away, and then said "zip."

"So it's paid for and supported completely by the family," and he noticed all the men around the table were nodding their heads. "If Roland here decided he fancied a set of wine glasses, or Samuel's sterling silver dresser set, or even one of the kilim rugs from the music room, could he pick them up and take them out of the house?"

Terry spoke up, "Not without Wilton having a heart attack." All the men laughed, and Terry continued, "To be clear, Roland or any of the family members could, in theory, appropriate items from the house for their own use, and there is actually a process in place. Everything - the house, the property, the outbuildings, the family-owned businesses - is part of the Bakerhurst Trust. The trustees for the trust meet quarterly and consider any requests, and in general, when items from the house go off the property, they go as long-term loans to individual family members. Long before Roland walked in with a box and newspapers to take home his wine glasses, Jennifer would have produced the appropriate paperwork, and I would have received notice he was coming to remove the glasses. It would be Jennifer's responsibility to assure that what is taken from the house is what is supposed to have been taken."

Roland jumped in, "And I wouldn't be bringing a box and newspapers. Jennifer and Wilton would have appropriate packing materials at the ready, and one of these gentlemen would most assuredly be on hand to see that only what is supposed to go in the box goes in the box."

"And what happens if one or more of the wine glasses breaks while they are in your possession?

"Then I hear about it from everyone - Mum, Dad, Wilton, Jennifer, Hercules, and Terry."

"He's right about that, but we all understand that items like wine glasses are meant to be used and they do break. The Bakerhurst isn't a vault. It isn't a showplace frozen in time. Wine glasses were meant to hold wine, not to sit in glass cupboards for people to observe them. That's our philosophy and we all understand that." Again, Terry seemed to be speaking for all the men and they nodded in unison.

"Visitors to the house are carefully observed, but family members are, well- they're family, and ultimately it's their house. I grant you, Dr. Cocktail, the situation is unique, but since this is the only museum most of us on the guard staff have ever worked at, this is normal for us."

Conversation turned at that point to a discussion of the basic security measures for the property, which inevitably led to a series of entertaining stories about guest - and staff - behaviors. A new guard had accidentally locked Jennifer in one of the attics one summer evening. She had managed to craft a white flag out of a pair of old bloomers and an ancient curtain rod and finagled it out through the bottom few inches of one of the windows to get someone's attention. The windows in the attic open only partially for security reasons.

The guards discussed the favorite places on the property for young couples to make out. The heavy woman who lagged behind a group once to see if, fully clothed, she liked the size of the ancient bath tub and got herself stuck. Joe noted that most of the stories were told with good humor and affection, not with any sense of pettiness or spite. The Bakerhurst welcomed visitors as part of the life of the museum, not as commercial necessities to be tolerated.

Joe enjoyed sharing coffee around this table as much as he'd enjoyed the more formal coffee with Sophia that morning. The day had flown. He felt comfortable at this table swapping stories of his own experiences with these men.

Throughout the conversation, Terry, or one of the other Bakerhurst security men, had occasionally glanced up at a Tambour mantel clock over the fireplace, and eventually Terry finished his coffee and said, "I hate to bring this to an end, Roland, but it's time for late afternoon rounds." They put their cups in a small dishwasher in the kitchen area and then put the cribbage board carefully away before wiping down the table. Joe shook hands all around and thanked the men for their time. Frank spoke for the group, "It was our pleasure, Dr. Cocktail, and we'll look forward to seeing you around."

Joe wondered whether Frank was referring to the fact that Joe would be spending a half-day at the museum tomorrow morning, or whether the security staff had just given Joe their stamp of approval. Joe found himself hoping it was the latter.

Roland and Joe hopped back into the Bonneville, and Roland, once clear of the Bakerhurst drive, put the pedal to the metal and zoomed off into the fading light towards town. A light snow was falling as they made their way down the main street, where after turning left at a stoplight, they pulled into an alley behind the cheerfully lit storefronts directly into a modern parking garage. "I thought you might want to drop your things and see your bed for the evening before we head off to the house for dinner. Dinner will be casual. My parents own dogs so you might want to change and get a little more comfortable."

Roland lived above a pipe tobacco and smoke shop. Joe could smell the rich mingled scents of the various tobaccos as they climbed the stairs to Roland's apartment. The layout was much like Joe's own apartment, only much, much larger. The outside door opened onto a good-sized living room lined with bookshelves. In addition to the shelves, there was also a heavy library table piled high with books. The space was double the size of Joe's own living room, and Roland explained that he had taken two apartments to create his own.

The conversion had also provided Roland with a good-sized kitchen, a formal dining room, and an alcove with a wet bar. Roland showed Joe into a guest bedroom with an attached modern bathroom - a significant improvement over Joe's own apartment - and left him to unpack. Joe washed up and changed into a pair of grey flannel slacks and black turtleneck sweater, his only option other than his pajamas and clean dress shirt and change of tie for tomorrow's meetings. He'd brought running clothes and running shoes too, but wasn't yet sure if he'd run. The weather was messy, and not knowing the area, or specific plans for tomorrow, he thought he just might hold off on running until he returned home.

He found Roland at the library table, nose in a book, a glass with two fingers of pale amber liquid at his side. He had also changed out of his suit and into a pair of slacks and long-sleeved polo shirt. Roland looked up. "Care for a cocktail? Glass of wine? Single malt?" and he indicated the contents of his own glass.

"Bourbon, if you've got it."

"Coming right up," and Roland headed towards the hallway leading to the bar.

Joe walked over and scanned the shelves of the filled-to-overflowing bookcases while he waited. Roland returned with his drink, and the two men took seats in front of a gas fireplace. Joe took a sip of his drink and allowed himself to relax. They spent the next hour companionably discussing their research and getting to know one another a little better. Roland talked a bit about his family and explained who would be at dinner that evening - his mother and father, brother Hercules and his wife, sister Isolde and her husband, himself, and possibly Uncle Ambrose.

"It shouldn't be too grueling for you, Joe. Then you'll have met everyone but Helena, which is a shame, because she's the best of the bunch."

Drinks finished, they reluctantly got to their feet and donned their cold-weather gear before heading off to dinner with the Bakerhurst family.

Roland drove out of town and into the countryside, where the farmland eventually gave way to forested areas. Turning onto a dirt road, they ended up in front of a large modern wood frame structure. Tall narrow windows projected shafts of light onto the snowy yard, and a wide drive led up to shallow steps. As they approached the front door, large panes of glass at either side allowed Joe a view of a foyer and steps leading into a great room. There was something about the house Joe couldn't quite place. It reminded him a little of alpine ski resort settings in 1950s movies.

Roland opened the door and the two walked in, Roland shouting, "Mum, we're here."

Roland took Joe's coat and his own and dumped them on the stairs in front of him. As he did so, Sophia appeared and looked pointedly at the coats. "Okay, okay," Roland said and picked the coats up and headed down a hallway to what was surely a coat closet or an extra room.

Sophia took Joe by the arm and walked him downstairs into the great room proper. An older man, not unlike Roland in looks, but bigger and broader, was making cocktails behind a wheeled cocktail cart. He smiled and looked up when Joe and Sophia approached. "I'm making a round of martinis. Will you have one, or has my n'er-do-well son been feeding you single malts already?"

"I won't, if you don't mind, sir. While I like a good martini, I started the evening with a bourbon and probably shouldn't mix my liquors."

"Quite right and quite wise. How about a Manhattan then?"

"That would be grand."

"Duncan," Sophia said wryly, "you might try introducing yourself to Dr. Cocktail before you start plying him with liquor."

The man immediately set down his cocktail shaker, wiped his hands on a small towel, and stepped from behind the cart. "Of course, my dear. Dr. Cocktail, Joe if I may?" Joe nodded. "I'm Duncan Bakerhurst. De facto patriarch of this motley bunch, although I suppose Ambrose could also lay claim to the title if he had even the remotest interest in it. I've heard a lot about you," the man continued, "and am familiar with some of your work. So glad you could join us here tonight," and he stuck out his hand.

"It's nice to meet you too, sir," Joe took the man's hand and was surprised by the firmness of the grip.

"The others haven't arrived yet, but should be here any minute. How's the day been? Like the old place?"

"Unbelievable, and yes, it's a remarkable property and quite a family."

Duncan smiled like a child at the compliment. "It's true, isn't it? We are quite a family, but you know we couldn't do it all with just family members. We need fresh blood in every generation to keep things going." He stopped for a moment and considered what he had just said. "That makes us sound like vampires, doesn't it? I don't really mean fresh blood, I'm trying to say we need new people with

307

new ideas in every generation, not just Bakerhursts. We need people like Wilton, my wife, Miranda, Jennifer, and Chef, particularly Chef," and, here, he patted his stomach. "And possibly, you." He looked quizzically at Joe as if he wasn't quite sure Joe was the right size to fit in an office.

The conversation was interrupted by new arrivals. Joe looked up to see a giant of a man with a full head of salt and pepper hair, mutton chops, beard and mustache, and immediately thought Dicken's 'Ghost of Christmas Present' had entered the room. Behind him came a slim woman in a slinky and expensive-looking suit with a slightly tired, bored expression on her face. *Hmm, here's an individual that doesn't fit the Bakerhurst picture; I wonder how that happened?*

Chapter Fifty-Two

The giant man turned out, as Joe had expected, to be Roland's elder brother and the director of the museum, Hercules Bakerhurst. The slim woman was his wife, Heidi. As they removed their coats, the door opened once again, bringing Uncle Ambrose and another woman, who was undoubtedly a Bakerhurst. She, however, was tall and bony, where Hercules was tall and broad, but she definitely shared features with both of her brothers, marking her as a Bakerhurst. She was accompanied by her husband, a good-looking Irishman, who was introduced as "Major." Ambrose greeted Joe heartily and Roland formally introduced Joe to his brother, his sister Isolde, and their respective spouses.

At that point, Sophia walked back in from what was presumably the kitchen or dining area and shooed them all into the great room for some pre-dinner conversation. After that the evening seemed to fly by for Joe. The Bakerhurst family was loud and boisterous and argumentative in a good-natured way. Isolde's husband seemed to keep up his end of the conversation. Joe gathered he was an attorney and was somehow engaged in the family business, though not the museum, but with contracts and work-related issues. Clearly, he and his father-in-law and brothers-in-law got along. Joe had already been told that Isolde was the horsey member of the family; she and Joe had briefly engaged in a conversation about horses and riding. He felt that he had somehow disappointed her by admitting that he was not a rider, but redeemed himself by conversing intelligently about dogs.

Hercules's wife seemed to brighten up and lighten up after one of Duncan's martinis. She didn't say much, but Joe noticed nothing escaped her. She was clearly smart, just not terribly interested in joining in the conversation. Roland had mentioned in an aside to Joe that his sister-in-law, a clinical research psychiatrist, wasn't a big one for talking. This was probably a good thing, thought Joe, since everyone else in the family was quite keen on talking, usually all at the same time.

Hercules had been perfectly polite and charming upon meeting Joe and seemed to vaguely understand that Joe was in town interviewing for a job at the Bakerhurst, but he wasn't particularly interested in Joe or his credentials. Hercules seemed to be mostly interested in himself and his activities. Clearly, he had inherited the polymath gene from his ancestors, because through the course of the evening Joe heard him discuss an upcoming trip to France to study with a famous pastry chef; news of the latest research into the olfactory abilities of fish; a charity event where he had been asked to perform a solo jazz piano selection; the monthly meeting of his cigar and wine club; and some research he'd been pursuing on 19th century *son et lumière* events. *The rest of the family treats Hercules like a precocious child, someone they enjoy and humor, but don't take very seriously. No, that's not quite right. It isn't that they don't take him seriously. He's clearly happy living in his own little world of endless activities and, as long as those activities don't harm him or endanger the family in any way, the family encourages him to do as he pleases.*

Joe was surprised at how quickly the evening was passing. Sophia, rather than standing on formality, had served a family-style dinner - no appetizers or removes, just vast quantities of cold-weather food. Throughout the meal, the family talked about the events of the day, and the events of the past couple of weeks; apparently, a regular family meal was the rule rather than the exception. Everyone made sure to include Joe in the conversation, and even Hercules's wife shared an interesting anecdote about a new intern who had shown up late and confused the psychiatry lab with the physics lab.

Hercules wasn't completely oblivious to the estate and the museum, and, for Joe, one of the best parts of the evening came as the family members shared their early memories of the house. They told stories about family gatherings, their holidays together, and daring summer vacation escapades. Isolde reminisced, "We used to play this rather horrible game called, oh what was it, yes, 'Guerilla Conkers,' with all the cousins. It's kind of like those paintball games people play today."

Roland chimed in, "Except that we never wore protective padding and the darned buckeyes hurt when they hit you." He picked up the story from his sister, "The goal was to gather and fill your pockets with fallen buckeyes, and then move off into the woods, while trying to hit others and not get hit yourself. If you got hit, you were dead. The last person standing was the winner and then it started all over again. Of course, we all cheated like mad. Pretty pointless really, but fun - except you usually ended up with bumps and bruises all over."

Hercules joined the conversation. "Much to Mum and Dad's dismay," and he looked at his parents, "Uncle Ambrose taught us all to shoot buckeyes as soon as we were old enough to want to pick them up."

"My dear boy, you were born able to hit a target, but I thought it only fair to give the younger ones an advantage as soon as possible. Call it a little assist in your "Lord of the Flies" Game. I felt compelled to do something to even the playing field out a bit."

"Remember when we stopped playing the game?" Roland asked his siblings.

"I do," said Hercules grimly.

"That was the year we changed the rules so tree-climbing was allowed," Isolde added.

"It was a real David and Goliath story. Our sister Helena, the youngest of us, used a makeshift slingshot to aim a buckeye at the back of Hercules's head. He fell like a rock."

"And I broke my arm and couldn't go rock climbing that summer," Hercules pointed out. He looked annoyed for a brief moment and then wistful. "But it was a great game."

Sophia looked at him incredulously, "It was not a great game and you idiot children are lucky you're all still alive. We'd have never known what was going on had you not fallen out of that tree, Hercules. It was sheer luck that you suffered nothing worse than a broken arm. Children will be children, but you were always inventing new and imaginative ways of getting into trouble over there."

Joe enjoyed seeing the motherly side of Sophia. He could imagine his mother responding just as earnestly, decades later, to stupid things he and his sibling had done in years past. Isolde looked slightly affronted at her mother's chastisement. "But Mother, Helena wasn't trying to kill Hercules; she just wanted to knock him out of that tree."

Joe thought to himself that the unknown Helena was becoming more and more interesting. Duncan, as if aware of Joe's thoughts, explained that his youngest daughter, in addition to her professional work, was quite an accomplished archer. "Comes from reading too much Robin Hood as a child," he suggested. "All the children were athletic. Hercules, quite appropriately, wrestled and Roland is still a runner."

Joe was glad to hear Roland was a runner. It gave him another thing in common with this man he had known for only a short time. Maybe he'd suggest a run tomorrow morning.

Duncan continued, "Isolde is our equestrienne, and Helena our archer."

"You'd have most of the prizes locked up at a county fair," Joe suggested.

"Indeed, we would."

Dessert consisted of apple dumplings with whipped cream, freshly whipped by Sophia herself. She had excused herself and closed the door behind her to mask the noise of the electric beaters. You could hear the sound even so, and Duncan, smiling, said, "That's the sound of dessert to me, my wife whipping cream. When I hear it I know that I'm just a few minutes away from something wonderful."

His children and Joe all smiled at his obvious affection for his wife and his sweet tooth. When everyone had been served dessert and their choice of coffee or some other warm beverage, the conversation turned to the museum and, one after another, the family told stories. After a while, Joe found himself contributing his impressions of the museum and the estate. Eventually Sophia brought the evening to an end, suggesting Joe had more than likely had a long day. The party broke up, family members departing in the order they had arrived. Sophia arranged for Roland to have Joe at the museum by 9:00 the next morning and the two men departed.

Chapter Fifty-Three

The drive back to Roland's apartment was accomplished in a companionable silence. Joe knew the evening had been a test, an opportunity for the family to see if Joe was the kind of person who would fit in. He was pretty sure he had passed on the table manners and social conversation part of the evening, although he felt he should have brought a bottle of wine or flowers to his hostess. Roland broke the silence, "Did you have a good evening?"

"Yes, but this has been the strangest job interview I've ever experienced. I know you're looking me over, and I'm supposed to be looking you over, but mostly it feels like I've walked into some utopian museum world that isn't quite real."

Roland laughed, "Oh, we're definitely not utopian at the Bakerhurst. I shall point out our flaws so you can judge the situation a bit better. I'll begin with my flaws. I only want to work on the projects I want to work on. Mostly, I just want to be left alone to pursue them in peace and quiet. I dislike it on the rare occasions when I have to get involved in the day-to-day business of the museum, and so I'd like them to hire you so you can pick up the slack in that area.

"Moving on. Hercules, well, Hercules is our figurehead. He's good on the marketing and show side, but I don't think he really believes anyone but himself is real. The rest of us are all just members of his audience. There's no harm in him.

"Isolde flutters around the periphery worrying about animals and trying to engage us in various rescue missions and save-the-world schemes. She's got a big heart and zero in the way of organizational skills. She's good with animals, not so much with people. People make her skittish. Major is a good man and understands the situation. He protects her and shields Isolde, as much as he can, from the baser elements in the world. You could easily sell her all the swampland in Florida if you could convince her that it would make the world a better place for animals."

"And speaking of animals, Father is a woolly lamb. Like me, he just wants to be left alone to do his work. Mum manages the whole place, top to bottom. She's a taskmaster, but doesn't ask more from us than she gives of herself. I will say this for my mother, she knows how to hire good people and let them do their jobs."

"Wilton has been with us forever. I think Ambrose hired him. Wilton thinks he owns the place and, in a sense, he does. We may all have memories and a fondness for the past, but Wilton owns the past. Every detail is there at his fingertips. You may have noticed he is completely OCD about the house and its contents?" Roland made his comment a question.

Joe acknowledged the statement with a nod of his head.

Roland went on, "We have a local firm we use that comes in and cleans the house on a regular basis. Most of the staff we've known, and they've known us for years. They added a new woman a few years ago, very efficient, and a good cleaner, but a natural born organizer and declutterer. Normally, Wilton is on hand for these cleaning sessions, but for some reason he was out that day. She started putting things away. Luckily, Jennifer happened to walk in on her and put a stop to it, but not before she'd already been through three rooms. Wilton blew a gasket and now hovers like a mother hen when the cleaning crew are in the house. He drives us, them, and himself crazy."

As Roland was finishing this story, he pulled into the parking garage and the two men headed inside. Joe tried to stifle a yawn to no effect and Roland clapped him on the back. "Get some shut-eye, Joe. I'll wake you at 6:00 a.m. and we'll get in a run before we need to be back to the house."

With no further encouragement needed, Joe headed towards the guest room. Fifteen minutes later he was fast asleep.

Chapter Fifty-Four

The next morning began with a brisk run. Despite Roland's promise of a hot fried breakfast, the two men had opted instead for freshly-baked croissants and hot cups of coffee from a small family-owned bakery a few storefronts down from the apartment. Joe finished breakfast a bit sticky from his croissant, but energized for the day ahead. He showered, packed his things, and the two men were soon on their way back to the Bakerhurst for Joe's morning meeting with Sophia.

Roland dropped him off, as Ambrose had, by the front door. This time Sophia wasn't waiting to meet him, but Roland had told him to head towards the kitchens; Joe was sure to find his mother there. "Ambrose is out at the farm today so I've got chauffeur duty. I'll see you after lunch and then we can take off for the airport around 1:00 p.m., if that suits you?"

"That's terrific, but don't you have work to do? I can easily call a cab."

"You could, but that's not really the way we work here. We treat our guests right." Roland's eyes twinkled, and Joe thought he looked very much like his uncle and his father. "Mind you,"

Roland cautioned, "once guests become employees it's a different story." He winked at Joe and drove off towards the back of the house.

Frank opened the door and reconfirmed Roland's instructions. "Mrs. Sophia is waiting for you in the kitchen. She says you don't need to get rid of your coat just yet, she's going to take you on a tour of the property."

Still a few minutes early, Joe took his time working his way to the kitchen. Looking at an original gaslight fixture here. Stopping to examine a fine inlaid table there. Reaching out to gently trace the pattern on a piece of fabric. He felt a strange kinship for this place and wondered if it was just because the past 24 hours had proven such an antidote to his real life. His real life. It seemed curious to think how unreal his real life seemed as seen from inside the Bakerhurst house.

He wasn't looking forward to going back to the museum and wondered what he had missed. *Had PFM taken over the running of the museum? Would there be a formal funeral and memorial service to attend this week? Had the police discovered exactly what had happened to cause the accident?* And then a slight chill coursed up his spine. W*as it really an accident?* There had been a few too many accidents or events in the past week for Joe to be completely sure of anything. *Why had someone tried to destroy his files? Who had disabled the security cameras? Who had poured bleach onto Katherine's costumes?*

For just a moment a thought flashed across his mind; *someone had said something to him recently. Was it yesterday or last night that had made him think differently about the events of the past week? Now what could it have been?* He shook his head. Whatever thought had been there was gone now. He'd leave it alone and perhaps it would come back to him.

Joe glanced at his watch and, as usual, his dawdling meant he needed to pick up the pace. He wound his way through the house and found himself once more in the cheery Italian kitchen. Today there were more students and Chef was there, holding a wicked-looking knife, and they all turned to see who had entered. He gave Joe a brief salute and returned to his demonstration of the best way to breast and skin a duck. Sophia was at the coffee urn filling a paper cup with coffee, and when she saw Joe she reached for another cup and motioned him over. "Grab a quick cup and we will go on walkabout and see something of the property."

Joe did as instructed and they headed out the back door. The morning passed like a whirlwind. Sophia sped Joe through the garages, allowing him to catch a glimpse of, but not stop and admire, the Bakerhurst automobile collection. She took him through the living space for unmarried male servants above the garage. Apparently, the unmarried female servants had lived in rooms above the kitchen. At some point, the garage rooms had been converted into dormitory spaces for kitchen interns and the occasional visiting scholar, with private baths, a communal kitchen, and living space.

They walked through the kitchen garden, the simple garden, and the rose garden. Ambrose's beloved roses were hidden underneath large plastic cones, protected now against the winter weather. There was a greenhouse and even an old-fashioned icehouse modeled after one created for a 16th century Medici prince. Samuel had seen the original on one of his trips to Italy.

Shielded from view of the main house by a thicket of trees stood a compound of long, low buildings that Sophia described as the workshops. They reminded Joe of buildings he had seen at Shaker villages. Here too, Sophia explained, the buildings had been converted to provide dormitory-like living space above for craftsmen-in-residence. Each workshop housed a different type of activity, but the living spaces above were similar to those above the garage with a private self-catered apartment for the master and communal bathrooms, kitchen, and living space for the apprentices.

Despite the cold, the workshop area was a beehive of activity and sound. Joe saw the foundry, a printing press, wood-workers, and people working and running to and fro everywhere. In the foundry, they ran into Ellen, Head of Education, and had a quick chat before moving on. Sophia seemed to know everyone by name and no one appeared to be annoyed at having their work interrupted by their visit. The atmosphere was something between a working farm museum and a medieval faire.

Hidden from the workshops by yet another thicket of trees was a parking structure. Sophia explained there was a private drive to and from the parking structure, which allowed the temporary residents, and visitors on the days when the workshops were open to the public, to come and go freely without having to circumnavigate the main house. Sophia spoke with him about the administrative organization of the workshops, funded by the Bakerhurst Foundation; they were jointly administrated by a board of directors made up of faculty and staff from the college and the masters of the workshops. Sophia sat on the board as well, and she expressed her hope that their new hire would join her there.

Leaving the workshops, they walked down a path, which led to a small lake, with a dam at one end and a fish hatchery at the other. Skirting the lake, they followed a well-groomed path through some woods and, after a short while, reached a clearing with a large log cabin, which turned out to be the sugar shack for gathering and processing the sap from the maple trees on the property. As they walked, Sophia talked to Joe about the various ongoing concerns of the estate and property, how things were managed, and their plans for the future. By the end of the walk, a chilled and cheerful Joe was all but certain Sophia would offer him the position, and though he planned to go back home and think about it, he was all but certain he would take the job.

Chapter Fifty-Five

They headed back to the house, making two brief stops, one to take a quick look at the barns, and the second to toss their paper coffee cups and pick up fresh mugs of coffee in the kitchen. Instead of heading down to the office, Sophia walked Joe upstairs to Samuel Bakerhurst's private library and office. Given what Joe had learned about the man in his short visit, he doubted Samuel really had a private anything. The man seemed to thrive on a constant stream of visitors and family members.

Someone, presumably Sophia, had made sure there was a fire in the large fireplace, and she motioned for him to sit down across from her in one of the huge over-stuffed chairs. After a few moments, Sophia spoke. "Well, Dr. Cocktail, what do you think? I still need to do my due diligence and check your references, but you've made quite an impression on Wilton and Roland and the rest of the staff. How do you feel about the Bakerhurst?"

Joe hadn't expected Sophia to beat around the bush; she just wasn't that kind of person. He'd expected an offer was going to be extended, but now that it was, he felt, well, he felt slightly giddy. "I feel like I belong here," he said simply.

She smiled. "Good. We feel you do, too. There are lots of details to be worked out, but an inclination to join us is the most important aspect of the process. My guess is you couldn't start immediately?"

"No, I'm due to teach a course this coming semester and have projects at the museum that I'd like to see completed. I could have everything wrapped up by mid-May. The earliest I could start would be June." He panicked for a minute. "Why, do you need someone sooner?"

She smiled again. "Relax, Dr. Cocktail. The Bakerhurst is an ongoing concern. As long as there are family members, there is all the time in the world. We aren't going away and can afford to wait for the right person." After that the two of them got down to the business of negotiating. Joe was relieved to discover that the salary they were offering was not just commensurate with his current salary, but a good deal more generous. The benefits were good- all employees had the traditional holidays off as well as three weeks of vacation plus an additional week annually as they continued with the museum, up to six weeks a year. Travel and expenses for museum-related travel were covered by the Foundation.

Every fourth year employees earned a three-month paid sabbatical to pursue individual research. Joe could hardly believe his good fortune. Museums were notoriously under-resourced, and when he'd headed down for this interview he'd rather expected, and been willing to take, a slight or perhaps even a significant salary cut if he found the job interesting. Given the offer on the table, he felt no hesitation at all about accepting the position. By lunchtime most of the significant details had been ironed out, and they both headed down to the kitchen well pleased with one another.

Today's luncheon party included Duncan and Ellen, Head of Education. When Sophia and Joe walked into the room, everyone stopped speaking and looked up at the two expectantly. Joe felt as if he had walked into a scripted ritual. Even Chef looked up from his task and motioned his busy students to be quiet.

"Ladies and Gentlemen, Dr. Joseph Cocktail, the soon-to-be newest member of the Bakcrhurst staff."

Everyone got up from the table and came over to congratulate Joe. Duncan and Roland both thumped him on the back. Chef came over, wiping his hands on a towel over his shoulder, and gave Joe a big handshake. Wilton clapped his hands together and smiled seraphically. Jennifer and Miranda hugged him, and Ellen, whom he had only just met that morning, smiled too. Joe felt like the prodigal son home at last.

The lunch that followed was as fine as it had been on the previous day, but Joe was so elated at having accepted a new position that he hardly noticed what he ate. Far too soon, Roland pointed out it was time for them to leave if Joe was to make his plane and hurried off to fetch his car. There was another round of hand-shaking, felicitations, and goodbyes. Sophia accompanied Joe to the front door in companionable silence, but once outside she turned and regarded him with a calm and confident gaze. "I'm glad you are coming to join us, Joe." And he realized it was the first time she had addressed him by his first name. "I think you'll be good for us, and we will be good for you."

Joe tried to think of something he could say that would come close to approximating how he felt at that moment. *What could he say to this woman who was soon to be, despite the organization chart at the museum, his real boss?* So he simply said what was in his mind, knowing she would understand. "The past two days have been terrific. For me, that's a pretty good sign this is where I'm meant to be. The hard part, now, is going back and being completely present in my old job for the next six months, especially given the events of the past week. If I could, I'd start here tomorrow..." And here, he smiled at her and looked around the house, "but I've got to go back and get things in ship-shape condition for whoever follows me as associate curator."

"You've got a lot on your plate right now, and I suggest you use the thought of your place here, and how much we are all looking forward to working with you, to help you through the next six months. Don't hesitate to give any one of us a call as questions arise, and feel free to come down and see us anytime you like. We'll be in touch, of course, about contracts and other details, but for now it's time for you to depart."

They shook hands one last time, and Joe jumped into the front seat of Roland's car. On their way to the little regional airport they talked about this and that, projects the museum and staff were involved with, plans for the future. The only disconcerting moment of the drive came when Joe asked Roland for some advice on looking for a place to live. Roland turned to look at Joe. "Didn't Mother mention that housing for your position is included?"

"No," said Joe, puzzled, "she didn't mention it."

"Well, she must have had her reasons, and I won't spoil her fun, and of course you can always find something on your own if you'd prefer, but if I were you, I'd wait and see what Mother offers you before looking around." After that, despite attempts by Joe to engage him on the topic, Roland refused to say another word, and the conversation shifted back once again to the work of the museum.

At the airport, Joe's flight was already boarding, so he said a quick goodbye, wished Roland happy holidays, and said he hoped to see him again soon. He grabbed his carry-on bag from the back seat of the car and made a run for the plane; luckily the airport was small, and he had no problems boarding on time. As he climbed up the stairway to the plane, he turned and waved goodbye to Roland, who was parked by the fence in the exact same spot as Ambrose had been parked - was it only yesterday?

He'd brought a book to read on the plane, but found after lift-off he couldn't focus. He eventually put the book in the seat pocket in front of him and considered what had just happened. He'd come to Leighton yesterday morning, seen the museum for the first time, and now, or at least very soon, he was going to be an employee of the Bakerhurst museum and Leighton was going to be his home. He looked out the window at the snow-covered fields below. Though they were already far away from the little town, he thought about how eventually he'd get to know these roads and perhaps – as he made out a few cars and trucks traveling on roads below – perhaps, he'd soon make the acquaintance and possibly become friends with someone in one of the vehicles below. The whole situation made him feel slightly like an alien in his own mind and body. *Who was this new Joe? Would he be different?*

Forget that, his conscience suddenly reminded him, *forget what you might become, you've got a lot to figure out before you can become that new guy. Projects to finish, people to tell about the new job. When would be the appropriate time to tell PFM? Maybe she wouldn't want him to stay for another six months, maybe she would want him to leave sooner, as she had suggested last week. I'm going to have to tell Charlie and Katherine. They'll both be pleased for me, but it means that the days of beer and wings at the Fox are numbered. Mr. and Mrs. Watson will be pleased as well as distressed. I'll miss my apartment and the fresh-baked cookies. I wonder what Roland meant about housing being included?* Joe's mind was racing now and he realized he needed to relax. *This position is a good thing and I've got plenty of time to figure out the details over the next few weeks. I'm not going to resolve anything sitting on this little commuter airplane.* And with that thought, Joe leaned his seat back and promptly fell asleep.

Chapter Fifty-Six

Wednesday morning was a uniform grey and Joe woke up slightly grumpy, despite his status as a man looking forward to a new job. He realized he wasn't excited about going into work. *Probably because there wouldn't be much work accomplished.* He didn't know what had transpired in the time he'd been gone, but certainly there would be any number of people stopping in to his office today to give him their version of events. He decided to sneak in a quick run, which would get him into the office slightly later than he had planned, but he knew he would be in a better mood if he had some exercise under his belt.

He quickly dressed and was out the door after stretching. He knocked off a quick three miles and was soon back at his apartment showering and getting ready for work. As he was leaving, Mrs. Watson came to the door. "Good morning, Joe. Did you have a nice trip?"

"It was fantastic. Hey, would you and Mr. Watson like to join me for dinner tomorrow night? I'll tell you all about it."

"Why don't you come over and I'll make dinner?"

"Nope, I'm taking you out for dinner."

"Well, if you insist, but..."

"No buts, Mrs. Watson. Tomorrow is a cooking-free night for you. We'll go out and have a real slap-bang dinner to celebrate the holidays. We'll need to have our strength up for the weekend. Your holiday thrift sale is this weekend, isn't it?"

"Yes, indeed. Will you be able to help out?"

"I wouldn't miss it for the world. Hey, do you mind if I bring my friend Katherine along to help out on Saturday?"

"Not at all, Joe, we can use the extra help." Joe left for work feeling much better. He was glad he'd thought to ask Mrs. Watson if Katherine could join them on Saturday. He had a plan in mind and he thought it was high time that Katherine met the Watsons; he just hoped that Katherine would be free. After all, the holidays are the busy season for performing-arts folk.

Driving into the museum garage a short time later, he pulled in just behind Charlie. *Strange; Charlie is normally an early bird.*

His friend had just gotten out of his car and was waiting for him. Joe noted that he looked tired. "What's up, Charlie? You okay?"

"Aww, nothing. I'm just tired. It's been a long couple of days. Glad to see you back. Katherine told me about your trip. Have you heard any of the news yet?"

"Nope, haven't talked to anyone. Just got back yesterday afternoon."

"PFM's been named interim director. But boy, she has her hands full. We had a senior staff meeting yesterday morning and there's an all staff today. Bradley Boehm is on administrative leave for tampering with the *Helt Diadem*, because his bloody joke may or may not have been partially responsible for the Director's death. Scott Theodore is on administrative leave, because the police found dish soap on the cloud platform and an empty bottle of the same kind of soap wedged behind a cabinet in Scott's office." And here Charlie looked at Joe. "Along with an empty bottle of bleach. So he may or may not have been partially responsible for the Director's death. Scott says he doesn't know where the bottles came from and denies putting them there."

Charlie continued, "Someone is in big trouble and Katherine is frantic because the equipment was tampered with under her watch. Meanwhile, the Dragon-Lady was closeted with PFM and Rita Avi for most of the afternoon. Grapevine says that both women left the meeting hysterical. Nobody knows what went on in the office, but Rita has apparently checked herself into a clinic, and Dragon-Lady's taking some time off. The result is that half the bloody place has taken administrative leave, and to top it all off, the police are still nosing around the museum.

"Detective Weber and his colleagues have set up in the small conference room, but he seems to prefer having his discussions over coffee in the cafe. He has set up kind of a satellite office at a corner table and just meets and talks with people. I'm not sure exactly what's going on, but when I spoke with him yesterday, he clearly knew about and had questions concerning the night your files were tampered with and the security cameras disabled. My guess is he will want to get your take on events sometime today. He seems to be a pretty sharp guy. He's already figured out that just about everyone had reason to dislike the

Director, some more than others - Scott, Boehm," he trailed off, and looked at Joe.

"And me," acknowledged Joe, "and let's not forget PFM, the Dragon-Lady, who was mad as hell at him that day outside his office, as was his wife, and, of course, one of the three witches suggested a drop into a vat of boiling oil."

"And me," agreed Charlie, "he'd been rather openly disparaging about the work of the Information Technology Department lately."

"So we all had a reason to dislike him, that doesn't mean any of us tried to kill him, does it?"

"No, but apparently a lot of people have been vocal about wishing him dead. Bradley and Scott both planned 'practical jokes' meant to embarrass and humiliate the Director in a public setting. And the fact is the practical jokes were two too many and may ultimately have led to his death."

Joe nodded. "I still don't see why they think there might be a link between what happened in my office and with Katherine's costumes and the Director's death."

"I don't know what they think, Joe. I just know they're asking a lot of questions of everyone. Marcus Richards has stepped up to take over as interim head of the Board of Trustees. He's a criminal defense attorney you know, and he's got some experience in these matters. He asked me to search through the email archives for certain key words."

"You can do that?" Joe was surprised. "Isn't that a violation of privacy?"

"Not on a work computer. Anything you do on that computer can be searched at any time if necessary. In the non-profit world, the administration is a little, let's say, more respectful or more tolerant of an employee's workspace, but business is business. I have to do this kind of task on occasion, although in the past the cases have typically been related to HR firing issues and not criminal cases per se."

"So, it's definitely a criminal case now?"

"No one has said anything definite to me, but it sure looks like it."

"I don't mean to be morbid or to make light of the situation Charlie, but what kind of keywords or phrases do you expect to find? 'I'll murder the bastard.' 'Kill-kill-kill,' or something like a to-do list that includes the notation 'buy poison?'"

Charlie smiled wryly. "You aren't far off, though I wouldn't expect to find anything that blatant. They've asked me to search for keywords that could indicate suspicious activity and that might, if handed over to the police, provide grounds to further pursue the case. As far as I know the police haven't approached the Board asking for our assistance in providing or searching for this information; I think Richards is preparing for the eventuality. The problem is, Scott did threaten to kill the Director at the gala - and the Director died at the gala. So Richards is doing the right thing. If it does happen, the police will have their own computer forensics folk and they will want to gain access to our systems, primarily our email archives. At that point I need to be able to ensure that nothing has been altered.

"What I'll have to do today is freeze the accounts for Bradley, Scott, and the Dragon-Lady, and ensure that the email archives are intact and accessible for the e-discovery process." He thought for a moment. "I'll probably need to do the same for the Director's computer, now that I think about it. This is going to be another long day."

The two men had stopped in the parking lot to catch up and had been greeting other staff as they filed past on their way in to work. Now they entered through the security doors and headed towards their respective offices. They agreed to meet for lunch or later in the day to continue catching up, although Joe knew Charlie would not be able to share any of the details he might find in his keyword searches.

Joe did have a chance to talk to Detective Weber later in the morning when he went up to grab a cup of coffee. The Detective was sitting in his corner, looking thoughtful, and tapping a pencil on the corner of the table. Joe got his coffee and walked over. *Might as well get a difficult conversation over with and maybe learn something in return.*

The detective looked up at his approach, "Dr. Cocktail, I'm glad to see you back safe from your travels. Good trip?"

"Very. Do you mind if I sit down?"

"Not at all, I was hoping to speak with you when you returned. If this is convenient for you, it's convenient for me."

"Am I allowed to ask you questions?"

Detective Weber looked amused. "Of course you may ask me questions. I just may not be able to answer them to your satisfaction. You don't mind if I ask you a few questions in return?"

"Not at all." And the two men began to talk.

The conversation with Detective Weber raised more questions than it answered in Joe's mind. Joe wasn't able to shed any more light on why he thought his files had been tampered with, but told Detective Weber that, even though incriminating bottles had been found in Scott's office, Scott's grudge was against the Director and not Katherine or himself. *At least I managed to convince Detective Weber that Scott's threat to harm the Director had been made under the influence and that he hadn't really intended to murder him - at the gala or anywhere else. But if not Scott, then who did murder the Director?*

Chapter Fifty-Seven

Saturday morning dawned bright and clear and unseasonably warm. *All in all, a great day for the thrift shop's big holiday sale.* Mrs. Watson had been sorting through the donations that appeared as people cleaned out their houses to make room for the guests and gifts that would appear during the coming holidays. But even so there was plenty more to do, and that was one of the reasons why Joe had invited Katherine to come help. *She'll get along with the Watsons and I'd like to spend more time with her.* He had yet to tell Katherine or the Watsons the news about his new job at the Bakerhurst. *There's plenty of time for that after the holidays.*

He'd told Katherine to come by around 8:00 a.m. for some of Mrs. Watson's coffee and baked goods. The store would open at 10:00 a.m. and that would give them a couple of hours to get everything ready for the opening. He showered and dressed; a little while later he headed downstairs and found Katherine and Mrs. Watson already seated at the little table in the back room, chatting as if they'd known one another forever. Joe was not surprised to hear they had already discovered a number of friends and acquaintances in common.

Mr. Watson had been sent off to gather last-minute donations from a few of the donation boxes placed strategically around town. He came in a few minutes later and Mrs. Watson put them all to work. Joe and Mr. Watson set up a long table for coffee, tea, hot cider, and cookies on one side of the shop. Then the two men carefully moved the holiday window displays to either side of the window and set up another table, where members of a local Girl Scout Troop would giftwrap packages for a token donation.

Meanwhile, Mrs. Watson and Katherine busied themselves emptying and sorting the items from the boxes Joe and Mr. Watson had brought in from the van. Mrs. Watson kept up a running commentary throughout the process, explaining to Katherine how to look carefully at clothing and objects, indicating how she should put aside those that needed to be cleaned or repaired and check the pockets to make sure they were empty. She told her, "If you find change, or money, or something valuable, see if there is a label in the item and we will try to return it. If not, it goes into the cash register."

Most of the clothes went straight from the boxes into a washing machine in the back room, so that items on the shelves in the store were always clean. Shoppers had no worries about finding bugs in items from Mrs. Watson's store. Often donations required special cleaning, or dry-cleaning, and Mrs. Watson had connections at several dry cleaners around town that donated their services. She was careful not to take advantage of local business people and made it her business to redeem these services as infrequently as possible. But some items came out of boxes so frightfully dirty or cracked or broken or otherwise useless that Mrs. Watson would just shake her head sadly and wonder out loud about the way "some people did things."

They had all been working quietly and companionably when Katherine, sorting clothes, gave a yelp. Joe and Mr. Watson, who had been hanging a few mirrors on a wall designated for display purposes, turned and looked at her, startled. Her eyes were bright. *Had she cut herself on a pin stuck in some fabric?*

He turned and walked over to where she was sitting. Mrs. Watson stood behind her looking concerned. Katherine's lap was covered in deep purple velvet that seemed vaguely familiar. As he moved closer, he knew immediately why it looked so familiar: The dress draped across Katherine's lap was the dress the Director's wife had worn the night of his death, but the dress didn't seem to be the focus of Katherine's attention. As Joe approached her, she held out her hand to him. In it were three clear marbles and what looked like a handful of large rubber bands with some thread and fabric attached.

"Katherine, what's wrong? What is it?" Although he had known she was upset by the Director's death, he couldn't imagine the dress and marbles alone had triggered this kind of response.

She handed him the marbles and the rubber bands, and took the medieval pointed sleeves of the gown in her hands, and displayed them to him - the left-hand sleeve had a small silk loop, designed to fit over the middle finger of the wearer to keep the point tight across the back of the hand; at the end of the right-hand sleeve, where the silk loop should have been, something had been ripped off the gown and the fabric was torn. He looked down at what Katherine had handed him; in his hands with the floral marbles was the catapult device for a slingshot. Joe knew immediately what had happened to the Director, and he knew Katherine understood as well. And while her knowledge came from an understanding of Elizabeth, Joe's insight arrived in a flash as little bits and pieces of things he had seen and heard over the past week came back to him.

Katherine in the bar the night they'd taken Scott home, talking about the Director's wife: *"She and her older brothers were the kinds of kids who tortured animals--rocks, sticks, BB guns, slingshots, a magnifying glass, whatever they could use to make something or someone miserable, they practiced until they were perfect."*

The ice balls, the same size as the floral marbles. Mysterious little spots of water on the marble floor of the rotunda, and then, most recently, what had someone said at dinner that night at the Bakerhurst home, was it Roland? *"Our sister Helena, the youngest of us, used a makeshift slingshot to aim a buckeye at the back of Hercules's head. He fell like a rock."*

Katherine looked up at him and said, "What do we do?" He looked at her, at Mrs. Watson, watching both of them concerned and not quite sure what had happened, and then glanced up at the clock. In just a few minutes the store would need to be opened. He could already see a few die-hard thrift shoppers waiting outside the door. He made the decision for all of them. "What we have to do can wait until the end of the day. Mrs. Watson, do you happen to have a clean plastic bag for this stuff?" He held up the floral marbles and the catapult. "And how about a zip-up dress bag for the whole shebang? We'll need to get it out of the way and put it someplace safe for the time being."

"Of course, Joe." Mrs. Watson hurried away.

He spoke to Katherine quietly. "There's nothing we can do right now. This afternoon we will call Detective Weber, hand the items over to him, and explain what we think you found and why."

"You're thinking what I'm thinking, aren't you Joe?"

"That she nailed him with a floral marble or intended to nail him with a floral marble, yes, that's pretty clear."

"Oh, Joe." Katherine put her face in her hands.

"Do you want me to take you home? Mrs. Watson will understand. She won't ask any questions until one of us is ready to explain."

"No, I want to stay. It will be good to do something normal. Be a part of something positive and festive. It was just an unexpected shock and then, when I realized what I was looking at, the world seemed to go fuzzy for a minute there."

Mrs. Watson came back at that moment, and Joe placed the marbles and the catapult into the plastic bag and sealed it and handed it to Katherine, who folded the velvet dress around it and placed the whole package into the dress bag and zipped it up.

"Give it to me, Joe," said Mrs. Watson. "I'll put it in the cabinet in the back room." Mr. Watson joined them at that moment and announced it was time to open the doors. He gave them all a big wide smile, blissfully unaware of the recent turn of events, and went to let in the shoppers.

Chapter Fifty-Eight

The day passed quickly. The store was flooded with shoppers looking for holiday deals. Katherine and Joe were too busy to worry. Young men and women from the college came in and tried on scores of sweaters, shirts, blouses, slacks, jeans, and dresses before leaving with bags full of gifts for friends and family. Mothers and grandmothers came in looking for gently-used toys and books. An antique dealer from down the street wandered in and perused the knick-knack and glassware shelves, hoping to find collectible pieces that could be marked up and placed on display in his own store window. Joe and Mr. Watson fetched and carried. Mrs. Watson rang up purchases and bartered with the customers, always willing to make deals so that mostly everyone went away happy with something they wanted or needed.

Katherine kept the cookie plates and the cider and coffee urns filled. She moved through the store, straightening a shelf here, putting clothes that had fallen to the floor back on hangers, and folding items that needed folding. During the first hour, Joe surreptitiously watched her to make sure she was ok, until she hit him and told him to stop. *Guess I wasn't all that surreptitious about it.* Katherine recovered beautifully from her shock and seemed to be enjoying herself, freely bantering back and forth with Mr. Watson and helping customers find items.

Joe noticed Mrs. Watson watching Katherine as well. He saw her smile approvingly as the girl helped two young brothers try to find a gift for their infant baby sister. Katherine skillfully steered them away from the plastic tractor toward one of the many stuffed animals or soft books Mrs. Watson had lovingly cleaned or refreshed.

The store was too busy throughout the day for them to stop and have lunch together. Around noon, Mrs. Watson set some sandwiches, chips, fruits, and soda out on the table in the back room, and they each took turns grabbing a solitary quick bite to eat before returning to the busy store.

Every hour on the hour three new Girl Scouts would arrive to serve their shift wrapping packages. They did a great business and had already emptied out their donation tin twice. Mrs. Watson had learned from long experience that people who felt they had gotten "deals" on her merchandise were more than willing to spend a little something extra in the way of a donation for having their packages wrapped.

At one point in the afternoon, Joe passed Katherine on her way to fill the cookie plates. "Where do all these cookies come from? Does she do nothing but bake cookies when she's not working in the store?"

"You may well be right, but I think a lot of these have been donated by Mrs. Watson's friends. She has a fairly wide network she can call upon. There was a lot of activity down here late yesterday afternoon. I imagine she calls in all her cookie favors for this event."

Finally, at a little past 5:00 p.m., just as it was beginning to get dark, Mr. Watson closed and locked the door behind the last customer of the day. They all breathed a sigh of relief.

Mrs. Watson was over the top. "I think if we sold nothing else for the rest of the holiday season we would still be ahead of last year's numbers. Wasn't it wonderful today?" She beamed at all of them and clearly still had energy to spare. "Let's get this place straightened up and then the two of you can go off and do something more entertaining than hanging around with two old people."

"Don't say that, Mrs. Watson. Today was so much fun. You and Mr. Watson are the youngest old people I know and I'm so glad Joe asked me to come help today. I can't think of when I've had more fun on a Saturday." Then Katherine stopped and frowned. Joe knew she'd remembered the dress and objects in the dress bag in the back room.

"Oh yes, you and Joe have another chore to get done today, don't you," Mrs. Watson commented.

Joe had taken her aside earlier in the day and explained the situation. "I've got his number, I'll call. He's probably going to want to talk to Mr. Watson too about which donation box the dress came from."

"That's easy enough," said Mr. Watson. "I keep colored bins in the car, one for each donation box. Do you know which colored box it came out of, Katherine?"

"Well, I was working on emptying out the yellow and the blue bins, and Mrs. Watson had the red and green bins. It could have come out of either one of them, but wait, it was the second bin, and I like blue better than yellow, so I'd started with the yellow bin and saved the blue for last."

They all laughed at Katherine's rationale for sorting.

"The blue bin comes from the box over at the eastern edge of town, on the road towards the big old houses."

"That would make sense," Joe added. "That's out near where they lived. Or at least where she lives now. We might as well get this part over with, don't you think?" he asked Katherine.

She agreed, but looked anxious, and he gave her a quick hug with one arm and then ran up to his apartment to get the number the detective had given him.

He was surprised when Detective Weber picked up the phone himself after the second or third ring. Joe identified himself and apologized for calling the detective on a Saturday evening. He gave the detective a quick rundown of the events of the day. Detective Weber listened, asked a few questions, and asked the group to stay put at the thrift store. Joe promised they'd wait there and went back downstairs to deliver the news.

While they waited, the four moved around the store cleaning up, straightening, and moving more items from the back of the store onto shelves, replenishing stock where they were able. Katherine wiped down the tables and carried the empty coffee and cider urns back to the little kitchen. Mr. Watson and Joe swept the floors, and Mrs. Watson cleaned and organized the gift-wrapping area, depositing little piles of half-eaten cookies and cookie crumbs, scotch tape ends, and bits of unusable ribbon in the trash. Soon Detective Weber arrived with a junior officer in tow.

"I'll make a fresh pot of coffee and bring down some of my own cookies," offered Mrs. Watson and bustled off. Katherine and Mr. Watson sat down at the table in the back room with the two detectives. Joe fetched the dress bag from the cabinet and set it on the table in front of the two men.

The detectives asked them to tell their respective parts of the story. Katherine unzipped the bag and brought out the contents, explaining that it had only taken a moment to recognize the dress as the same dress worn by the Director's wife at the gala the previous Saturday.

Detective Weber asked her why she'd looked in the pockets of the dress, and Katherine explained Mrs. Watson's rules of order. She had first checked to see if there were pockets in the dress. Once she located them, she had pulled out the contents of the plastic bag containing the floral marbles and catapult.

Detective Weber stopped Katherine at this point and wanted to know how the dress had come to be in the store in the first place. Did Katherine have any idea how long it had been in the store? Mr. Watson took up his side of the story, explained about his last-minute visit to each of the donation boxes that morning, and his bin system for organizing donations. On occasion, a wife might get rid of a pair of a husband's much-loved pair of pants, not realizing that car keys or a wallet might still be in the pockets, or library books sometimes get donated, and at that point it helped to know just exactly what bin he needed to look through.

Having clarified that part of the story, Detective Weber asked Katherine to continue. She again related her theory of sorting based on her favorite colors; both of the detectives grinned at that part of her story just as Joe and the Watsons had earlier. Mrs. Watson confirmed that the dress had come from either the blue or yellow box, and not from the red or green bins that had been her responsibility. Joe confirmed that he, too, had recognized the distinctive dress as unmistakably having belonged to the Director's wife. Feeling slightly embarrassed, Joe shared his and Katherine's theory about what they thought had happened.

As before, Detective Weber listened patiently and looked thoughtful. He made an occasional note in his own notebook. The junior officer was taking copious notes. "I'm going to ask Sgt. Wilkins here to type up the statements you've made here today, and then sometime tomorrow I will ask you to read them and sign them. Meanwhile," and here he addressed his remarks to Mrs. Watson, "I'm going to give you a receipt for these items. It is important, please, that you say absolutely nothing to anyone about what you found today. Say nothing to family members, friends, and particularly nothing to any of your co-workers at the museum. Do we understand each other?" Joe and Katherine both solemnly nodded their heads. "These items may mean something or they may mean nothing, but you can leave it in our hands now."

Chapter Fifty-Nine

The next weeks were busy. Mr. and Mrs. Watson dealt with the increased shoppers and increased donations that came with the holiday season. They seemed to be busy from morning until night. Mrs. Watson was never too busy to make cookies or cupcakes or to stop and offer Joe a cup of coffee in the evening when he came home from work, though.

The museum held a formal and uneventful memorial service for the Director. The Director's wife was in attendance, pale and lovely, dressed all in black. She was sitting with her parents and brothers in the front row, but seemed somehow apart from them. Katherine, Charlie, and Joe all sat together in the back of the auditorium. Joe noted Detective Weber's presence as well. Marcus Richards gave the primary eulogy, though PFM and several trustees also made brief remarks. Lori, the Dragon-Lady, Scott, and Bradley Boehm did not attend. Neither did Rita Avi, who, according to rumors, was still recovering from the shock of the gala.

After the memorial, events returned to normal at the museum. The winter holiday season was always a busy time for museums as families gather and college students come back home for long winter breaks. Museums are places to escape from the confines of home and one of the few places where inter-generational activities still take place in a community. The galleries were busy. Joe expected and enjoyed calls from trustees, patrons, and friends who wanted special tours of the museum for out-of-town guests and family members. Katherine was impossibly busy managing the performance aspects of various special events - choirs performed in the atrium and galleries. There were special events and the annual Members' Holiday Party, which the trustees decided not to cancel. Design and Installation prepared a tasteful sign displayed near the entrance indicating the party was being celebrated in memory of the Director.

Scott was back at work, but keeping his head down, and, according to Charlie, making a successful stab at sobriety. There had been no further discussion, at least that Joe heard, of any role Scott might have played in the Director's death, or that his job was in danger. Bradley Boehm's administrative leave had been extended into the New Year, when the Board of Trustees would meet and discuss his situation. Rita had officially resigned as President of the Board of Trustees; Marcus Richards had officially been named in her place. The Dragon-Lady had also not returned and there seemed to be some mystery attached to that, but Joe was too busy, and frankly, too uninterested to pay much attention to the gossip going on around him.

Joe had been in touch with Sophia Bakerhurst and they had come to a final agreement about salary and benefits. Joe brought up the housing issue and Sophia suggested he plan a return visit in late spring, and they could discuss his housing choices and when to announce his appointment then. Joe hadn't wanted to bring up his cryptic conversation with Roland, so he agreed and left the conversation at that. In the meantime, he decided he would keep his news to himself for the time being. He might tell his family at Christmas, although his mom would worry about the change from a large museum, and the move, and all the other bits. Perhaps he would just sit on this and tell everyone in the spring.

It wasn't until the 22nd of December that Joe was finally able to convince Katherine and Charlie to meet him after work for a drink at the Fox. Katherine's evening events and responsibilities were done until after Christmas, and Joe knew Charlie had taken the week between Christmas and New Year's off to go visit his family in Illinois. As Joe drove to the bar, he thought about their last event-filled evening together. Had it only been a few weeks ago? So much had happened in the interim.

Joe parked. No familiar cars in the parking lot. Again, he was first on the scene. Pushing open the door, he looked over at the bar and saw Scott Theodore and his wife, Judy, sharing a plate of wings and drinking soft drinks. Joe waved and called out "Merry Christmas" to them. Charlie and Katherine arrived just at that moment and, after a brief conversation with Judy and Scott, they headed to the back of the bar and found a convenient table. Sylvia brought them menus and took their drink order. The three of them settled back in their chairs. Joe imagined his friends were also remembering the last time they'd been at this table.

When the beers arrived Katherine said, "Charlie's got an announcement to make."

Joe looked at Charlie expectantly.

"I'm leaving the museum in mid-January," Charlie said. "My brother-in-law does some consulting work for a big firm in Chicago. They needed a CIO. I interviewed last week and they made me an offer today. The museum is changing and it's time for me to change, too."

"That's terrific. Congratulations, but what a loss for the museum."

"I don't know. I think it's an opportunity for them to try and find a senior staff member who has a little more of a feel for the mission of the museum. I've enjoyed my time here, and I understand the museum world better than when I started - a whole lot better, in fact. But I still think it would be a good idea for them to find a CIO who has a real affinity for the job."

He looked at them. "You two are in this because you love the institution. I liked the challenge of the job, and the money, but never really felt like I was a part of the mission. Maybe if I'd served under a different kind of director, but who really knows?" He laughed a little ruefully. "This job made a nice change from the for-profit sector, but I'm ready to go back. I'm tired of the constant battles."

That had been a long speech for a man who was really only voluble when discussing software, gadgets, hacking, or his most recent hobby.

Katherine spoke up, "We'll have to find someone to take your place at bar night. It's going to be lonely this winter with just Joe and me."

Joe felt briefly guilty, knowing that it was going to get much lonelier after he left the museum in the early summer. "Let's not get melancholy tonight. Remember what Lorenzo de' Medici said," and he quoted in a singsong voice:

> *"Youth is sweet and well*
> *But doth speed away!*
> *Let who will be gay,*
> *To-morrow, none can tell"*

"Lorenzo de' Medici, give me a break. See, that kind of stuff is why I don't really belong in a museum. How about quoting John Lennon or Elvis Costello? Or at least someone from the past century." Charlie rolled his eyes and they all laughed and clinked their beer mugs together. They enjoyed the rest of the evening in a spirit of uncompromising good fellowship. There might not be many more evenings like it to enjoy one another's company.

Chapter Sixty

Joe, like Charlie, took the week between Christmas and New Year's Day off, although as a curator he kept in close contact with the curatorial staff at the museum in case he was needed to facilitate any last-minute gifts to the collection. There were people who, just after Christmas, started thinking about their tax situation and scurried to offload works of art to museums in the hopes of future financial benefits. He spent the week with his family and visited a couple of old friends from school that he kept in touch with who were also home to visit parents.

Joe returned to work in the New Year full of plans to make the most of his five months at the museum. He wanted to leave everything in perfect order and his collections in the galleries looking their best upon his departure.

Charlie's last day of work at the museum was the end of the first week in January. There was the official mildly cheesy thank you and going away coffee for him on Friday morning. Lunchtime brought a rather more entertaining IT staff event to which Joe and Katherine were invited. The IT staff "deaccessioned" and presented Charlie with a collectible plate bearing the picture of Captain James T. Kirk of the Starship Enterprise. After work the three friends went to the Fox for one final round of beers. The evening began a little awkwardly. It seemed they had been saying goodbye to Charlie all day and there really wasn't much left to say. They might exchange Christmas cards, or an occasional phone call, but this was the end of the close camaraderie the three had shared. Joe was not really surprised to hear that Charlie was packed and headed off to Chicago the next morning.

Katherine had a piece of news she wanted to share with the two of them. "Did you hear about Elizabeth?"

Both men looked at her, waiting.

"The police arrested her this morning - for manslaughter."

Clearly Katherine wasn't going to refer to their role in the process, and Joe didn't bring it up either. He and Katherine exchanged a glance, and then both looked at Charlie. Charlie was looking into his beer and not at the two of them when he finally spoke.

"I was sleeping with her," he announced.

"What!" Joe exclaimed, surprised. He looked at Katherine. She didn't seem surprised.

"It was a mistake. I do, did, I mean, a lot of my work after hours, when everyone was out of the building and off of their computers. Beth was often in the building killing time before dinners and special events. She started stopping by the office. She was attractive and it was exciting. You know she always carried those giant bags, and she always seemed to have a bottle of something - wine, vodka, gin." Charlie had still not looked up from his beer; Katherine and Joe glanced at one another as another piece of the puzzle slipped into place. She carried a giant bag big enough to hold a bottle - of gin, or bleach, or cleaning solvent.

"The guards didn't bother to check her bag. It was more trouble than it was worth to mess with Beth. She either charmed them or made their lives miserable." He looked up for a moment, and neither of them said a thing; they didn't know what to say, so he continued.

"At first, she'd just come in and look over my shoulder, and ask me questions about my job. You know the sort of thing I mean. 'Charlie, you are so smart,' he spoke in a recognizable imitation of Elizabeth's husky voice. 'How do you program the computers? What's a network? Can you actually see what people are doing all over the museum? How do the cameras work? What happens if they stop working?' It all seemed fairly harmless at the time. I bought into her flattery hook, line, and sinker. It's one of the reasons I'm leaving. Not because of the arrest, but because I let myself get completely taken in by that woman. I can't escape the fact that I bear some responsibility for the Director's death. I don't know what eventually led to her arrest, but I became fairly certain that she had to have been the one behind the damage to your costumes," and here he looked at Katherine and then continued, "and your office, Joe."

"But why, what did that have to do with the Director?"

"Nothing," Charlie said flatly.

"I don't understand." Joe was confused. "Why would she go after Katherine and me?"

"She was jealous," Katherine said softly, and Charlie nodded.

"That evening we were headed to the Fox, the evening we found Scott and took him home, you remember?" Charlie asked.

"Of course, you were both running late."

"She called me just as we were headed out with a, let's just say, an offer I couldn't refuse. She was waiting for me in my office and I told her we needed to make it quick because I was meeting the two of you. She didn't seem angry at the time."

"She wouldn't," added Katherine. "Elizabeth always liked her revenge to come as a surprise."

"And it was revenge on all of us. The more I looked into the disabling of the security cameras, the more it seemed that the only place it could have originated was from my office. It just didn't make sense and I was still too blind to put two and two together. Of course Katherine didn't discover the bleach in the costumes until a day or two later, so I didn't even really connect the two incidents, until I saw the size of the bottles used."

"The bottles they found in Scott's office, the one with traces of bleach, and the other with the dish liquid. They were like the ones used in your office and they were about the size of a one liter water bottle. She carried them in her purse. If any of the guards had stopped her, she could have said she was taking them home and had been shopping. But, nobody did stop her. Listen, I don't know for sure this is what happened. It's what I think happened, but I'm sure she did it."

He sighed. "And I'm sure, somehow, she was behind what happened to her husband. She hated him. Hated him for having an affair with Lori. Hated him for having an affair with Rita. She didn't want him, but she didn't want anyone else to have him either."

"I'd intended to approach her about the bottles and the security cameras. But, after the Director's death, it seemed like the wrong thing to do at the wrong time. The police came and talked to me just before Christmas. Someone, and I'd guess it was Beth, had suggested to them that I was behind the vandalism. I told them what I knew, or thought I knew."

"You know," he continued, "after the Director's death I tried to call her. I wanted to help. I wanted to see if she needed anything, but she wouldn't return my calls. I still haven't seen her. She used me." Charlie looked a little lost and angry. "When this job in Chicago came up, I jumped at it. I've got to get away," he repeated. "The police are okay with me leaving, but I'll have to come back if there's a trial. I guess I shouldn't be surprised that she had something to do with the Director's accident – I guess she soaped his shoes or something?"

Katherine and Joe nodded understandingly, not knowing what to say, and still feeling bound by their promise to Detective Weber. Katherine put her arm around Charlie and Joe gave him a friendly punch on the shoulder - it was the best way they had at the moment to express their concern and support. Joe knew it had been hard for Charlie to confess his part in recent events, but at least they had another piece of the story. Soon after that, they called it an evening. Joe said goodbye outside the Fox. Katherine and Charlie had driven to the bar together; they'd been friends for a long time. Joe guessed they had some unfinished business to take care of before they said goodnight. He left them to it.

362

Chapter Sixty-One

On a grey afternoon in early February the phone on Joe's desk rang. Mrs. Watson spoke on the other end. "Joe, Detective Weber just called and asked if he could stop by on Sunday afternoon. He's bringing some clothing donations from his mother and, naturally, I invited him to stay for coffee. He suggested it might be pleasant if you and Katherine came too. He was quite emphatic about including the two of you."

Joe understood, without Mrs. Watson having to spell it out. Detective Weber wanted to speak with them, off the record. "I'll call Katherine and let her know. I'm pretty sure it won't be a problem," he said.

Sunday afternoon they were gathered once again around the table in the back of the thrift shop. There was an enticing plate of warm cookies and a pot of fresh coffee on the table with a second pot percolating on the stove. Detective Weber eventually opened with the subject that was on everyone's mind.

"Your friend Charlie called and told me he'd spilled the beans about his affair. Although it's highly irregular, I thought you deserved to hear a little more of the story, given your thrift store find played a pivotal role in her eventual arrest."

"Is the poor woman going to go to jail?" Mrs. Watson asked.

"No, I don't think that will happen, unfortunately."

"Oh Ted," Mrs. Watson chided him.

"Mrs. Watson, I've no doubt you see a lot of different types of people come through your thrift store. You are a genuinely nice lady. So nice, I daresay, that if you knew this young woman as thoroughly as I think I do, you wouldn't feel quite as sorry for her as you do now. I'm glad there are people like you in the world. I'd like to think that you'd be just as forgiving of me for my sins."

"Teddy Weber, you've no more serious concerns on your conscience than apologizing someday for that pie you and the other boys stole from my kitchen during your senior year."

The detective looked blindsided for a moment, and then he laughed out loud. "I should have known you'd remember that. Well, as Scrooge's nephew said to Bob Cratchit, I'm heartily sorry for it."

"Apology accepted; now, go on with your story."

Detective Weber looked at the group around the table with that familiar twinkle in his eye. "And it was a very good pie, too. Apple, as I recall."

"Peach, and I had to serve day old cookies to my Bridge group the next day when I discovered the theft," she scolded.

"I'll make it up to you, I promise. Now where was I? Once we had determined, fairly early on, that the fall was not quite the accident it appeared, we started looking for motives, and opportunities, and suspects. As you both know, there were quite a number of people at the museum with reasons, good reasons, to dislike the man. That said, disliking someone is not the same as murdering them, and so from a long list of suspects, including the two of you," and here he indicated Katherine and Joe, "we narrowed it down to those with real motivation."

"Me?" Katherine squeaked. "I didn't like him, but what reason did I have to kill him?"

"Well, to be honest, the Director's wife had suggested that you and Joe might have been in cahoots on the accident. She even went so far as to suggest that you, Joe, and Charlie had planned the damage to your areas and the disabling of the security cameras."

Katherine hissed an unpleasant word. Mrs. Watson looked a little shocked, but quickly recovered.

"That fellow Scott Theodore, the Director's wife, and Bradley Boehm were the most likely candidates from the very beginning. We eliminated Boehm early on in the process. He certainly hated the Director, but when we talked to him, he was clearly so terrified that he might have somehow caused the fall with his juvenile prank that we quickly discounted him as the actual killer. He might have been a clever actor, and he was certainly quick to point out others who had just as much of a reason to be angry as he was. So, we were obviously missing something."

Here Detective Weber stopped and looked at Joe. "Boehm, too, mentioned you as a likely suspect. Your name came up on several occasions. I considered the idea that you and your friends set the whole thing up, including the damaged property, but that solution just felt a little too complex. You told me you didn't like the Director, but it wasn't until a day or two before that you'd had any good reason to actually want to do him physical harm. Frankly, you seem more like the kind of guy who would pop him one in an angry moment than plan an elaborate scheme to off him during a gala."

"That's true. It's taken me a lifetime to learn to control my temper."

"Now, let's talk about Mr. Theodore. He was the only one of my suspects who'd actually threatened to do in the Director at the Gala - and he did die at the gala. He said it in front of witnesses. You and the bartender at the Fox."

"Yes, that's right," said Joe. "Sylvia was near us when he talked about it."

"And he'd apparently been talking about it a lot that afternoon. He's a man who thinks out loud when he's drunk. You told Katherine and your friend Charlie what had happened, so you could say that the threat was already common knowledge around the museum by the next day."

Katherine started to say something, and then stopped. Joe thought he knew what she might have said. They were all guilty of gossip at one time or another.

"The problem with Scott Theodore as a suspect is he didn't really have a motive for trashing your property -unless it was to divert us from looking too carefully at him as a suspect for the murder, and besides, he was already at the bar drunk when your files were tampered with. And as he himself explained, as an event planner, he wouldn't have messed with Ms. Harding's costumes. They had been partners and friends during the horrendous week leading up to the gala."

"What about Rita Avi, and the Dragon-Lady?" Joe asked and then blushed and corrected himself, "Lori, I mean."

"Well now, this next bit is completely confidential and if I hear a whisper of it in the big world I'll come and arrest you all. Do you understand?"

They all nodded somberly.

"It's off the record, because this part of the story helped us make our case, along with your discovery, and your friend's confession of his affair and subsequent events. You see, both Rita Avi and your Dragon-Lady planned to be married to him, the Director, in the New Year."

"What, both of them?" asked Mr. Watson. "He was going to marry both of them?"

"No, no, and here's where it got sticky. Apparently, the Director had shifted his interest to Ms. Avi from your Dragon-Lady and she, Lori, I mean, was frantic in the weeks leading up to the gala. You see, she's pregnant."

"What?" Both Katherine and Joe nearly shouted.

"Simmer down. Yes, pregnant. It all came out during an encounter between the two women in Prudence Fenn-Martin's office on the Monday following the gala. Both women ended up hysterical. Dr. Fenn-Martin correctly brought this information to our attention. We talked to each individually and both were quite clear that your director had already asked his wife for a divorce and was enforcing her good behavior by threatening to reveal her own adulterous activities and naming himself as the wronged party. Whether that would have worked is debatable, but we understand he was a canny investor and had hidden most of their assets. If they divorced she would have lost her status in the community as well as the lifestyle to which she was accustomed. She denied that he'd asked her for a divorce and asserted Ms. Avi and your co-worker were making things up."

"So," now Katherine spoke, "to use mystery novel parlance, you had motive, but you didn't know the means and opportunity."

"Exactly. And that's where you and your friend Charlie came through for us. We think, between the three of us, you've provided a pretty fair picture of the events leading up to the gala. We can't prove anything, but the evidence is pretty compelling. With that said, judges and juries are notoriously easy on pretty women. The best we can hope for is manslaughter, but I've no doubt she achieved exactly the results she intended."

"How sad," Mrs. Watson said, looking with affection at her own husband, "for both of them." She looked down then and noticed the cookie plate, empty except for a few crumbs, and with the brisk efficiency Joe loved, she stood up and headed for the little thrift store kitchen, "I'll get some more cookies and who wants another cup of coffee?"

Chapter Sixty-Two

On a fine morning in May, Joe carried a box up the stairs to his old apartment. He nudged the door open with his foot and maneuvered his way into the dining room, where he put the box down with all the other boxes on the floor and looked around. His action was greeted by a complaining meow from the top of a nearby box. Copyright was taking stock of his new home and wasn't a bit happy about the change. "Don't worry, Copyright," Joe said, "I bet Mrs. Watson will start keeping cat treats now that you are here." Copyright just glared at Joe for a second, turned his back, and jumped behind a box out of sight.

Joe wondered where everyone had gone. Then he heard a sharp pop like a cap gun coming from the direction of the front room. Katherine called out, "Joe, come quick."

He sprinted into the front room and there found Katherine and the Watsons. Katherine held an open bottle of champagne and was pouring it into the glasses on a tray held by Mrs. Watson. They all smiled at him and Mrs. Watson pointed out, rather obviously, "It's a toast." They each took a glass and Mr. Watson, doing the honors, announced,

"To Joe, a great neighbor," and here Mr. Watson tipped his glass towards Joe, "who, in leaving, has provided us with our next great neighbor." He nodded to Katherine. "Here's hoping the Bakerhurst job turns out to be everything you desire a museum job to be, with good colleagues and good friends," and, before they could raise their glasses to their lips, he finished enthusiastically, "and completely murder-free."

About The Author

Holly Witchey has a Ph.D. in European painting and sculpture and 30 years of experience as a museum professional.

Her research interests currently focus on North American perceptions of museums prior to the building of the nation's first great museums in the late 19th century.

Made in the USA
Monee, IL
17 October 2020

45409751R00207